Across the Salted Plains

MEGAN LONGMEYER

ISBN: 979-8-9910470-0-5 (e-book)
ISBN: 979-8-9910470-1-2 (Paperback)

Printed in the United States of America
First printing edition 2024

For rights and permissions, please contact:
Megan Longmeyer Books
meganlongmeyerbooks@gmail.com

www.meganlongmeyerbooks.com

Contents

To my twelve-year-old self, who was never afraid to dream.

This is for you.

I love you.

PROLOGUE

A WAVE OF COOL air breaks free from the canyon, clouds of loose dirt rolling upward, bursting into the early morning sky. For a moment it's completely silent, the dust and debris drifting aimlessly, mingling with an infinite tapestry of stars. It's such a beautiful, peaceful moment; so beautiful, in fact, that I'm sobbing, dry herbs and earth settling in my lungs as I struggle to breathe, my strangled cries ricocheting off the rocks below. As I start to gather myself, the wind picks up again, my sadness drifting away, echoes of my heartache howling through the canyons like someone screaming against the tide.

I've dreamt of visiting this place for the last six years, this dry, desolate patch of earth at the very top of my bucket list. I knew seeing it in person would be enchanting, magical even, but I think I secretly hoped it would be more than that, like the wild, untamed desert would release something in me, a longing buried beneath the sand. So far, no such luck; the canyon is just a canyon, and right now I miss him more than ever.

Annabean, my father says, his voice calling to me through the darkness, his warm, velvety baritone slicing through my ribcage, flaying me down to the bone.

Smearing tears across my cold cheeks, I focus on the horizon, trying my best to ignore him. It's pointless, really, considering he's a figment of my imagination, that his absence from this place is the reason I'm so sad. Still, this trip isn't about him; I'll be damned if I'm going to let one weak moment ruin one of the best weeks of my life.

Dream big, baby girl, he whispers, his memory relentless, his familiar words breaking through my resolve. I whimper, fresh tears streaming down my face as I pinch my eyes shut, desperate not to let him in. The man who taught me about adventure, who raised me to want a big, beautiful life. The person I miss the most but hate more than anyone; that bitter coward, that selfish son of a bitch.

Burrowing deeper into my heavy coat, I'm fighting to regain control when I realize that the sky is brighter, the clouds overhead tipped in gold as I slowly open my eyes. My breath catches, the past fading away as the first signs of light begin pooling on the horizon.

The sky lightens, the sparse clouds overhead a mixture of hazy lavender and shimmering pink. Tendrils of blue mist dance between the canyons, filling them up, turning the landscape into a mystical terrain of colored earth. The horizon shifts red, then orange, and finally a buttery gold, the rocks and shrubbery enveloped in a blanket of golden light. Everything pulsates, coming alive all at once, the peaks and crevices of the canyon as velvety and rich as an oil painting.

I smile, happiness seeping into my veins as I marvel at the spectacular view. This is what I came here for, this exact moment, the beauty of the desert so raw and pure that it is felt as much as it is seen. Maybe I can't forget the past, the disappointments and the betrayals, but if my life is filled with moments like this, I can at least look forward to the future.

The sun finally breaks the horizon, the entire landscape glowing an iridescent gold. I close my eyes again and spread my arms wide, my tears evaporating as the sun warms my skin, its heat sinking into my bones. I sit this way for a long time, breathing in the crisp morning air, embracing a level of joy and freedom I haven't felt in a long time.

My eyes are still closed when I hear something behind me; a small sound, like the snap of a twig. I ignore it, soaking in the early morning sunshine until, a few moments later, I hear it again. When it happens a third time, I finally recognize what it is: the click of a camera shutter.

I slowly open my eyes, squinting into the harsh daylight. Shifting my weight, I turn to see a man a few yards away, peering at me through a camera lens. For a moment I panic, a startled scream building in my throat until my eyes adjust and I realize it's just Graham, holding my own camera.

"Good morning," he says, his face lined and sleepy. His hair is a frazzled mess, his dark locks sticking up in every direction, a condition made worse by the wind. He lowers the camera a bit but he doesn't put it away, the lens still pointing straight at me.

"You know I don't do pictures," I say, arching a brow in his direction. I turn back toward the canyon and listen as he walks toward me, loose rocks crunching beneath his hiking boots.

"I know," he says, sitting down beside me. Even after an entire day outdoors with no shower, he still has a bold, peppery scent, like he's just walked through a Moroccan spice market. He hands me the camera, the weight of it familiar and comforting, the cool metal warm from his touch. "I came to give you this, but when I saw the sunrise coming up, I just couldn't resist."

"If you say so," I tease, nudging him with my shoulder. He doesn't budge, his body somewhat stiff, his lanky frame lean but solid.

"Trust me," he says, his eyes sweeping over the landscape, the rocks now fully bathed in warm sunlight. "You'll be glad I took it."

I nod, feeling the weight of his gaze as his attention shifts toward me, his pale honey irises glistening in the morning light. A shadow moves over us and I look up to see a hawk flying overhead, its striped wings outstretched as it glides effortlessly in the wind. We watch as it drifts away, silence wrapping around us as it moves off into the distance. "Your turn," I say, sweeping my wind-battered hair to the side as I place the camera strap around my neck. Picking up the bulky device, I point it at him, adjusting the lens to focus on his face. I snap a photo, his angular features softened by the jagged nature of the terrain. "One thing about digital cameras, you have to replace the battery," I say, frowning as the LCD screen goes black. "I'm pretty sure it just died."

"Want me to go grab another battery?" Graham asks.

"No," I say, looking out at the canyon below us, the rocks and valleys stretching on for miles. "Not yet. Right now, I just want to see it... I've waited so long just to see it."

The sun ascends quickly, bearing down on us, the morning chill shifting to a warm, dry heat. I unzip the bulky coat from around my body, stretching my legs out, fresh air tickling my skin as it sizzles under the desert sun. Graham stares at my legs for a second too long before quickly glancing away, his cheeks flushed as he motions toward my coat. "Glad that kept you warm this morning," he says. "Even if it is a little big on you."

"It did," I say, his oversized jacket hanging loosely on my slim shoulders. "Sorry I didn't ask first, I was planning to be back by the time you woke up."

"It's fine," he says, shrugging his shoulders. "Don't want you getting hypothermia in the desert, that's just embarrassing."

I laugh, my joyful cries echoing through the canyon below us. I sit up a bit, attempting to remove his jacket, but Graham stops me, securing it back in place.

"It looks good on you," he says, his hands lingering on my shoulders, the weight of his palms pressing through the layers of fabric. Flickers of last night flash through my mind, a tangle of sweat and heat, and I flush in spite of myself, my vulnerability on full display. Even though he's the same old Graham, everything we were has changed, or perhaps we're simply becoming what we were always meant to be.

Both of us are silent for a long time, our bodies reaching toward one another, his pale brown eyes searching my face. He slides his hands down my arms, my skin prickling beneath the slow, methodical movement until he takes my hands in his, his thumb gently caressing the top of my fingers. "I wish you had been there this morning," he says, his voice smooth and intoxicating, each word its own rich melody. "Last night... I wasn't sure if it was real. Hard to tell when I've already dreamt about us so many times." I glance down at our intertwined fingers, unsure what to say, every stroke of his thumb sending shockwaves through my body. I feel like I'm on fire, the desert sun looming over us, heat building in my chest as I struggle to breathe. I look up at him and he's watching me, his expression serious. "I meant what I said, Avery," he whispers, his voice low but clear. "I meant every word."

I swallow, the sincerity in his eyes burning straight through me. "I know," I say.

"Do you?" he asks, his eyes scanning my face, his jaw is tight. If I didn't know him so well, I wouldn't realize how nervous he is right now, his emotions mostly hidden behind a mask of cool indifference.

I turn to face him head-on, my foot inadvertently kicking a few rocks toward the cliff's edge. They tumble over the side, the sound ricocheting off the canyon walls as I scoot closer to him, his warm scent filling what little space is left between us. "Yes, I do," I say, holding his gaze, pushing away whatever hesitation or fear I have left. "I meant what I said, too, Graham. For me, it's always been you... always."

Graham studies me for a moment, his eyes glowing like amber as he slowly leans in and kisses me. I sink into him, pressing myself into his chest, our bodies warm and fluid, a combustion engine of desire and heat. His kiss is warm and deliberate, dirt and sunscreen clinging to the edges of his lips, his touch so tender that I become light-headed, sighing into his mouth. He gently pulls away and wraps his arm around my shoulder, his cheek resting against my hair as he brings me in close. For the first time in years, I feel happy and whole, my heart overflowing as I lean into Graham, my love for him as rich and wild as the desert around us.

Little do I know, by the following morning, I'll be headed east and we will be all but over.

CHAPTER 1

No signal. Why is there still no signal? I hold my phone up, pacing anxiously around the wide, manicured lawn, hoping for the millionth time today that I'll finally get a few bars. But my phone is lifeless, staring back at me with no calls, no texts, the blank screen seemingly unbothered by my need for service.

I need a signal. I need to make sure she's okay.

I bite down on my lip, hard, attempting to ground myself, an exercise I know will be useless. *This is why I don't do travel jobs*, I think, cursing as I trip over a sprinkler head hidden in the grass. I can't focus on my work if I'm constantly worried about being unreachable.

I'm busy shuffling back and forth when Leah approaches from behind me, carrying two plates of food. One holds a hefty portion of chicken, green beans, and mashed potatoes; the other is a fairly large piece of chocolate cake. "Thought I'd grab you some dinner before the guests devour everything," she says, holding out the plates. "We're back on in ten minutes."

I frown, my stomach growling as I turn back to my phone. "I'm trying to get a signal," I say as I take a step away from her, balancing the device on my outstretched fingertips. "Do you have one on your phone?"

"Nope," she says, looking out at the vast sea of lush, green trees below us. "I'm not surprised, either. They said it would be a remote location, and this is *definitely* remote." We'd driven three hours to shoot a wedding at Sugar Maple Lodge, a sprawling contemporary cabin built deep in the Ozark Mountains. With breathtaking views along the cliffs of the Buffalo National River, we'd been working non-stop to capture this location from every angle, trudging around the property with the bridal party in tow.

I'm walking in circles, my arm shaking from exhaustion when Leah finally intervenes, reaching up to snatch the phone from my hand. "Okay boss, you're done," she says, tucking my phone into her back pocket. She points at a nearby retaining wall, my dinner sitting on top of the smooth, tan stones. "Go take a break and I'll keep trying." She spins on her heel and walks away, moving to another part of the yard before taking both of our phones out and continuing the search.

Feeling defeated but grateful, I walk toward the retaining wall, squirming as I sit on its hard surface, the stones sweltering after hours under the afternoon sun. I glance toward the wedding reception, a line of white pop-up tents shifting in the breeze, the soft sound of voices, music, and clinking cutlery drifting across the yard. I don't really feel like eating but I know that I should, the reception guaranteed to last at least a couple more hours. I look down at the two plates beside me, my eyes shifting back and forth, contemplating what to eat first.

"Screw it," I say, reaching for the chocolate cake. I break off a big piece and shove it in my mouth, the spongy filling and thick icing soothing my frazzled nerves. I take several more large bites until the tension in my shoulders subsides, my stress coming down to a manageable level. *Just a couple more hours*, I think as I take one last bite and set the plate aside. *She's okay, everything is going to be okay.*

***

By the time Leah and I start loading up the car, it's dusk, the stars emerging overhead as we break down our camera equipment and shove it into the trunk. I'm checking one of my lenses when Jillian, the wedding planner, approaches us from the party. She's wearing a sleek gray dress, her red hair silky and vibrant, even in low light. She's beaming as she walks up to me, pulling me in for an unsolicited hug, like usual. "I'm so thrilled you were able to make it today," she says, squeezing me once more for emphasis. She pulls away and I catch a strong whiff of her perfume, an expensive Italian brand she often wears to these events. "I mean, what a dream location! It just wouldn't have been the same without you."

"It is an incredible venue," I agree as I put the camera lens away. I really don't want to talk to her right now, but considering she hired me for this job, I figure I owe her a few words. Zipping up my camera bag, I turn to face her, forcing myself to smile. "I appreciate you having me."

"Oh, of course," she says, batting away my words. "You're my go-to photographer! I know it's not our normal gig in Branson or Springfield, but I just couldn't have done it without you. When I showed the bride and groom your work, they wanted you, too... cost be damned!"

I smile politely, shifting my weight as my patience starts to wear thin. I am anxious to get on the road, desperate to get back to cell service and civilization. “Well, I appreciate the recommendation,” I say. “It was a bit of an adventure getting up here, but I’m glad we could do it together.”

“Speaking of adventure,” Jillian says, her eyes flashing with excitement, “I have another wedding for you... something pretty big.”

“Oh yeah?” I say, tilting my head to the side. Working with Jillian always brought in a good paycheck, but lately she’d been booking some pretty high-end clients, couples with money to burn and very deep pockets.

“It’s my biggest client yet,” she whispers, excitement pouring off of her. “I had a wedding back in January and one of the guests liked it so much, she booked me to do her wedding, too! It’s in Aspen just before Christmas, *400 guests*! Can you believe it?!”

I try to match her enthusiasm, but my smile falters. “In Aspen?”

“I know, it’s just so exciting!” she squeals, her shiny hair swaying side to side as she bobs back and forth. “They have a huge budget, I get a whole *team* of people to help me manage the day, and the bride is just dying to meet you.”

“Me?” I say, my smile completely crumbling. I barely agreed to do this job, let alone a location that's easily a day or two away. “You told her I would do it?”

“Not exactly,” Jillian says. “I told her you don’t do travel work, but she is absolutely *obsessed* with your pictures. She offered to triple your rate, plus cover all travel expenses for you *and* Leah. I mean, I know it’s far but how could you not do it?! It’s such an incredible offer!” She grabs my hands and squeezes them, shaking me a bit as I stand there, completely dumbfounded. “It’s going to be so much fun - we can go skiing together while we’re there!”

I feel sick, partly from the job offer but also because I'm not halfway down the driveway by now. "Jillian, I can't go," I say.

Jillian laughs, unbothered by my response. "You weren't sure about doing this job, and look, you're here! It's such a great opportunity, and it's just a few days–"

"No," I say, turning away from her. I shut the trunk, my eyes catching Leah's as she finishes loading more gear into the backseat. There's an odd expression on her face, her mouth drawn downward in a look of concern and possibly pity. She finishes loading the gear and shuts the rear door, climbing into the front passenger seat without saying a word.

Frustration and guilt roll over me as I turn back toward Jillian. Even in the dying light, I can tell that I've hit a nerve, her generally sweet features twisted into an expression I can only assume is anger. I've never seen her truly upset before, so it's difficult to tell. "I'm sorry, I just... I can't," I mutter. "It's too far away, I'll be gone for too long."

She straightens, shaking off the rejection, her stiff shoulders loosening a bit as she works a smile back onto her face. "Listen," she says, "I get it. I know travel isn't part of our normal deal. I just wanted to include you, because they *really* do love your work. If the money isn't enough, I can counter with another offer, whatever makes you comfortable."

"It's not that," I say, shaking my head. I'm trying to keep my composure, but I can tell by her soothing tone that she thinks I'll cave, that she can talk me into this job, too.

"Well, just take some time to think about it," she says, her brilliant smile practically glowing in the dark. "You said you were looking for more work, so—"

"I don't want to think about it," I say, cutting her off. "I don't need to. There's nothing for me to consider, Jillian - the job simply isn't for me." I close my eyes for a moment, unable to look at her, my frustration matched only by my embarrassment. "Thank you for having me today, it was a lovely wedding. But I just can't and... I need to go." I turn around and beeline toward the driver's side door, shaking as I jump inside and slam it behind me.

Silence settles over the car as I sit frozen in the driver's seat, my clammy hands gripping tight to the steering wheel. I glance in the rearview mirror, noticing the sour look on Jillian's face as she turns and stomps away, her long hair swinging wildly behind her. I want to go after her, to apologize and make things right between us, but now is not the time. Instead, I put the key in the ignition, feeling my body exhale as the old car roars to life.

Leah is watching me, her brow scrunching together in concern. We've worked together for years, so she's aware I don't take travel jobs, she just doesn't know why. "You okay?" she asks, tilting her head to the side to look at me, her short, choppy haircut becoming more asymmetrical than it already is.

"Yeah," I reply, smiling weakly. I look at the horizon, the last bits of orange and yellow light grazing the evening sky. After a few moments, I reach for my seatbelt, buckling myself in as I put the car in reverse. "Let's go home," I say.

I maneuver the car out of the gravel parking lot before turning left onto the main road, the two of us winding down the mountain into the night. I crack my window a bit, cool air washing over me as Leah turns on the radio, a twangy, southern melody coming through the speakers. Already I feel lighter, calmer, my mind and body finally able to relax. After a few minutes, my phone starts buzzing in the cup holder, emails and texts slowly come through. *Finally*, I sigh. *A signal.*

"Can you send her a text?" I say, glancing over at Leah. She picks up my phone and types out a quick message. Within seconds, my phone pings and she picks it up again.

"She says to drive safe, that she'll see you soon," Leah says, tossing the phone back in the cup holder. She leans her seat back and closes her eyes, the soft rumble of her snoring overpowering the radio within minutes.

I settle into my seat, feeling the weight of the day slide off me as we make our way down the winding hill. *I'm on my way*, I think, looking out at the twinkling lights in the distance. *I'm coming.*

CHAPTER 2

I HURRY UP THE sidewalk, fumbling with my keys as I reach the front door. I quickly unlock the doorknob and the deadbolt before giving it a shove, my shoulder pressing into the worn wood. It doesn't move, doesn't even budge, the thick oak panel holding steady against the warm night.

Damn it, I think, pushing on it again. *She locked the sliding bolt.*

Adjusting the bags in my shoulder, I turn to walk to the back of the house when I hear movement from behind the door. The muffled jingle of a dog collar, the click-clack of heavy paws on the dining room floor, the sound of whining as Hank, our dog, catches my scent. He lets out a few menacing barks, and while I know that he's a complete marshmallow, I'm glad that he at least sounds intimidating to strangers.

After a few seconds, I hear the creak of our old sofa, followed by the sound of footsteps as someone makes their way toward the door. The interior bolt slides clear and the door swings open, the front porch flooding with soft, yellow light.

My mother, all five-foot four of her, is sporting her worn, turquoise slippers, a thin blanket draped over her shoulders. Her curly hair looks wild in the backlit doorway, a clear indication, other than her pajamas, that she'd been sleeping. Just the sight of her loosens something in me, my anxiety shifting from high alert to a dull roar. She yawns, smiling sleepily, then shuffles to one side to let me in, her cane thumping softly against the hardwood floor.

It's still odd for me to see her with a cane. My exuberant mother, who once loved to hike and attend dance classes; now she struggles to leave the house, her movements rickety and slow. Mostly I hate the cane because it's a reminder of how much pain she's in, how much her life has diminished over the last five years. She's always in good spirits and does her best to stay active in our community, but the sight of it simply makes me ache.

"Hi sweetie," she says, giving me a tender hug as I step inside. She smells like fresh jasmine and coconut, the heady fragrance rolling off of her slightly damp hair. Hank works his way between us, jumping and yelping, excited by my late arrival. "It's about time, Hank was just about to doze off. It's way past his bedtime."

"Is that so?" I say, bending down to give him some love. He smiles at me, pushing his head into my thighs, his fluffy tail happily swishing back and forth. I scratch his ears, his chin, all eighty pounds of him leaning into me as he basks in the one-on-one attention. "You wouldn't sleep on the job, would you, Hank?"

My mother closes the door behind me, securing the locks before returning to the couch. "You know better than anyone that he's less 'guard dog', more 'house cat'. Eating, sleeping, and lying around are what he does best." Hank, unaffected by her insult, nuzzles into me one last time before licking my hand and trotting after her. He goes straight toward his massive dog bed beneath the television, collapsing onto it with his full weight, the familiar thud rattling the nearby coffee table.

I chuckle, setting my bags down before following them into our living room. It's always been the heart of our home, a cozy space with blue floral curtains and wide windows, its floor-to-ceiling bookshelves filled with used paperbacks and garage sale trinkets. My mother lowers herself onto the couch, propping her leg up on a mound of plush pillows. She rubs her thigh a bit, and I know without asking that her leg is hurting her.

"So," she says, scooching over a bit so I can sit down beside her, "how was it? Did the old death trap make it up the mountain in one piece?

"Barely," I say, smiling. We've had the same beat-up sedan for over ten years now, and it's only lasted this long because we rarely take it out of town. "It definitely didn't enjoy the ride up, that's for sure. Honestly, I was afraid the engine would blow just driving up the foothills."

She laughs, adjusting her position on the couch. Her expression is warm but I can tell that today has been a rough day for her, her pain evident by the way she's carrying herself. Guilt ricochets through me, pinging against my ribs and landing squarely on my heart. *I should have been here*, I think, watching her as she adjusts herself once again. *I can't help her if I'm not here.*

Reaching for her injured leg, I massage her foot for a few minutes before working my way up her calf. I gently press into her scar tissue, manipulating the affected skin, loosening the layers of disfigured muscles and fascia. My mother stiffens, wincing as I rub the burnt tissue, my hands gentle but firm. After a couple of minutes, I return to massaging her foot and she relaxes, her head rolling sideways against the couch.

"Did you take any meds today?" I ask as I dig into the sole of her foot.

"A couple hours ago," she murmurs. She closes her eyes, her face peaceful as I move from one foot to the other.

"How about a bath?" I ask. "Or some pain cream?"

She smiles, but doesn't respond. After a while, she opens her eyes again, her body languid and relaxed. "So tell me about the lodge," she says, changing the subject. "Must have been a fun place to shoot."

"It was alright," I mutter. "I got some cool shots, and Jillian seemed happy until I pissed her off as we left."

"Jillian, really?" she says, her expression skeptical. "How? I thought that woman was joy incarnate."

"She offered me a job in Aspen and I turned it down," I say, reaching for her CBD cream. I take a big glob out of the jar and place it on her scar. "I mean, I barely agreed to do this wedding and it was in the state! I just don't get it, she knows by now that I don't do travel jobs."

My mother nods, watching me as I massage her leg. "You've worked together a long time, honey. I'm sure she just wanted to include you, bring you along for the ride."

"I get that, but I'm fine," I say, working the medicine into her leg. I press a little too hard and my mother twitches, a gentle reminder to slow down and watch what it is I'm doing. "I like the work I do here, I like my local clients. I don't need to travel halfway across the country for a job."

She studies me for a moment before looking away, reaching for her water on the coffee table. I catch a glimpse of her other scar, a deep laceration across her cheek, hidden strategically by a layered, messy bob. She prefers to tell new clients that it's from her most recent accident, but I know better. She had it the day she pulled me out of school, but I still don't know how it happened - only who's responsible. "I'm just saying, it could be fun," she says, taking a sip of her water. "Maybe it's time to spread your wings a little, go try some new things."

"I'm *fine*, Mom, " I say, pulling her pant leg down over her scar. I give her a warm smile, reassuring her that I'm happy with this decision. "I promise. Now, can we relax and watch some TV? I need to unwind from this ridiculously long drive."

"Fine by me," my mother says. She glances over at Hank, who's now fully sprawled out on his dog bed, snoring as his limp paws dangle in the air. "See... house cat."

***

We spend the next hour on the couch together, flipping through infomercials and old reruns. It's become a nightly ritual of sorts, the two of us chatting about actors and news events as my mother channel surfs, our feet smooshed together between the couch cushions. Even on warm summer nights, we like to drape a blanket over ourselves, huddling together in spite of the heat. She is my absolute favorite person, my God-given best friend. I don't know what life would look like for either of us if I weren't here by her side.

Around one o'clock, my mother yawns for the millionth time and slowly rises to her feet. "Alright," she says, bracing herself on the arm of the couch, "I'm exhausted. Good night, sweetie - get some sleep." She leans down and kisses me on the forehead before making her way down the hall, her fuzzy slippers scraping against the worn wooden floor. Hank, awakened by her movement, struggles to his feet, yawning as he stretches out his stiff muscles. He trods after her, bits of loose fur falling to the floor as he dutifully follows her down the hall.

I stare after them, wondering if she'll sleep through the night. I used to hear her thrashing back and forth sometimes, reliving old, painful memories. Now her nights are a series of interrupted dreams, the discomfort in her leg amplified by lying in one position for too long. Occasionally I wake up at night, the soft light of her bedside lamp peeking under my door, and I go to her, climbing into her bed as she reads or does crossword puzzles. I like to think that my presence brings her some kind of comfort, but I don't know that it does; maybe it just makes me feel better.

I flip through the channels for a few more minutes, then turn off the television. Climbing to my feet, I do a quick pass through the house, checking all the locks and windows before turning off the lights and heading to my room.

My room, like the rest of the house, is small, my full-sized bed tucked against the left-hand wall, a tiny wooden desk resting on another. Pictures from popular magazines are tacked up everywhere, stacked over one another like roofing shingles, unique photos I found interesting or inspiring. A narrow bookcase sits at the end of my bed, filled with photography books and old camera gear, discarded equipment that I still love but now rarely use. It seems like a lot of stuff for such a small space, but it's really only a fraction of my things. The rest of it was left behind when we moved here, when we started over.

Pulling on my rattiest pair of pajamas, I throw my hair into a messy bun as I take a seat at my desk, the ancient wooden chair creaking beneath my weight. Grabbing the laptop and camera out of my bag, I begin downloading today's images, backing them up on a hard drive before saving them to the cloud.

I study the pictures as they transfer over, a part of me truly mesmerized by the elaborate setting that Jillian created. She has improved so much over the years, her signature style transformed from clean aesthetics to unconventional yet elegant decor. We did an event last Christmas where she was asked to create a frozen *Alice in Wonderland,* and the resulting party was an overwhelming success. She got three more bookings out of it, and I was able to piggyback onto two of them as her event photographer.

As I look through the images, I wonder if she'll stay in Missouri or if she'll eventually move on, taking her talents with her. My heart aches a bit, knowing how rude I was toward her today. We've always worked well together, and the fact that she was willing to offer me a job of that caliber is nothing short of amazing. Still, I can't do these long distance jobs she's getting booked for, and the sooner she accepts that, the better.

I pick out a few exceptional photographs, including a breathtaking shot of the bride at sunset, and make a copy for editing. I work on the bridal photo for an hour or so, adjusting the contrast and color profiles, smoothing skin and removing blemishes. Fatigued and slightly delirious, I save it to the cloud then grab my phone, yawning as I lean back in my chair and open up social media.

I go to my business page, my account an impressive twenty thousand followers, even though I never tag other people in my work. Selecting the bride's photograph, I quickly list out my equipment and rattle off a few professional hashtags, then I scroll to the bottom and hit 'Submit'. I chew on my fingernails as it uploads, a surge of anxiety and dread rushing through me as the image appears on my page. Every time I post something, it terrifies me, my mind restless over who will see it, if my work will compromise our safety. As much as I love my career, I don't want my work to jeopardize us, to be the end of the cozy life we worked so hard to rebuild.

Pushing my fears aside, I navigate back to the home page and switch over to my personal account. Travel images flood my newsfeed, an endless loop of beautiful scenery, location recommendations, even resort and hotel deals. Places filled with adventure and promise, far away from the endless monotony of small town life.

I bop around for a while, each post a painful reminder of the life I wanted, of how small my world has become. Jealousy and pity well up inside of me, catching in my throat, and I quickly shake my head to keep myself from crying. I don't know if it's my exhaustion or Jillian's offer to work in Aspen, but tonight the sting of longing is deep, penetrating to my very core.

Frustrated, I click over to my personal profile, a collage of odd images that I've pieced together over the years. Random objects, obscured shots of my face, a memory box full of trinkets and treasures precious only to me. They don't really make any sense, but I enjoy looking at them. Like my professional work, they're little pieces of my soul out in the real world, hidden in plain sight.

I see the picture from our morning at the canyon, my arms spread wide, the background full of color and light. As I look at it, I can feel Graham sitting beside me, his lips soft and urgent, his rough hands trailing over my skin. I close my eyes, replaying this moment over and over again, his memory fulfilling a primal urge, a high I can't get any other way.

Scrolling to the bottom of the page, I click on one of my favorites posts, a close-up of an old Polaroid. It isn't obvious from the photograph, but it's the day that changed everything for us. Meeting Charles at the diner on our first day in town, and his famous fried peach pies.

I smile fondly at the photograph, then I turn off my phone and get ready for bed.

CHAPTER 3

Twelve years old, five days after "The Incident"

THE CAR IS SMOKING as we roll into town on our first day, the tired engine overheating after nine straight hours on the road. We had stopped frequently, Mom refilling the radiator with watered-down coolant until we eventually made it to our destination.

To be honest, we're in worse shape than the car at this point. We're both running on fumes, our clothes rumpled and dirty from sleeping in motel parking lots. More than anything, I'm scared, our lives uprooted overnight, everything I've known and loved gone in an instant.

My mom didn't have much of a plan when we left, just the car, a few baskets of clothes, and a sizable stash of cash. She did grab a few personal items for me, including my new camera, but I still haven't taken any pictures yet. The truth is, I can't bring myself to document the trip because it just doesn't feel real. So I hold it in my lap instead, cradling it in my sweatshirt like a baby.

My mom parks the car on the other side of the street, a block away from the diner. She checks her makeup in the mirror, her hand shaking as she applies a fresh coat of rose-colored lipstick. It's hard to look at her, to acknowledge the yellow bruises beneath her foundation, the still-puffy skin around her eye. Worst of all, her once-flawless face is now gnarled by a deep cut, slicing along her cheekbone toward her ear. It's impossible to hide but she cut her hair to conceal it, a last-ditch effort to keep people from asking questions.

After a quick once-over and a slight hair adjustment, she turns to me. "Okay," she says, giving me an anxious smile, the super glue on her cut bending and buckling. "Let's run it again. What's your name?"

"Avery Walters," I say.

"And what is mine?" she asks, her blue eyes piercing, her expression serious.

"Mom, or Penny, if someone asks."

"Good," she says. "And where are we from?"

"Cherry Creek, South Dakota."

"That's right," she says, nodding her head in agreement. She's trying to act normal but I can tell how nervous she is, her foot tapping incessantly on the floorboard below. "And if something isn't *right*, if we need to leave, what do we do?"

"We walk out of the restaurant and turn away from the car," I say matter-of-factly. "We'll circle back to it from a side street, making sure we aren't being followed."

"Good honey, that's good." She looks at the diner, then glances around us at the other buildings. There are several small businesses on this street, one butting up against the other, customers and employees running around behind strategically-lit window displays. An elderly couple strolls along the sidewalk, meandering past an athletic-looking woman who's talking on the phone while pushing a double-wide stroller. A few other patrons litter the street, but overall, it's pretty deserted.

My mother checks the time, only two minutes till 11 o'clock. "Okay," she says, turning toward me once again. "Are you ready?"

I look at the quiet street, taking it all in. This place is so different from Seattle, from everything I know my home to be. It's hard to imagine a life here; it's hard to imagine feeling safe. "Do you think they can help us?" I ask, looking up at her.

She gives me a half-hearted smile, her eyes glassy and tired. She ducks her head, squeezing her palms together as she takes a couple of deep breaths. I can't tell if she is panicking or praying. "I don't know," she says, looking up at me. "But we won't know the answer unless we go inside. We'll take it one step at a time, okay?"

I nod, the two of us holding hands for a second before we open our doors and jump out of the car. Once we're on the sidewalk, we crash back together, her arm wound tight around my shoulder, my Polaroid camera bouncing against my belly. As we get closer, my heart starts to race, the bright red awnings and bucket of fresh daisies near the door doing nothing to calm my nerves.

The diner is deafening as we step inside, the room buzzing with chatter and the sounds of a bustling kitchen. The smell of coffee and fried potatoes fills the air, and I'm instantly starving, my stomach so hungry it forgets how to growl. My mother is extremely tense, her body twitchy and rigid as a hostess approaches us.

"Table for two?" a waitress asks, grabbing a few laminated menus from the host stand. Her wrist is overflowing with colorful, handmade bracelets, and her Miranda Lambert t-shirt has a red-and-white checkered name tag on it that identifies her as *Tanya.*

My mom peeks around her into the dining area, checking out the other customers. "I'm looking for Donna, I'm supposed to meet her here at eleven."

The woman looks back and forth between me and my mother, taking in our frazzled state before giving us a warm smile. "Follow me," she says. She guides us through the busy restaurant, local patrons pausing their conversations as we pass, their curiosity obvious and unapologetic. It's unnerving, to say the least, and my mother's strong grip tells me that she doesn't like it, either. When we arrive at our booth, there's no one there, but the table is set with a pitcher of lemonade and a plate of what appears to be cookies. Setting our menus down, the woman smiles again as she motions for us to sit. "Take a look at the menu and let us know if you have any questions. There's some homemade pie here while you wait, it's fresh out of the oven."

I start to sit but my mother stops me, her fingernails digging into my arm. "We're just here to see Donna," she insists, keeping her voice low.

"I understand," the waitress says, her smile impossibly sweet. "Please, take a seat. Charles will be out in a minute, he had to step in the back to talk with a vendor."

"He?" my mom says, fear flickering across her face. Her eyes dart back and forth, scanning the kitchen and the front door before snapping back to the hostess.

"It's okay, darling," the woman says, her voice calm. "Just take a seat, he'll be right out."

We sit down on the squishy booth, my mother still clinging to me as she glances around the room. She looks scared, borderline feral even, her composure completely deteriorating. I'm staring at the plate in the middle of the table, the fresh smell of butter and pie crust filling my nostrils. "Mom, can I?" I ask, nodding toward the plate. We haven't eaten since yesterday, and I'm curious to see what this "pie" tastes like.

"I don't know," she says, her eyes on the front door. "Maybe this was a mistake."

A few moments later, a tall, gangly man exits the kitchen, his salt-and-pepper hair neatly combed, his striped long-sleeve shirt buttoned and pressed. He moves slowly around the counter, his body hunched over like he's ducked under one too many doorways. He approaches our table, squatting down on cracking knees to take a seat. He doesn't speak at first, just smiles at us, his face cheery and relaxed as my mother stares back apprehensively.

"You must be Penny and Avery," he says, his voice gravelly, like he's smoked one too many cigarettes. He looks down at the untouched food. "Have you tried the pie yet?" he asks. "It's my specialty, peach and lemon custard. Kind of a staple around here."

"No," my mother says, her mouth a thin line of frustration. She still has a hold of my arm, and I can tell by how tense she is that she wants to rip me out of this booth and leave. "We're here to meet Donna. Is she available, or do we need to come back at another time?"

"Please," he says, gesturing toward the dessert, "have a pie. I'll explain everything." My mother studies him, her eyes sharp and appraising. After a minute, she releases my arm and nods, giving me permission to try one. We each take a pastry, and as I cautiously bite into it, the gooey sweet flavor of peaches fills my mouth, followed by the tang of lemon. I eat faster, devouring the flaky dessert, the pie somehow sweeter and more fulfilling with every bite.

I quickly grab another but my mother refrains, carefully setting hers on a plate after only one bite. "Thank you," she says, gingerly dabbing at her mouth with a napkin. She sets the napkin on the table, her rosy lipstick bright against the white linen. "They're very good."

"I know," he says, still smiling. "They're a good ice breaker, helps people feel more comfortable."

"I see," she says, holding his gaze. "So, what's going on, who is Donna? We were told to meet her here."

"Donna is my wife," he says, leaning back in his seat, his palms folding over his belly. "And she's been dead for six years."

"Oh, I'm sorry," my mother says, shifting uncomfortably. She glances down at me, then back at Charles. "So, we aren't here to meet *her*, we're here to meet you."

"I'm afraid so," Charles says, his expression apologetic. "Before we met, Donna was married to a terrible man, absolutely brutal. After she left him, she wanted to help other women, so we signed up as an emergency housing contact, providing refuge for displaced families." He bows his head, his cheerful smile fading a bit. "After she died, I decided to carry on what she started. I kept her as the contact person, though - people can get a little spooked when they hear that I'm a man."

My mom nods, relaxing a bit more into her seat, the tension draining from her stiff limbs. "So you've been doing this for a long time, I take it?" she says.

"Yes," Charles replies, nodding. "For over twenty years now. We rehoused dozens of women and their kids, did a lot of good together. It was important to her, so it's important to me."

Tanya approaches our table, smiling sweetly at Charles before turning toward us. "So, what did you two decide for lunch?" she asks.

"Oh no, we're okay," my mother says, waving her hand. She looks down at her uneaten pastry, clearly hungry. "These are plenty, we can eat lunch later."

"Get them the special," Charles says, smiling at Tanya. "They'll love it." Tanya nods, her bracelets jingling as she scurries away toward the kitchen. "Okay, so here's the rundown," Charles says, his voice low but serious. "I've got a studio apartment set up for you, it's right down the street. Nothing fancy, but all the essentials are there. I've stocked it with a few groceries, too, just to get you started. Do you have any money?"

"A little," my mother says, her cheeks turning red as she looks down at the table.

"That's good," he says. "The rent is covered for three months, so that's taken care of. After that, you can decide what to do next. Get a different place, move to a new town - it's up to you."

"Do people usually move again so quickly?" my mother asks.

"Some do," Charles says. "They get nervous about staying in one place. I don't judge, and I don't tell people what to do. I just offer what I can so they can figure out their next move."

My mother nods, then reaches down to grab her pie. She takes a bite and exhales, a big sigh that seems to move through her whole body. "Thank you," she says quietly. "We have nowhere else to go, so... thank you."

Just then, a young girl close to my height enters the diner, marching right past the host stand. She goes up to the counter, climbing up on a high chair to peer into the back of the kitchen. "Mom, you back there?!" she yells, moving from side to side. She surveys the dining room, grinning as she spots Charles at our table. Climbing down from the chair, she walks over and plops down beside him, her blonde ponytail bobbing back and forth. "Hey Charles!" she says, her voice loud and chipper.

"Hey Rach," Charles replies, giving her a little nudge. "You making trouble for your mom?"

"Of course," she says, reaching across him to grab a pastry. She shoves it in her mouth, a glob of bright yellow custard dripping down her chin. "I'm going to Sarah's house, I just need to let her know." Rachel looks at the two of us, my mother and I silent on our side of the booth. "Hi, I'm Rachel! Have you tried Charles' pies?" She proudly thrusts the pastry toward me, as though she made it herself.

"Yeah," I say, glancing over at my mom. I've been quietly listening to my mother and Charles' conversation, so it's a bit jarring when she addresses me directly. "They're good."

"They're famous around here," she says, finishing off the gooey pastry. She's about to grab another when a different waitress approaches, a plump woman with hoop earrings and bright red lipstick.

"Rachel, those aren't for you," the woman says, her voice stern while her expression reads as slightly amused.

"Sorry mom," Rachel says. "I'm going to Sarah's, our school project is due. I'll be home later, okay?" Rachel gets up to leave, leaning over our table to steal one more pastry. Her mom swats her hand away before gently smacking her on the butt.

"Eat something decent at Sarah's house," the woman says, watching Rachel as she happily skips away. "No candy and popcorn like last time."

"Okay, Mom. Love you!" Rachel cries, giving her mother an angelic smile before turning to walk out the door.

I watch as Rachel moseys down the sidewalk, curious what grade she's in, when Tanya reappears with our food. Tender meatloaf and crispy roasted potatoes cover our plates, the smell so intoxicating that I instantly forget about the girl. Charles chuckles, leaning against the table as he rises to his feet. "Enjoy your lunch, relax for a bit. I'll come back when you're done so I can walk you over to your new apartment." With that, he walks around the counter and disappears into the kitchen.

My mom and I sit there for a moment, dumbfounded, trying to process everything that just happened, the gift we'd just been given by a total stranger. For the first time since we walked in, my mother smiles, a shocked laugh of relief and gratitude escaping out of her. She leans over, kissing me on the side of the head, then grabs her napkin and places it in her lap. "Ok, sweetie," she says, "let's eat."

Seeing the relief on her face, her first genuine smile in days, I reach down to pick up my camera. Leaning over the plate of pastries, I adjust my angle and snap a picture, the Polaroid slowly rolling out of the front. I grab it, giving it a good shake before setting the picture aside, the two of us smiling at one another as we pick up our forks and start to eat.

CHAPTER 4

GOLDEN RAYS OF SUNSHINE spill in through the open windows as I walk into the dining room the following morning. I was careful while getting ready not to make too much noise, hopeful that my mother was still asleep. Now that I'm in the dining room, I can see instantly that she's not. Like most Saturdays, she's sitting in our living room, drinking black coffee and reading a magazine while fighting Hank for a majority stake of the couch.

I walk up behind her, giving her a kiss on the cheek, a hint of jasmine still lingering on her skin as I pull away. "Good morning," I say. "I'm headed to the studio for a bit. What are you up to today?"

She flips through her magazine, landing on an article about at-home facials. "I'm not sure yet. I was thinking I might run over to see Susie."

"Again? Didn't you see her last weekend?"

My mother shrugs, flipping the page yet again. "Yeah, but I enjoy visiting her on the weekends. I basically just sit around, drinking iced tea while she works in her garden."

I laugh, knowing full well that Susie's "iced tea" is actually afternoon margaritas. I like that she has somewhere to go while I'm busy, though, someone around to look out for her. "Sounds like a perfect day. I'll text you, but I should be home by lunch." I give her a gentle squeeze, her soft, blonde hair tickling my cheek. Then I grab my bag and head for the door, smiling as I step out into the beautiful spring morning.

***

The main street of Selene is already bustling with locals; young moms running errands, couples and their children enjoying the local park, elderly folks meeting for brunch. I park on a side street and make my way toward Buttercrust, the town's main source of pizza, pasta, and endless gossip. It's not technically open yet, so I head to the back door, using my key to quietly slip inside.

I head straight for the rear stairwell, but as I'm rounding the corner, I nearly slam into Harold, the restaurant's assistant manager and head chef. He's carrying what appears to be a vat of tomato sauce, the red slurry sloshing back and forth. I'm beyond grateful that it didn't spill on me, or worse, splash into my camera bag.

"Good morning Harold!" I say cheerfully. "Looks like you're busy already."

He smiles, shifting the heavy pot in his hands, his chest and forehead glistening from the heat of the kitchen. "You know how it is, all prep work and no play. How about you? Working on a Saturday, too, huh?"

"Yeah, I'm on a deadline," I say, shifting my camera bag. "Had a big event with Jillian yesterday, so I need to start sorting through all the photos."

Harold moves around me toward the kitchen, the massive pot starting to get the best of him. "Okay, well have fun! If you're hungry later, just pop downstairs and I'll make you something."

"Thanks Harold, you're the best!" I shout as I climb the narrow steps to the second floor. The wood floorboards creak and moan, each carefully-placed step a familiar tone. When I get to the top of the stairs, I take my keys out and unlock the door, my mind already thumbing through my tasks for the day as I let myself inside.

My studio is a very small space, a single room with a tiny kitchenette and the smallest bathroom any reasonable person would ever want to use. I've made it a bit more chic with colorful furniture and some artsy photographs, but overall it's still a bit of a lemon. I don't care, though, because I love it; it's one of my favorite places in the world.

My mom and I had lived here when we first moved into town, this tiny, unconventional space both our sanctuary and our salvation. We'd spent our nights playing cards on our shared queen-sized mattress, eating leftovers that the kitchen gave us from downstairs. We lived here for more than six years before we finally moved out, partially because we couldn't afford anything else, but mostly because we didn't want to let it go.

I shut the door of the apartment, the smell of garlic and fresh bread thick in the air. Setting my bag down, I cross to the far wall, opening three large windows one-by-one, the cool breeze refreshing in the small, musty room. Sitting down at my desk, I pull out my laptop and start sorting through the photos from yesterday's event, losing myself in my work. I'm about to start tackling some social media posts for a local client when I hear a female voice float up through the open window. "You better not be hosting a party up there," the woman yells, her sarcastic words bouncing off the brick walls.

I walk to the middle window, kneeling down to poke my head out. Rachel, my closest friend, is standing on the sidewalk, her long blonde hair a rat's nest on top of her head. She's wearing a patchwork denim jacket and holding a large cup of coffee, her oversized vintage sunglasses shielding her face from the sun. It's hard to tell from her appearance whether she's had an all-nighter at the hospital or a bar. "Nah, no party," I say, smiling down at her. "Just a baby goat yoga class."

"Barnyard aerobics, sounds promising," she says, taking a swig of her drink. "Didn't think you had enough room up there for something like that."

"I don't," I laugh, shaking my head. "It's a work in progress."

Rachel nods, her messy bun swaying back and forth. "I'm headed to the square if you want to take a break. I've been itching to do some shopping that I can't afford."

I glance at the clock on my desk, surprised but not shocked to find that it's after 1 PM. "Okay, but I need to be home by three."

"Deal," Rachel says, chugging the rest of her coffee before tossing the paper cup in a nearby trash can. "Wrap things up and get your ass down here."

"Give me five minutes," I say, retreating back into the room. I close the windows and the blinds, throwing the studio into darkness. Pulling my phone out, I send a quick text to my mom. *Walking to the square with Rach, be home by 3. Need anything?*

I repack my bag, slinging it over my shoulder as I head for the door. As I'm locking up the studio, a text pings on my phone. *All good sweetie, have fun.*

Shoving my keys into my pocket, I turn and head down the stairs.

***

"Oh, these look cool," Rachel says, rummaging through a table of porcelain vases. We're currently at her favorite antique shop a few blocks from my studio, a dumping ground for spring cleaners or unwanted garage sale merchandise. She has a basket full of home decor pieces, each item featuring an interesting shape or texture.

I have no idea how she's going to arrange them together in her home, but I know the end result will be creative and trendy. She's constantly changing her aesthetic, which is something I love about her. One day she's wearing something chic and sophisticated, the next she has a relaxed, boho farmer vibe. She is completely unpredictable, a breath of fresh air in our quiet little town.

I pick up a set of glass coasters, the silver trim catching the light. "What about these?" I ask.

Rachel studies them before giving me a disapproving look. "Those are boring," she says flatly. "Come on, Avery, you're an artist! Look for something bold, quirky, different."

"They are different," I say, putting them back on the shelf next to me. "They're vintage."

"Vintage doesn't mean interesting," Rachel says. She picks up a simple, white vase, frowning as she turns it over in her hands. "For example, this is your typical milk glass vase, I've seen dozens if not hundreds of them. Sure, it's pretty, but we're looking for something unique."

"I'm not looking for anything," I point out. "I have plenty of stuff at home, more than I know what to do with. I don't need flashy, fancy things - practical is fine by me."

Rachel rolls her eyes as she continues to pick her way through the antiques. "Well, I think it's time you shake things up a bit," she says as she leans down to place her basket on the floor. I can tell by her expression that she's up to something, that this shopping trip is about more than vintage home decor. "Speaking of shaking things up, do you remember those pictures you showed me about a month ago? The ones you took at The Grand Canyon?"

"Yeah?" I say, thrown off by her question. I'd never really talked to her about what happened on that trip, but I'd recently sent her some of the final edits of my photographs. They were pictures I took on my last day there, fractured light streaming through an afternoon mist, the smooth sandstone glowing orange and purple. I'd spent years editing this work, perfecting the colors and tones; to this day, I still consider it some of my best work.

"Well, you know how much I loved those pictures," she says, tripping over her words, a nervousness to her voice that isn't like her. "Anyway, I just thought that they deserved to be celebrated, so..." She reaches into her purse and pulls a large, white envelope, a noticeable crease running through the middle of it. "I submitted them," she says, handing the envelope to me, her green eyes locked on my face as she awaits my reaction.

I look down at the envelope, my body going still when I notice "The Ashford Institute" in the upper left-hand corner, its name embossed in silver. In the middle of the envelope is my name, the letters inky black against the crisp, white paper. I run my fingers over it, every ounce of air sucked out of my lungs. "You sent them in?" I ask, my mind spinning. The Ashford Institute holds a massive photography competition every year, a prestigious event for the best photographers in the world. We had talked about it many times, but I'd never dared to send in my work.

"I did," she says gently, sensing the panic in my voice. "You're *in*, Avery. One of your pictures was chosen as a finalist for 'Photo of the Year.'" She turns the envelope over and pulls out the bunch of papers, a thick stack of informational content with my congratulatory letter resting on top. "You're in the running for the biggest prize of fifty thousand dollars!"

I look down, taking it all in, the papers from the packet a blur in front of me. I run my hand through my hair, unable to think, unable to breathe. "I don't understand," I whisper, shaking my head.

"It's two weeks from now in Miami, right before Cinco de Mayo. And..." Rachel digs into her purse again, pulling out a smaller envelope, this one with an airplane logo on the side. "I'm going with you! We're gonna have so much fun, it'll be like a girls' trip!"

I look at her, completely stunned. Not by the trip, necessarily, but by the fact that she still has no idea what she's done. "Wait, you bought us plane tickets, too?"

"Well, yeah!" Rachel cries. "You talk about this competition every year, of course I'm going to be there with you! You've watched every presentation, taken all their online workshops. I just know you're gonna love it! Plus, it's a huge prize! You could use it for your mom's treatments." She stands back, beaming, her smile working overtime to convince me this is a good idea.

I close my eyes, breathing deep, my hand gripping the table beside me for support. My anxiety is rising fast, blood and heat rushing to my face, but I'm trying my best to stay calm. When I look at her again, her smile is faltering, the enthusiasm draining from her face. "You know I can't go," I say quietly, hoping that I don't have to elaborate further.

Rachel studies me, her broken smile morphing into a frown. "Avery, you have to go. It's a well-respected competition in your field that people would kill to be a part of. You can do this."

"But there will be vloggers, press, live panels," I say, shaking my head. "It isn't safe."

Rachel shoves the paperwork under her arm, grabbing my hands and placing them between her own. "Look, I know I've pushed you to do some things in the past that you didn't want to do, but this isn't about me. This is about you, Avery, you *deserve* to be a part of this competition." She holds my gaze, her expression serious. "Plus, I could really use some time away with my best friend. I think this trip could be good for both of us, get us out of here for a little while."

I stare at her, speechless, my chest raw and heavy. Rachel has always been understanding about my reluctance to travel, but things came to a head two years ago on her 21st birthday. Rachel was planning a big trip to Atlantic City and I was adamant that I couldn't come. We had a huge, blowout fight, and to salvage our friendship, to explain to my best friend why I couldn't be there, I told her the truth about my past. Not everything, not any of the details, just enough for her to understand.

However, it's clear from this conversation that she doesn't understand. She doesn't get that my reaction isn't anger or concern over my career; it's fear. Fear that this competition could uproot our lives, fear of undoing everything we've already been through. Fear of him finding us and having to start all over again.

Rachel takes the plane tickets and shoves them back in her purse. She gathers the rest of the paperwork, tucking it back in the envelope before handing it to me. "Just think about it," she says. "Your new baby goat yoga business can wait."

CHAPTER 5

My drive home is a blur, a sequence of familiar streets and predictable turns. Rachel and I had shopped a bit longer in relative silence, her excitement about the announcement extinguished by my inability to celebrate it. A part of me wanted to scream, to dance and cheer and celebrate this achievement, but I couldn't. All I could think about as I wandered through the aisles of discarded artifacts was my mother.

I pull up to the stop sign on our corner, my head throbbing, my fingers itching as anxiety pulses through my veins. I start to creep forward until a horn blares on my right, snapping me out of my reverie. I slam on my brakes just as a silver minivan rolls through the intersection in front of me. "Sorry!" I cry, waving my hand at the driver, apologizing for my poor driving skills. The man gives me a dirty look and drives on, speeding up the street as my lower lip starts to quiver.

I breathe in, leaning back against the upholstered seat. Why would Rachel do this without asking me, why would she even consider it? It's baffling to me that she somehow thought this was a good idea, that she thought I would be happy. What's even more frustrating is that I know deep down that she had good intentions. I've been talking about this competition for years, going on and on about the sponsors and the huge cash prizes. Winning it would certainly go a long way towards my mother's recovery, especially with our insurance cutting off her laser therapy treatments after only three sessions.

I open my eyes and notice an elderly woman staring at me from her lawn, her puzzled expression mostly hidden by a large sun hat. It takes me a moment to realize that she's staring because I'm practically parked in the middle of the intersection, my car idling for more than a minute. I straighten, checking my side mirrors before driving on. I wave at her as I pass but she turns away from me, bending down to trim an overgrown rose bush.

When I arrive home, I park the car and stumble toward the house, my mind a sea of jumbled thoughts. Reaching into my bag, I take my phone out and attempt to call my mother. It rings and rings, the phone pressing into my ear as I unlock the door and step inside. Hank clocks my entrance but he doesn't get up, his head barely rising as he remains curled up on his dog bed. "Some guard dog," I say, shutting the door and locking it behind me.

My call goes to voicemail. No answer. I try again, letting it ring through, but she still doesn't pick up. I open my messages and send her a quick text. *Call me back*, I say, not alerting her yet to the problem at hand.

I look around the empty house, the tranquil setting making me anxious, the silence grating on my nerves. It's too quiet, too peaceful for how upset I am, for how uneasy I feel. I double over, grasping one of the dining room chairs, the tension behind my eyes so excruciating it feels like my head is about to explode. Taking a deep breath, I force myself to calm down. *It's not that bad,* I say. *You can figure this out, you can fix this.*

I stand up and walk to my room, throwing my bag down on the bed and pulling out my computer. I turn it on, chewing on my thumbnail as it comes to life. Opening my web browser, I click on a folder labeled "PHOTOGRAPHY" and scroll down till I find what I'm looking for. I click on the link, holding my breath as the website starts to load.

The Ashford Institute website pops up in front of me, its sleek layout and elegant imagery representing one of the most respected artistry foundations in the world. I scroll down the page, my heart racing as soon as I see the link: The Ashford Institute International Photography Awards. I click on it, hoping for anonymity, for my work to be displayed subtly behind the other nominees. I realize pretty quickly that that isn't the case.

My submission appears boldly near the top of the page, sandwiched between the other nine finalists. Below the image, my name appears in all caps, the words *AVERY WALTERS* jumping off the page. I click on my name and a biography appears, images of my work filling the screen. Most of the photos are shots from my website; luckily there is no profile picture, just a copy of my logo in the frame where my photo ought to be

I stare at the biography in horror, my blood pressure rising, every fiber of my being screaming for me to panic. This level of exposure is my absolute worst nightmare. Although none of the images are outwardly recognizable, they wouldn't be impossible to identify. If someone *really* wanted to, they could track me down - they could find us.

I click on my submission photo, longing and sadness piercing through me as the ethereal image fills the screen. The photograph had happened by accident, the result of Graham and I getting caught in an afternoon squall. I can still feel the rain soaking through my clothes, Graham's arms wrapped tight around my waist, his warm breath on my neck as I steady myself and take the shot. It's so real and vivid in my mind, as vibrant as the colors in the picture. But I never meant for these photos to be seen, especially by so many people. They were only meant for me, because I wanted to remember; I wanted to keep this moment alive, to pretend that it still meant something.

Grief crashes through me, the past and the present mingling into a cocktail of emotions I cannot bear. Tossing my computer aside, I lean forward and put my head between my knees, breathing deep as acid rises from the pit of my stomach. I want to scream or cry, just to get the emotions out, to feel some kind of relief. Instead, I sit alone in my empty room, trembling in fear as the silent house pushes in on me from all sides.

I don't know what to do, how I can possibly fix this. My work and my life have just been made very public, and there's no way to keep people from digging deeper or asking too many questions.

***

The room is dark by the time my mom pulls into the driveway, her headlights flashing through the window. I hear her key in the lock, the sound of Hank's frantic whining as she opens the door and steps inside. She calls out to me, her cane thumping against the wood floor as she wanders through the house. I lie on my bed, staring up at the ceiling, debating on the best way to break the news.

She knocks once and opens the door, peeking her head inside. "Avery? Are you in here?" she says, flicking on the overhead light. I shield my eyes, the sudden glare from above making my head throb. My mother pauses, noticing my fragile state, her brow creasing with concern. "What is it?" she asks, hovering near the door, unsure whether or not to come in.

I glance at her, swallowing hard. I motion toward my computer, which is now plugged in on my desk. "Take a look," I say as I wipe at my blotchy, tear-stained face.

She hesitates for a minute before hobbling toward my desk and taking a seat. She hits 'ENTER' and the computer screen lights up, revealing the website and my bio. She looks over it for a few seconds before turning to me, her eyes bright with excitement. "You got in?" she says, her voice bordering on ecstatic.

I sit up on my elbow, realizing that this news isn't a shock to her. "You knew about this?" I ask.

She nods, looking back at the computer. "Rachel told me about the contest a while ago. She said you were a shoo-in, that she wanted to submit you." My mom shakes her head, a stunned laugh rising out of her. "I just didn't know she actually went through with it."

"Well, she did," I say pointedly. "And now I'm plastered across the front page of the biggest photography contest in the country." I roll onto my back, closing my eyes as blood pulses through my temples. The room feels too hot, my skin clammy and itchy beneath my clothes.

My mother watches me for a moment before turning back to the computer. She scrolls through my bio, examining the photograph that Rachel sent in. A small smile creeps across her face, the tiny lines around her eyes deepening. "This is beautiful, honey. When did you take it?"

I don't look at her, afraid that she'll acknowledge my pain, that I'll break down all over again. "A few years ago," I say. "At the Grand Canyon."

She nods, then stands and walks over to my bed. She sits down next to me, her cool hand resting on my leg. "You should go," she says, her voice steady. "You deserve to go."

"Mom, I can't. It's a huge event, there will be press and social media–"

"I know," she says, her voice calm. She squeezes my leg, looking at me with conviction. "Go."

I gape at her, my eyes wide and fearful. I understand what she's saying to me and I shake my head in protest. "It's not safe, someone might recognize me. I look just like you, other than my hair."

"And your eyes," she says, brushing a lock of hair away from my face, her expression sad as her fingers lightly graze my cheek. There's an intimacy between us that's hard to describe, a shared history that no one else could understand. She takes my hand, squeezing it gently. "You need to do this, Avery. I need you to go. Do it for me, please."

She kisses me on the temple, her fresh jasmine scent folding around me. Then she stands up and walks out of the room.

CHAPTER 6

Eight years old, four years before "The Incident"

The gentle twang of melancholy guitar fills our kitchen as my father stands in front of the stove, a steady stream of Johnny Cash and Hank Williams echoing through the quiet house. It's become a Sunday tradition of sorts, my mother and I waking to the smell of coffee and sizzling bacon, the three of us a happy-groggy after a Saturday night of movies and popcorn in the family room. I sit at the counter, my knees tucked under me as I perch on one of the high chairs, scribbling in an old coloring book. I peek over at my dad, giggling as he dances around the kitchen, his grease-stained apron reading "World's Okayest Cook".

"My Annabean, my country girl, she likes to dance and spin and twirl," he sings, shimmying side-to-side on the tile floor, his spatula doubling as a microphone in between flipping pancakes. Walking over to the counter, he tosses a fresh pancake on top of an already impressive stack, grinning as he reaches out with the spatula to playfully poke me in the ribs.

"Daddy, stop it!" I cry, laughing as he continues to tickle me.

"Oh, I'm sorry!" he says, pretending to be remorseful. "I swear, there was a spider on your shirt!" He walks over to what's left of the pancake batter, tapping the spatula against the side of the bowl. "Maybe I'll just throw it in here, good source of protein."

I shriek, covering my face with my hands as he stirs the bowl, a low chuckle rumbling out of him as I howl in protest. I always enjoy Sunday mornings with my father, blissful moments when it's just the two of us, him typically messing with me for sport. I toss a crayon at him, the waxy pencil bouncing off his apron and falling to the floor with a thud. "That's gross, don't do that!"

After a couple good stirs, he pops the spoon in his mouth, his lips pressed tightly together as he pulls it out, the spoon completely clean. "Tastes good to me," he says, smacking his lips. "What do you think, Annabean?" He moves closer, dipping the spoon in the bowl once more before sticking it in my face.

"Ew, no!" I scream, shoving his arm away. "No spiders for breakfast!"

"You're missing out," he replies, licking the spoon one last time before tossing it in the sink. He winks at me as he starts cooking again, each of us clearly enjoying his silly antics.

My mother strolls into the kitchen, the belt of her silky blue robe tied tight around her slim figure, her blonde hair a mess of tangled curls. Even fresh out of bed, she's one of the most beautiful women most people will ever see in person. "Good morning," she says, her eyes half-closed, a sleepy smile on her face as she walks over and kisses me on the head.

"Good morning, love," my dad says, kissing her on the cheek as he hands her a fresh cup of coffee. I watch as she reaches up to caress his face, playfully scratching at his unruly beard. She goes to stand next to him as he cooks, sipping her coffee while he drapes his arm around her, his hand resting on her hip. I love seeing them together, their interactions always the same, their love and tenderness never wavering. My dad kisses her again and I look away, concentrating on my coloring book, the current page nearly complete.

My dad finishes up the last of the cooking, untying his apron as he turns off the stove. "Okay gang, we're good to go," he says, hanging his apron on the side of the fridge. Scrambling down from my chair, I skip around the counter, waiting in earnest as he grabs the stack of pancakes and sets it in my hands. "Now be careful with those, Annabean. You've got the main course!" he says, slowly letting go of the plate.

"It's Annabelle, Dad," I say, peeking around the pancakes to give him an exaggerated scowl. I know my comment won't deter him; he calls me Annabean every chance he gets.

"Oh yes, that's right," he says, smiling as he gathers up the plates and silverware. "Lead the way, kiddo."

My mother steps aside as I hurry into the dining room, shuffling over the sunlit wooden floors, the southern-facing windows painting the faux vintage wallpaper a yellow-gold. I set the pancakes on the table and climb into my seat, waiting patiently as my father arranges our place settings and my mother pours fresh orange juice, the glass pitcher casting prisms of light onto the white tablecloth. We dig in, our mouths full and our hearts happy as we eat breakfast together as a family. "Well, what's the plan for today?" my dad asks, pouring a generous amount of syrup onto a pancake. "Any errands or playdates? Or are we just staying home today?"

"I don't know," I say, shrugging as I shovel a piece of bacon into my mouth. I turn to look at my mother, who simply shakes her head, holding a napkin to her lips as she chews.

"No plans," my mother grumbles, chewing her food a bit more before she swallows. She smiles at my father before turning back to me, her beautiful hair backlit by the morning sun. "Is there anything you want to do today, sweetie?"

"Not really," I say. I glance around the room, trying to think of something we haven't done in a while. "Maybe play some cards later?"

"You read my mind," my father says, his eyes lightly crinkling as he smiles, steam drifting in front of his face as he takes a sip of coffee.

We spend most of the day in our living room, reading story books and magazines, playing rounds of Slap Jack and UNO as a family. My father constantly cheats, grinning from ear to ear as he slips me cards under the table, his laugh booming through the house every time my mother calls him out. My father and I read *National Geographic* together from his vast collection, the two of us planning elaborate, implausible vacations, trips around the globe where we ride orcas or ski down Mount Kilimanjaro. By the evening, we're all exhausted, the three of us lazily watching reruns on the television. My father sips on a tall glass of whiskey, his arm cradling my mother as she burrows in next to him on the couch. I lay sprawling on the floor in front of them, relaxing on a makeshift bed of blankets as my dad intermittently nudges me with his foot. I roll away from him, laughing like a loon, an endless game of cat and mouse that I never get tired of playing.

By eight o'clock my mother is ushering us to bed, guiding my father off the couch and sending him down the hallway to their room. Rushing past him to my own room, I quickly throw on my pajamas before popping into the bathroom to brush my teeth. My mother comes in as I'm finishing up, her hair tied back into a loose braid, her newly-lotioned skin supple and smooth. She brushes my hair then walks me to my room, the scent of coconut drifting over me as she tucks me into bed. "Goodnight sweetie," she says, pulling the blankets up beneath my chin. She kisses me on the forehead then glides out of the room, her silky blue robe flowing gracefully around her feet.

My father pops his head in, wearing an old, ratty pair of pajamas, his movements slow and sluggish as he walks over to sit on the edge of my bed. "Goodnight, baby girl," he says, kissing me on the cheek, the smoky, sweet scent of liquor lingering on his breath. "Dream big."

I roll onto my side, smiling into my pillow as I fall asleep, the easy dreams of a little girl who has no idea what's coming. In just a few short years, the facade will begin to crack, the joy and laughter and cozy memories falling away, our happy life together shattering on impact.

CHAPTER 7

We spent the rest of the weekend lying around the house, ordering Chinese food and playing board games. I find myself watching my mother intently, waiting for her to panic like I did, but she's unphased, her mood cheerful all day Sunday. I, however, am not cheerful. All I can think about is the contest, how reckless it is for us, nervousness festering beneath my skin like a splinter. I try to talk to her about it, to make a case for staying home, but she dismisses my concerns, adamant that I should attend.

As we're leaving the house on Monday morning, my mother in a rush to meet a new client, she stops abruptly in the driveway, spinning around to face me. "Don't worry about the contest," she says, reaching out to squeeze my arm. "Everything will work itself out, you'll see." She opens her car door and climbs inside, waving as she starts the engine and backs out of the driveway.

I hop into the sedan, silence wrapping around me as I settle into my seat. I sit there for a couple of minutes, contemplating what to do. Finally, I reach into my bag and pull out the big, white envelope. Rummaging through it to find my acceptance letter, I get out my phone and dial the 1-800 number at the bottom of the page, my heart racing as it starts to ring.

"Hello, Ashford Institute," a man says into the phone, his tone way too cheery for a Monday.

"Hi, my name is Avery Walters. I'm a finalist for the International Photography Awards."

"Oh, hello Avery! Congratulations, it's an honor to receive your work," he says.

"Thank you," I say, pausing to consider my words. "I was wondering, can you walk me through the conference, explain to me how it works? All this paperwork is a bit confusing."

"Of course, happy to help," he replies, his happy voice singing through the phone. "The conference officially starts on Friday, with finalist introductions and a showcase of your individual work. There will be a launch party that night, which is usually a big event, followed by a judges' critique on Saturday, as well as a 'meet-and-greet' with fans. Then, Sunday morning, the official winners will be announced."

"Uh huh," I say, mulling over the information. "And will it be broadcast this year?"

"Yes, of course. We have several new sponsors, so this will be our biggest year yet!"

I frown, disappointed by the exciting news. "I see. And, what if I'm unable to attend? Would my work still be considered?"

There's a pause on the other end of the line, my question probably not one that he anticipated. "Unfortunately, no. You did agree upon submission that someone would be in attendance to represent your work, in the event that you were chosen. We need you or someone representing you to be there."

I sigh, leaning against the door, my forehead pressing into the window. "Okay, so if there's no one there to represent me..."

"... then we will have to withdraw your entry," he says, completing my sentence for me.

I stare out the window, looking at the freshly manicured lawns of my neighborhood, at the dazzling blue sky. As much as I know I need to do it, giving up this opportunity feels like I'm smashing my camera on the sidewalk. Something I want and love being destroyed, tossed away, and I'm the one doing it. The last time I did that, it damn near killed me.

The man, sensing my hesitation, finally speaks up. "Look, if you aren't able to attend, we understand. But please let us know by this Friday at the latest. We would hate to lose your work, but this is a big event - we need to keep the train moving."

"I understand," I say. "Thank you." I hang up and fall back against the seat, frustration and sorrow rolling over me like the morning breeze.

***

"You are *not* backing out," Rachel says, her face scrunched up so tight it looks like she just ate an entire lemon.

We're sitting in her living room, me crammed into her couch between her cat and a huge mound of unfolded laundry. She's fresh off another night shift, her scrubs already replaced with a baggy t-shirt and a pair of boxer shorts. Her blonde hair is ratty and dirty, and she's clearly in need of a cut-and-color. I'd brought her over a cup of coffee to butter her up, to talk this thing through with her, but she isn't listening to anything I have to say.

"Come on Rach, you know I can't do this," I say, scratching the top of her cat's head. "It's too risky. There's way too much press, too much exposure."

"What does your mom say?" she asks, folding her arms over her braless chest.

"She's on the fence," I reply, taking a quick swig of my drink. I try my best to hide my face; Rachel can always tell when I'm lying. "She wants us to be safe," I say, my second statement at least half true.

"You *are* safe," Rachel says, throwing her hands in the air. "You've lived here over a decade now, no one is coming to find you."

"You don't know that," I say, balking at her statement. It's honestly a fair assertion, even though I'm not going to admit that. "The point is, this is a *huge* event. It's going to be all over the internet *and* local news outlets will be there. It'll be broadcast everywhere, someone could easily recognize me."

"It's a photography competition, not the Grammys," Rachel says defiantly, leaning back in her chair. "Do you honestly think anyone even cares to find you at this point?"

I look away, unsure how to answer that question. By now I'm just frustrated and upset that no one seems to care about our safety but me. "I don't know, okay? But I can't be there, it's just too much." I pause, shifting in my seat. "There is one alternative, though. One way we can make this work."

Rachel leans forward in her seat, her face brightening. "Okay, what is it?"

"You attend the contest for me," I say, watching her as the offer sinks in. "If I win anything, I'll split the prize with you, fifty-fifty."

Rachel sits back in her chair, her face a look of pure shock. Then something in her shifts, her features going dark, her jaw locking into place. "No," she says, her tone almost hostile.

"No?" I say, honestly surprised by her response. "You've already booked the plane tickets *and* our hotel room. I'll even pay you back for them, if you want. You can take Daniel, turn it into a mini vacation with a cash prize at the end."

Rachel glares at me, my words somehow angering her more. "I said no, Avery."

"Why?" I say, shaking my head. "Give me one good reason."

She opens her mouth then closes it again, taking a deep breath before she finally speaks. "Because this is about you, Avery. It's your work, *you* should be the one taking credit for it, not me. You can withdraw if you want to, but I am not going to accept this award for you." She stands up, swiping her coffee off the side table. "I've got a lot to do today, I should probably get to it." With that, she storms off, leaving me dumbfounded on her messy couch, her fluffy cat purring happily in my lap, oblivious to our conversation.

CHAPTER 8

On Thursday night, after a few days of awkward silence, I invite Rachel over to the house. She shows up early, a bottle of wine stowed in her purse, her expression friendly but guarded. She takes a seat on our couch, pouring the lukewarm chardonnay into wine glasses, my mother's famous bundt cake sitting in the middle of the coffee table. I find it kind of funny that they're acting like this is some kind of girls' night, like I didn't bring Rachel over here for a serious conversation. It makes me wonder, since they know me so well, if they already know what I'm about to say.

I'd spent the last few days thinking about the contest, obsessing over Friday's deadline. Everytime I'd start to dial The Ashford Institute, I'd hang up the call, unable to give up my spot. The truth is, I want to do this; I've wanted to attend this conference for years. With my mother's support and Rachel by my side, I realized that not only will this be good for my career, it might actually be really fun.

I pace back and forth in front of the coffee table, waiting for my mother to sit and get comfortable. Hank watches me from his spot on the floor, displeased by my constant movement. "Thanks for coming over," I say, forcing myself to stand still as I address Rachel directly.

"I'm glad you called," she says, smiling. "I really needed someone to drink this wine with." She picks up her glass and swirls the wine before taking a generous sip.

I laugh, grateful that we're engaging in some light banter. "I've thought a lot about what you said, about how I should be the one to represent my work. So, after a *ton* of consideration, I've decided to compete in the competition."

Rachel jumps up, her wine sloshing out of the glass. It lands mostly on the rug but some of it hits Hank, who bolts upright in surprise. He licks his damp fur then recoils, unimpressed by the cheap chardonnay. "Oh shit, this is incredible!" Rachel cries. "Miami, here we come!"

My mother laughs, rubbing Hank's ears. "Congratulations honey, I'm so happy for you. This is exciting news!"

"Thanks," I say, blushing a little. I'm relieved to see my mother so happy, her face not showing an ounce of fear or regret. "But, I do have some ground rules," I say, glancing back and forth between the two of them.

Rachel sits back down, reaching for the wine bottle to refill her glass. "Okay, what are the ground rules?"

"First of all," I say, "you can't post about this trip. Like at all. It'll be like it never happened."

Rachel's face immediately falls. "I can't take any pictures?" she asks.

"No, you can take pictures," I clarify. "You just can't post them on social media. If anyone recognizes me, I don't want them finding you online and tracing us back to this town."

Rachel studies me for a minute, thinking. "If someone recognizes you, they'll just trace you back here through your work," she says.

"Maybe," I agree, "but it won't be easy. My online portfolio doesn't reference any of the local businesses I work for. It's mostly generic photos - product photography, commercial shoots, stuff like that. Plus, people can't tag me in anything. But *you* are connected to this town, to me and to my mom." I pause, taking a deep breath. "If we do this, you can't post about it. Also, I would prefer if you used a fake name while we're there, just to be safe."

Rachel frowns, turning her wine glass in her hand. "I don't think I'm going to be able to do that one, babe. I'm all about moving in the shadows, but I'm going to end up forgetting my own name... especially if I'm drunk."

I laugh, shaking my head as I reach for my wine glass. "Okay, fine. But no social media and no last names - just Rachel." I take a sip of my drink, the crisp sweetness smoothing out my rough edges. Next, I turn to face my mom. "The other rule is, you can't stay here alone while I'm gone. Knowing you're here by yourself will be way too stressful." My mom reaches for my hand, squeezing it like she always does. "You can stay with Susie for a few days or she can come over here, whatever works best for the two of you. I'm also going to get you a smart watch, so you can easily call someone if there's a real emergency."

My mother nods, the scar on her cheek bobbing in and out of view as her hair sways back and forth. "Of course, sweetie, I can do that. If it means you'll go, I'll do it."

I nod, smiling as the pieces start falling into place. "We need to check in with each other every morning and every night, and text a bit throughout the day. I know we already do that, but it will help me to not worry so much."

"That's hard to imagine," Rachel teases, raising her brows as she drinks more of her wine.

I flash her a light-hearted scowl, then continue. "Lastly, I need to look less like a carbon-copy of you, Mom. There will be photos and online panels, things I can't control. So, I think the best way not to be recognized is to really change up my look, starting from the ground up."

"How are you going to accomplish that?" my mother asks.

"A haircut," I say, "and a completely different color. Different makeup, big sunglasses, new clothes - whatever it takes. I still want to blend in, though, so we'll have to figure it out."

"Wow, you're going full-on spy mode," Rachel says. "Shall we call you Carmen and get you a big red hat?"

"Maybe on the next trip," I say. "This is a full undercover operation. I am going for the prize money and the experience, not the publicity."

"And for a kick-ass trip with your best friend," Rachel adds, raising her glass.

I laugh, smiling at her. "Yes, that too," I say. At this point, it feels like a pretty solid plan; I just hope I'm not forgetting anything.

My mom raises her wine glass as well, saluting me. "Congratulations Avery," she says, "you deserve this." We all clink glasses, sipping on wine as we relax into our respective seats, the serious part of the night over. Rachel's eyes rake over me, a mischievous grin creeping across her face.

"What?" I ask, curious what's going through her mind.

"This makeover is going to be fun," she says. "Just like old times." She salutes me once more then drains her glass, her eyes glistening with excitement. "We'll get started this weekend."

CHAPTER 9

Fourteen years old, two years after "The Incident"

"RACHEL, I SAID I would be there," I say, sifting through a rack of old hats, a majority of them stacked on top of one another like a Russian doll set. I dig deep into one of the stacks, trying on a silver-sequined baseball cap before quickly putting it back.

"I know you're going to the carnival, but you need to dress up!" Rachel says, rummaging through a bin of used purses. We've been wandering around the local thrift store for hours now, looking for accessories to add to Rachel's Halloween costume. "Putting on a werewolf mask and spending the entire night on the haunted hayride is not going to cut it. You need to get out there and participate. We need to get you a costume."

It's been more than two years since we moved to Selene, and while I'm polite toward my classmates, Rachel is my only real friend. It's understandable, though, considering I bury myself in oversized hoodies most of the time, I won't take pictures with anyone, and I never want to go anywhere. *No one wants to be friends with the weird girl,* I think, taking a deep breath as I attempt to minimize her expectations. "I told you, I don't want a costume," I say. "I'll bob for apples and carve a pumpkin, but I have no interest in wearing some big, elaborate outfit."

"Well, you need to wear something," she says, crossing her arms over her chest, her shopping basket hanging from the crook of her elbow. "My mom doesn't take costumes lightly and neither do I. So, what will it be? I'm sure we can scrape something together for you."

"By 'scrape together', you mean something free, right?" I ask, giving her a serious look. "I'm sure my mom's cool with me going out for Halloween, but she can't afford anything extra right now. She's saving up to get our car fixed."

"Why even bother fixing it?" Rachel says, tossing a pair of chunky bracelets into her basket. "She never drives, she lives like a block and a half from work."

"I guess she wants the *option* of a car," I say, giving her a shrug. She is right, though, this town is so small that you can walk to most of the major businesses from our apartment. "Not everyone wants to hand-carry their groceries home twice a week. Besides, she's been talking about going back to school, taking some college courses or something."

"Okay, well, whatever. We'll make it work with leftover stuff from my house." Rachel rounds a clothing rack and walks into the next aisle, still chatting with me as she sifts through a bunch of blazers and jackets, her face partially hidden. "So, the big question is... what do you want to be for Halloween, Avery?" she asks.

I think about it for a second, my mind stuck on one essential requirement. "Invisible," I say, stepping up to the rack and shoving the jackets aside, the two of us face-to-face again. I want her to know that I'm serious, that I have no intention of going through with this plan if I just end up looking like myself. "If I'm going to parade myself around town with you all night, taking pictures and whatnot, I want a full-on costume. *With* a mask."

"Deal," she says, reaching between the clothes to shake on it. I grab her hand and she smiles triumphantly, like she's just negotiated world peace or something. "As long as you're there, I'm happy. Tyler Jones tried to grope me last year, then spilled orange soda down my dress after I slapped him. I need a wing woman."

I roll my eyes, her version of events getting more and more dramatic every time she tells this story. "Okay, well, I'll be there. But just to be clear: no mask, no wing woman."

Rachel ponders this for a moment, frowning. "This might be harder than I thought," she says. "I was thinking a gypsy or a 70's disco dancer, but the mask would make those pretty weird."

After putzing around for another ten minutes or so, Rachel pays for her things and we head home, the two of us parting ways at the corner. Throwing my hood up, I scurry along the sunlit sidewalk, my body on high alert as I scan the quiet streets, my eyes darting back and forth. Ever since the incident that led us to this tiny town, I feel like I'm paranoid, constantly watching for threats or danger, hypervigilant about who or what is around me. I cross the street to Buttercrust, hoping to slip in the back door but it's blocked off, a produce vendor currently using it for an afternoon delivery. Hurrying around to the front, I jerk the heavy wooden door open, the smell of butter and garlic pouring out onto the sidewalk as I step inside.

The restaurant is dimly lit, the ambiance of candles and tungsten lighting making it difficult to see. As my eyes adjust, I notice someone sitting in a booth near the door, hunched over with his back toward me. I recognize him as Rachel's older brother, Graham, a stand-offish kid who works here frequently as a pizza delivery boy. I'm about to rush past him when I notice that he's drawing on the inside of a pizza box, a rough sketch that's already quite good. Taking a step closer, I peek over his shoulder, curiosity getting the best of me. "What are you drawing?" I ask, my quiet voice echoing through the empty dining room.

Graham jumps, glancing over his shoulder at me, his face a mixture of surprise and irritation as he tries to cover his work. "Nothing," he says, eyeing me suspiciously as he removes one of his earbuds, the sound of angsty rock music blasting out of it. I've never talked to him before but he doesn't seem particularly friendly, his guarded demeanor more similar to mine than to his sister's.

My eyes wander back toward the pizza box, his art intriguing me in spite of his sour attitude. It's a comic strip, cartoon characters arguing over which is better, breadsticks or cheese sticks. I study the individual drawings, the characters well-crafted, the highlights and shadows expertly done. "This is good," I say, not so much talking to him as I am talking to myself.

"Thanks," Graham says, his expression still guarded.

I look at the characters again, realizing that I've seen his work before. "We've gotten a couple of these on the smaller pizza boxes," I say. "Last week, our box had a guy carrying a pizza like a briefcase, something about edible handles... it was pretty funny."

Graham chuckles, clearly knowing which drawing I'm referring to. He looks at me, taking in my bird legs and baggy hoodie, his gold eyes flashing in the candlelight. "You eat here a lot?" he asks.

"I mean, I do live upstairs," I say flatly. "Frank brings us a lot of free leftovers."

Graham nods but doesn't respond. I begin to feel a bit awkward, embarrassed that I interrupted his work, so I change the subject. "Are you going to the Halloween festival?" I ask.

"Maybe," he says. "You?"

"If your sister can whip me up a costume," I say, nervously shuffling back and forth, hyper aware that my hands are empty after a two-hour shopping spree. "I can't really afford one, so..." Graham nods again, the silence between us stretching unbearably thin. He looks down at the table, his eyes refocusing on his work. I take this as my cue to leave. "Well, have a good night," I say, waving at him as I walk away.

"Goodnight," he says, peering at me once more before bending over the pizza box, his hand moving quickly as he scratches and scribbles. I hurry toward the back, busting through the kitchen's double doors to make my way up to our apartment.

***

"Whoa," I say, staring at the costume hanging on the back of Rachel's door. I'd gone over to her house early to get ready for the festival, and she'd been squealing and giddy from the second I walked inside. Now I know why.

"I know, isn't it great?" Rachel says, clapping her hands as she jumps up and down. "Honestly, I half-considered stealing it for myself."

"It's really pretty," I say, walking up to touch the delicate fabric. It looks kind of like a fairy costume, the tattered green dress covered in a thin mesh, its bodice and skirt adorned with feather-like patches. I run my hand over the silky material, excitement for the festivities buzzing through me for the first time. "How did you make this?" I ask.

"It was mostly my mom," Rachel says. "We found some old nightgowns of hers and ripped them a bit, dyed everything green before tacking on the appliques. I tried it on a few times so she could cinch it up, get a proper fit." She points at the floor, a pair of beat-up brown ankle boots lying next to the door. "I dug these out of my closet for you, they match perfectly," Rachel says, beaming with pride. "I'm so excited for you to try it on!"

"Me too," I say, still a bit cautious. "And what about the mask?"

"Let's get you dressed first," Rachel says. "Then we'll worry about the mask."

We shut the door and I take off my regular clothes, my heart racing as I slip on the forest green dress. I feel exposed, practically naked without my jeans and oversized hoodie, but my nerves quickly subside as I turn to look at myself in the mirror. I look incredible, the dress fitting nicely over my waist and hips, the top part flattering my modest amount of cleavage. Twirling back and forth, I admire my girly silhouette, a version of myself I'm not very familiar with anymore. After a couple minutes of spinning in circles, Rachel's mom, Maggie, comes into the room, sitting me down at Rachel's vanity to tackle my hair and makeup. Before I know it, I'm covered in shimmers and sparkles, my brown hair cascading down my back in braids and loose waves. Maggie and Rachel are ecstatic, each of them glowing as they marvel at my unique costume, proud of their joint creative masterpiece.

I stare at myself in the mirror, my final transformation met with a wave of dread. "Okay, Rachel," I say, "this is amazing, but you promised my costume would have a mask. So, where is it?"

"Here," a voice says from behind me. Turning around, I'm met with a large, looming figure standing in the doorway, his long, black cloak obscuring his features. I take a step back, panicking for a second before I realize that it's Graham, his all-black Halloween costume making him appear threatening. He walks into the room, lowering the hood of his cloak, his dark hair a disheveled mess as he presents me with a small shoebox. "It's a nymph mask," he says, handing it to me. "Figured it would go well with the dress."

I open the box, air immediately leaving my lungs as I gaze upon the exquisite mask. It looks like a piece of tree bark, moss and twigs accentuating parts of it, an asymmetrical design that almost looks like a crown. There's also a pair of pointy silver ear cuffs, the spun wire and beading incredibly intricate. "Graham saw us making the dress and offered to help," Rachel says. "Do you like it?"

I carefully pick up one of the ear cuffs, turning it over in my hand, admiring the craftsmanship while simultaneously wondering how long it took him to make it. "I do," I whisper, glancing up at him. "These are amazing, thank you."

"You're welcome," he says, nodding his head, a small smile flickering across his face.

"I'm so glad you're coming with us this year," Maggie cries, running over to kiss Graham on the cheek, a gesture he openly flinches away from. "It's been years since you've gone to the fall festival with us."

Graham shrugs, wiping at his cheek. "Well, I do graduate next year. Figured I should participate while I'm here."

"That could still change," Maggie says, a wistful tone to her voice as she pats him on the arm. "There's no reason to rush into adulthood, you're only sixteen."

"Well, we *do* need to rush if we want to make the festival on time," Rachel says, guiding Graham and her mother toward her door. "Avery may be ready to go, but this disco diva still needs to change."

Forty-five minutes later, after a safety pep talk and an obscene amount of photos in their living room, the four of us hop into Maggie's car, Rachel and I giggling in the back while Maggie sits quietly in the passenger seat, a plate of fresh brownies in her lap. Graham drives us toward Main Street, parking a block or two away as the streets become more congested. I glance around as we step out of the car, shocked by the sheer number of people this year, dozens of families wandering toward the festival, dressed up in their Halloween best. Feeling a bit nervous, I double-check in my reflection in the car window, making sure my mask is on tight, that I'm not easily recognizable. When I feel satisfied, I run around the car and grab Rachel's arm, holding on tight as we blend in with the rest of the crowd, Maggie and Graham not far behind.

As soon as we hit Main Street it's a madhouse, people and vendors and activities everywhere. There's a DJ on stage at the far end of the street, a huge crowd of people dancing below him, grooving to a mix of spooky techno music. The sweet smell of caramel apples drifts through the air, mingling with the scent of savory barbecue, hot dogs, and roasted turkey legs. "I'll see you kids in a little bit, be good!" Maggie yells, breaking away from us to drop off her brownie plate at the school's fundraising booth. We continue walking down the street as a group, Graham lurking behind us, shadowing Rachel and I like our own personal bodyguard.

As we're walking by the "Bob's 'Bobbing for Apples'" stand, a group of high school boys approaches, blocking our path. "Hey Graham, fancy seeing you here," one of them says, stepping to the front of the pack. "Didn't think you were invited."

"Didn't think I needed an invitation," Graham replies, his voice calm as he slides in front of Rachel and I. I recognize these guys from school, but I don't really know any of them.

"Go away, Blake. We don't want to talk to you," Rachel says, poking her head around Graham.

"Well, that wasn't always the case, was it?" Blake retorts, a fire in his eyes as he claps Graham hard on the shoulder. Graham flinches but he doesn't move, a tension building between the two of them that I don't understand. "We used to be such good friends, you and I."

"That's hard to imagine," I say, my thoughts slipping out by accident. I don't mean to insert myself into the conversation, but this guy seems like a bully, the worst kind of human, in my limited experience. I can already admit with confidence that I don't like him.

Graham smirks a little at my comment, but Blake isn't impressed. "If you knew the whole story, you wouldn't want to be friends with him, either," Blake says, glaring at me. He's a pretty big kid, and even from a distance I smell stale beer on his breath. "Besides, what would you know about it, anyway? You aren't friends with anyone in this town except for these two losers and your sad sack of a mother."

"That's enough," Graham says, stepping forward. He might look a bit more ominous in his dark cloak, but I know this guy could beat the crap out of him, especially with the help of his friends. "Leave her alone."

Blake lets out a maniacal laugh, clenching his fists as he comes toe-to-toe with Graham. He smiles at him, grinning wide right before shoving Graham, hard, Rachel and I catching him as he stumbles backward into us. "For now," Blake says, his smile fading as he glances around, clocking the large crowd of people. "But I'll see you again soon, you can count on it." Blake and his buddies walk away, disappearing down a side street as they exit the festival.

"What was that all about?" I ask, looking at Graham as he stands up straight, adjusting his costume.

"It's not important," he says, giving me a half-smile. "Now, where are the caramel apples?"

We wander around the festival, the three of us, bouncing from activity to activity. It's the first time I've felt like a kid in a long time, moving through the crowds without fear, my identity undetectable beneath my costume. We play carnival games, run through a spooky zombie maze, indulge in an obscene amount of candy and treats. After a while, we meander toward the main stage, the crowd of ghouls and goblins still dancing to the non-stop party music.

Tyler Jones walks over to us, smiling directly at Rachel. He's dressed up like one of the vampires from *The Lost Boys*, his bad-boy outfit making him appear extra smug. "Care for a dance?" he asks, his question coming out in a lisp from the cheap, plastic vampire fangs in his mouth.

"You're kidding me, right?" she says, crossing her arms over her chest. She cracks a small smile, though, clearly not as upset about the groping as she let on.

"Not in the slightest," he says, his smile unwavering as he waits for her response. She eventually nods, unfolding her arms and following him onto the dance floor, the two of them moving closer to one another as the crowd pulls them in.

I stand next to Graham, the two of us watching in horror as Rachel starts grinding on Tyler, an awkward display for either of us to watch. Graham frowns, shaking his head before turning toward me. "You want to dance?" he asks, gesturing to the raging mosh pit.

"No, that's okay," I say, my mask wobbling slightly as I shake my head.

Graham tilts his head to the side. "Not a dancer, I take it?"

"It's not that," I say, my neck and face growing warm as I look up at him, embarrassed. "You don't have to hang out with me, you know? You can go find your own friends, if you want to."

"Where are your friends?" he asks, his tone curious, sincere.

"Out there," I say, nodding at Rachel. "She's pretty much the only one." I sigh, thinking about my hometown, all the people my mother and I left behind. I look over at Graham, his eyes still on me. "Really, it's okay. I'm used to being on my own."

Graham stares at me, his expression unreadable. Just then, the song changes, another upbeat tempo with a very strong beat. Graham starts shrugging his shoulders, his movements building as he begins twisting back and forth, a weird, jolting dance that looks absolutely insane. I laugh, doubling over as he starts bouncing around, his bizarre moves catching everyone off guard. Without saying anything, he slides onto the dance floor, his eyes on me as he beckons me to follow him. I do follow him, something inside of me pulling me forward, a flutter deep in my belly that I've never felt before. I start to jump and spin, the music crashing around us as we dance freely, each of us whooping and hollering into the night. I don't even notice when he grabs my hand to spin me, both of us lost in the moment, having too much fun.

CHAPTER 10

"Wow," I say, staring at myself in the mirror. I'm sitting in the local salon, my newly-cut hair blown out and styled, a good six inches of length trimmed away. I keep looking for traces of the old me, but to be honest, I hardly recognize myself.

"You said you wanted to look different," Rachel says as she stands behind me, scrutinizing my makeover. We'd spent most of Saturday in Fayetteville, bouncing between shops for all the necessities. New outfits, sunglasses, a few professional dresses that were a step up from my normal "drab" clothes. Rachel even talked me into getting a light spray tan, although it seemed a bit excessive at the time.

"I said I wanted to blend in," I reply, touching my red locks, the feathered, shoulder-length haircut a far cry from the long brunette I've always had. I lean forward, lightly touching my makeup-caked face, my soft features hidden under layers of foundation and mascara. Even my eye color is different, the vibrant hazel now a soft murky blue thanks to a pair of colored contacts. I twist my head side to side, marveling at the transformation; I knew Rachel was good, but I didn't really expect the makeover to be this successful.

"Honey, you've never blended in," Rachel says. "A diamond in the rough is still a diamond." She reaches into her makeup bag, pulling out a couple shades of lipstick. "Okay, red or nude?"

I study the lipsticks, unsure if I even need it after everything we've already done. "Nude," I say.

"Let's try the red first," Rachel replies, handing me the silver tube. "It'll look good with the new hair."

I think of our first day in town, my mother dabbing at her rose-colored lips, her hand shaking as she concealed a small cut. I shake my head, pushing the memory away, then glide the color across my lower lip in one fell swoop.

***

As soon as I get back to my office, I launch into full-on work mode. Our plane leaves Thursday morning, so I have just three days to get my things in order before we take off. I send out an email to my regular clients, letting them know about the last-minute trip before I dive into some photo editing. I've only been working for about ten minutes when my phone rings beside me.

It's Cynthia, one of my neediest clients. She has zero photography or marketing skills, but she runs three separate businesses in town and she pays me generously to handle everything for her. As much as I hate dealing with her sometimes, she's an important part of my business' success. "Hi Cynthia, how are you?" I say, doing my best to sound chipper.

"Oh, Avery, I'm so glad I caught you!" Cynthia says, her voice breathy. I hear something thumping in the background and wonder if she's at the gym. "I got your email - you're going out of town?"

"Yes, just for the weekend. I'm participating in a photography competition, I should be back late Sunday night."

"Oh, how exciting!" she says, her enthusiasm sounding more forced than genuine. "I just wanted to check in, will you still be running our socials while you're gone?"

"Yes, I will," I say, doing my best not to sigh. "I am editing some of your product photos as we speak."

"Okay, well I just wanted to be sure," she says, her words coming out in a huff, her breathing labored. "Because it states in our contract that you'll post daily on each of our accounts. Once on each business page, three times per daily feed, which includes a video, of course!"

I clench my teeth, the demeaning nature of her words grating on my nerves. I hear this speech almost every other week, her need to remind me of our contract as pervasive as ever. "I know, I have no intention of letting you down."

"Well no one ever *intends* to let me down," she says, her words a little dramatic. "But with a last-minute trip like this, things can slip through the cracks." I hear a beeping sound, her winded breaths immediately slowing, an indicator that she's just finished her workout.

I lean back in my chair, pinching the bridge of my nose as I speak in my most professional voice. "Everything is under control, Cynthia. I won't miss a thing," I say.

"Okay good, well I just wanted to check in," Cynthia says, her voice returning to normal. "If you ever need any help, my niece just graduated from school with a degree in marketing. I'm sure she could take on a couple of your tasks if you ever get too busy." She has mentioned her niece once before, a passing comment about her "impressive design skills". I'm not sure why but these comments feel like a threat, a warning that she has someone waiting in the wings if I ever get tired of her antics. She is a tough woman to keep happy, though; I doubt her niece wants to deal with her any more than I do.

"That's not necessary," I say, "but thank you. All of your posts will be scheduled and uploaded for your approval by tomorrow."

"Okay great! Well, have a good trip... I'm sure I'll be checking in!" She hangs up immediately, the phone going silent without waiting for my response.

I set my phone aside, my mind lingering on the comment about her niece. As annoying as Cynthia can be, she is a big client, someone I need to cater to so I can maintain my monthly income. As much as I'd love to focus solely on photography, it isn't a dependable source of income in such a small town; combining it with social media, however, helps us to pay a lot of bills.

Around seven o'clock, there's a knock at the studio door. I get up from my desk, stretching my aching muscles as I walk across the room and open it. Frank, the owner of Buttercrust, is standing on the landing, his blue shirt and slacks pressed, a freshly-cut rose poking out of his shirt pocket . His beard is neatly trimmed, and I can smell a faint scent of cologne and lemon soap. It's unusual to see him dressed up like this, the tidy outfit making him look younger, dashing. "Hey, Frank, what's up?" I say, taking in his stylish appearance. "You look fantastic."

He steps forward, pulling me in for a huge bear hug, his strong arms shaking me enthusiastically. "I heard about your award!"

he says, stepping back while holding me at arm's length. "I'm so proud of you, kiddo! I always knew you'd do great things."

I laugh, shaking my head. Frank is someone I've really come to admire throughout the years, not just for his generosity but also his encouragement and kindness, the way he constantly lifts up everyone around him. "Thank you, Frank, but I haven't won anything yet."

"Well, award or not, you should be proud," he says matter-of-factly. "You always work so hard. For yourself, and for your mom."

"Thank you," I say, my face turning red from his sincere compliment.

"Why don't you come down, have some dinner? I made a special meal to celebrate." He lets go of me and gestures toward the stairs, urging me to follow him.

"That's really sweet, Frank, but I have a lot of work to do..."

"Come now," he insists, the corners of his eyes crinkling as he smiles. "It'll be quick, I promise."

I sigh, hurrying to grab my phone off my desk. I return to the landing, shutting the door behind me as Frank ushers me past him, his big hand grazing my back as I descend the steep stairs. As I walk through the kitchen and out into the dining room, a gathered crowd erupts in unison, a barrage of voices stopping me in my tracks. "Surprise!" everyone calls out at once, the room filled with friends, neighbors, and at the very front, my mom and Rachel.

My mother shuffles forward, wrapping her arms around me. "Surprise, sweetie! Sorry to spring this on you, but we needed to celebrate." She places her hand on my cheek, her skin warm and soft, her eyes misty with tears. "I am so incredibly proud of you, baby girl," she says, holding my gaze. "You are my greatest gift, no matter what happens."

I smile at her, resisting the urge to cry. "Thanks, Mom. I love you."

"Love you more," she says, kissing me once on the cheek before releasing me.

Rachel runs up and hugs me next, pushing a small bouquet of flowers into my hand. "It was all your mom's idea, and Frank's," she says, smiling at the two of them. "They wanted to see you off properly. I suggested money toward our bar tab in Miami, but this works, too."

Frank walks up behind me, grinning from ear to ear, pleased by his successful surprise. I hug him again, his jubilant laugh echoing through me as everyone claps and cheers. "Frank, this is incredible!" I say. "Thank you so much, you didn't have to do all of this."

"Yes, I did," he says. "You're family, little lady, and we celebrate family here." He turns toward the group of people, the room quieting down to let him speak. "Thank you everyone for coming, for celebrating Avery and her incredible work. Okay, who's ready for some dinner?!"

The crowd cheers as everyone turns around and walks toward the middle of the room. There are several tables overflowing with food, each one stacked with pastas, pizzas, and calzones, the room a bouquet of hearty aromas. There's also a table in the center with a large cake, the words "Congratulations Avery" written across it in blue and purple frosting. I stare at, famished and teary-eyed, my work upstairs suddenly the last thing on my mind.

Rachel, my mother, and I each grab a plate, the three of us sitting down with Frank in a booth near the wall. As we're laughing and enjoying our meal, one of the kitchen staff appears at the end of our table, a camera in his hand. "Everyone say cheese!" he says, waiting for us to smile.

I glance at my mother, who smiles back at me and nods. We both turn toward him, our smiles wide and joyful as he takes our picture. Then we go back to celebrating, the party lasting well into the night.

CHAPTER 11

"Hurry up Avery, you're going to be late!" my mom yells, her airy voice echoing through the quiet house.

I sprint out of the bathroom, awkwardly juggling an armful of lotions and toiletries. I've been up since 5 AM, my anxiety surrounding this trip waking me from a restless slumber, intrusive thoughts playing on repeat as I lie awake in bed. Now I'm so frazzled and tired that I've barely packed. I shove the liquids into a plastic bag, then place everything into a secondary bag in case something decides to spill out on the airplane.

My mother peeks her head into my room, an amused look creeping across her face as she rests against the door frame. "You're going for a weekend, Avery, not a month," she says, shaking her head as she examines the mess of clothes scattered across my comforter.

"I need options," I say, wheeling around to inspect my backpack. I sift through the contents again, making sure I have everything I need so I can tackle some work while I'm gone. *Laptop, hard drive, editing tablet; check*. My mother steps into the room and starts folding my disheveled clothes, gently tucking each item inside my suitcase.

"What time is Susie coming over?" I ask, glancing at her over my shoulder.

"She'll be off work at four," she says, setting my bag of toiletries on top of the folded clothes.

"And she's staying the whole weekend?" I ask, turning toward her, my arms folded over my chest as I scrutinize her response. She's always been a terrible liar, another trait I seem to have inherited from her.

"Yes," she says quietly. "She's going to borrow your bed, I hope you don't mind."

"I don't mind as long as you're not alone," I say, rushing over to stand next to her. I shove a pile of socks and underwear into a side pocket, hoping security won't feel the need to rummage through it.

My mother stops packing and sits down on my bed, her delicate frame barely moving the mattress. "Let's talk for a minute," she says, patting the empty space beside her. I doubt I have time for whatever this is, but I don't want to waste time arguing about it, either. I plop down beside her and she takes my hand like she always does, the calluses from her cane rubbing against my palm. "Avery, I'm going to be fine. It's just a few days," she says, her voice steady and calm. "I want you to go and enjoy yourself. Stop fussing over me."

I nod, my body deflating as I let out a big breath. "I'm sorry. It's just the last time I left..."

"It was an accident," she says, cutting me off. "A random car accident. I got dinged up a bit, a couple bumps and bruises, but I'm fine."

"Mom, you were trapped in the car and severely burned your leg," I say, gesturing toward her injured limb. "They almost had to amputate it, you were in and out of the hospital for months."

"That's true," she says, looking down at her cane, that slender piece of wood as much a part of her now as the injury itself. "But your being there wouldn't have changed anything, honey. This stuff just happens, that's how life works out sometimes." She brushes the hair away from my face, her fingers lingering on the choppy, rust-colored locks. "This weekend is about you, Avery, nothing else. I want you to enjoy yourself, to be twenty-three years old for once. Stop fretting about what *might* happen and just live your life."

I sigh, unsure how to respond. It feels impossible not to worry about her, considering our history.

"Here," my mother says, reaching behind her head, removing the heirloom necklace she's worn since I was a girl. "Take this with you. A little piece of me for luck and for love." She secures it around my neck, the purple glass stones glistening in the light. "And for God's sake, don't lose it—it belonged to your grandmother."

I laugh, gently touching the dainty jewelry. "Thanks, Mom. I'll take good care of it."

"If it makes you feel better, I have zero plans to leave the house this weekend," she says. "No open houses, no trips into town. I'm just going to hole up here with Susie the entire time you're gone."

I give her a weak smile, her words mildly reassuring. "Good, I like that plan."

Just then, the doorbell starts ringing in rapid fire, the sound so obnoxious that Hank breaks into a loud, high-pitched howl. My mom laughs, shaking her head. "Better go take care of that before Hank wakes the neighborhood," she says, pushing to her feet. She turns toward me before she goes, leaning down to kiss me on the forehead. "Everything will be okay, sweetie," she says. "I promise." She hobbles toward the door and disappears around the corner, the thump of her cane drowned out by Hank's incessant barking.

I close my eyes, breathing deep, trying to let my mother's words sink in. *Stop fretting, everything will be okay.* I cling to them, repeating them over and over again, the sound of her voice echoing through my head. Pushing my fears aside, I abruptly stand and shove the last of my stuff into my suitcase, then zip up the bag and flip it onto the floor. Grabbing my backpack, I scan my room one more time for forgotten necessities, then I spin my suitcase around and head for the living room.

Rachel is standing in the entryway, already in vacation mode, her big sunglasses and pink lipstick perfectly accentuating the bright yellow sundress wrapped around her. I realize in that instant that I don't need to worry so much about blending in. Rachel is mesmerizing, her bubbly charm and infectious smile lighting up the room, even from several yards away. She's going to be the one pulling focus wherever we decide to go, not me. "Ready for an epic girls' weekend?" she squeals, jumping up and down in her strappy, polka dot wedges.

I grin, her enthusiasm momentarily neutralizing my nerves. "Ready as I'll ever be."

***

By the time we get to the airport and through security, I am an absolute mess. Sweat pours down my back as we shuffle through the terminal, Rachel occasionally stumbling as my grip on her arm throws her off balance. I slink alongside beside her, cowering in my sweatshirt, my face obscured by a pair of large, tinted sunglasses. Every time we pass a new group of people, I jolt sideways, the sea of unfamiliar faces making me feel too exposed, too seen.

"Everyone is looking at me," I hiss, retreating deeper into my oversized hoodie.

"That's because you're acting like a rabid ferret," Rachel says, steading herself for the millionth time. It's a wonder she hasn't rolled her ankle by now in those strappy shoes. "The whole point of giving you a makeover was so you'd feel less recognizable outside of Selene. So far, your behavior is negating our efforts."

I shoot her a bitter look. "I am not acting like a rabid ferret," I say, resisting the urge to lean into her as we pass a family of five pushing a stroller.

"Well, you definitely aren't acting normal," she says, giving me a disapproving look. "We're supposed to be having fun. Besides, you need to start practicing being around new people. You're never going to win this competition if you can't handle meeting a few strangers."

I sigh, knowing in my heart that she is right. I lower my hoodie and take off my sunglasses, squinting at the bright fluorescent lights overhead. "How long till our flight leaves?" I ask, tucking the sunglasses into my pocket.

"Another hour or so," Rachel replies, smiling at me as I shake out my matted hair. We make our way through the bustling crowd, me continuing to cling to her side. I bump into her a few more times, causing her to wobble precariously on her wedges, but she doesn't let go of my arm. As we approach our gate, she spots an empty airport lounge on the opposite side of the walkway "Let's stop in here for a bit, have a cocktail before our flight."

"Whatever takes the edge off," I mutter, turning with her toward the open bar.

We head toward the far corner of the lounge, away from the crowded terminal, and take a seat at the bar on a couple of sticky, leather barstools. I unzip my hoodie, welcoming the cool rush of air as a bartender approaches us. He's surprisingly handsome, his edgy wristbands and styled faux hawk inconsistent with his boyish charm. "Hey ladies, what can I get for you?" he asks.

"We'll have two margaritas and two shots of tequila," Rachel says, laying on the charm herself. "We're on a girls' trip, need to kick things off properly."

"And some chips and guac," I say, glancing over at Rachel. "I'd prefer not to puke on takeoff."

The bartender laughs, a hearty, confident sound that I'm sure makes most of his patrons swoon. "You got it," he says, walking over to the computer to start us a tab.

"Puke on takeoff?" Rachel groans, rolling her eyes. "That is not the way to flirt with the hot bartender - or get us free drinks - on our first ever girls' trip."

"I'm not trying to flirt," I say. "I'm trying to stay alert and not barf on the plane later. I mean, I already feel nauseous as it is." The bartender returns, setting the shots and a plate of limes down in front of us before walking away to make our drinks. I stare at the shots, my stomach flipping. "Plus, you know I don't do tequila."

"Ok, well next time I'll order us Long Island ice teas," Rachel says, giving me a mischievous grin.

I laugh, smacking her on the arm. "You're a terrible influence!"

She cackles, her laughter bright and infectious. "Best friends are essential for unforgettable moments and poor decisions, Avery. You'll thank me someday." She picks up her shot and waits, her smile wide as I follow suit, grabbing mine off the bar. "To us," Rachel says, "and to many more shots this weekend! Preferably bought by sexy investment bankers."

"Not sure Daniel would approve of that," I say as we clink glasses and down our shots. The fiery liquor slides down my throat, smooth and hot, the intensity of it sending me into a coughing fit. I double over, wheezing and sputtering, gripping onto the bar as I regain control.

"Daniel won't mind," Rachel says, patting me on the back as she bites into a lime. "Besides, this trip is about *us*. If we choose to cash in on free drinks by grinding on some locals, then so be it."

"Or we could just pay for them," I laugh, her witty commentary making me cough even more. The bartender returns with our margaritas, setting them down with a wink. I eagerly grab mine and take a sip, the cool, refreshing beverage calming my throat. "Well, whatever happens this weekend, I just want to say thank you."

Rachel gives me a quizzical look. "For what?"

"For pushing me to go on this trip," I say, smiling at her. "For making it possible. You're the reason I'm here, that I'm in the contest in the first place."

"That was all you, babe," Rachel says. "You got yourself in, you're the one with the talent. Besides, I've been trying to drag you out of town for years. You need some time away from that place."

"We both do," I say. Rachel agrees, nodding in earnest as she drinks her margarita.

Our chips arrive a few minutes later, flanked by a side of guac and a ramekin of fresh tomato salsa. I grab a chip and scoop up the guac, moaning as I take my first bite. "Ok, I'm not sure if I'm tipsy or if I have a skewed view of airport food, but that guacamole is delicious."

"Everything tastes better with margaritas," Rachel says, grabbing her phone out of her bag. She picks up her drink and holds the phone out, angling it toward us. "Smile!" she says, grinning at the front-facing camera.

I hold up my drink, angling myself slightly as I smile for the camera. Rachel takes the picture and shows it to me, the two of us relaxed and happy, our smiles radiating through the screen. It takes me a second to recognize myself, my new, choppy haircut a far cry from what I'm used to. I'm not sure if I'll change it once this trip is over, but I must admit, the red color does suit me.

"Remember what we agreed upon," I say as I watch her edit and tweak the photo. "No posting online. This trip never happened, remember?"

"I got it," she says, waving me away. She taps her phone a few more times then sets it down on the bar, reaching for her drink. Within ten seconds it buzzes and she snatches it up again, laughing as she stares at the screen.

"Everything good?" I ask, popping another chip into my mouth.

"Oh yeah, it's just Graham," Rachel says, tapping away on the phone's keyboard. "He liked our picture, says I turned you into Raggedy Ann with all that red hair of yours."

I frown, my skin prickling at the mention of Graham's name. "I just told you that I didn't want you posting about this trip," I say, folding my arms over my chest.

"I didn't post about it, I sent the picture straight to him," she replies, glancing over at me. "That way he can spot us at the hotel."

I freeze, every ounce of irritation draining out of me. I stare at her, my mind drifting to the pictures she submitted, the photograph I'm nominated for. The click of my camera, the water-logged canyon bathed in golden sunlight. Graham's arms wrapped around me, the heat of his breath on my shoulder. "The hotel?" I repeat, my voice unsteady.

"Yeah," she says. "His company is sponsoring a booth this year, he's going as one of their lead representatives. He said he would touch base with us when he lands."

My mind is reeling, images of the two of us weaving through my thoughts. It's been years since I've seen him, not since the night I left. I flag the bartender down and he strolls over, flashing us a dazzling smile. "We're gonna need more shots," I say, pushing our empty glasses toward him. Rachel squeals in delight, bouncing up and down on her bar stool as I down the rest of my margarita in one, big gulp.

CHAPTER 12

Fifteen years old, three years after "The Incident"

"First I would buy myself some better lenses," I say, taking a big bite of pizza. I reach forward, moving a pepperoni slice diagonally across our make-shift checkerboard, Graham's latest idea for creating entertaining pizza boxes.

Graham frowns, his expression skeptical. "If *you* won the lottery, the first thing you'd do is buy yourself a set of camera lenses?" He picks up a piece of Canadian bacon, making his move.

"Well, I don't really have any," I say, shrugging. "I can borrow them from the school, but it's not the same thing."

"What about a trip?" he says, trying to conjure up a more creative answer. "Like an epic, 'circle the world in style' kind of trip? You're always researching different cities and countries, finding new places you want to visit."

"Yeah, I guess a trip would be nice," I say, moving another pepperoni. "But I would still need a decent camera. I can't go on an epic, multi-continent extravaganza with a basic point-and-shoot."

Graham laughs, shaking his head. I like it when he laughs, the deep rumble of his voice, the way his full lips curl over his mostly-straight teeth. "What about a bigger apartment?" he asks, gesturing around us, the metal table we're seated at barely squeezing between the kitchen and the bathroom door. "Hell, you could buy a freakin' house, have your own bedroom. Honestly, that should probably be priority number one."

"I don't know," I say, looking around the tiny, cramped space. It is small; so small, in fact, that my mother and I still have to share the queen-sized bed tucked into the corner next to the window. "I like it here. It's so close to everyone, and it's easy access to pasta and pizza."

Graham laughs again, looking down at the board. He moves another one of his pieces, hopping diagonally over several slices of pepperoni. Picking up the defeated pepperonis, he pops them in his mouth with a grin, bits of red sausage now sticking to his teeth. It's a true, authentic smile, the type of goofy grin he often reserves only for me, a smile that secretly makes me giddy, a rush of pure ecstasy. I scoff, pretending to be upset with him as I smack him in the arm with the back of my pizza. "You know, if I knew you were going to eat all my pizza toppings, I would have told you to draw something else," I say, snacking on some of the remaining pepperonis without actually making a move.

"Just trying to keep things interesting," Graham says, wiping pizza grease off of his bicep with a napkin. "Figured people are tired of my cartoons by now. There are only so many jokes you can make about pasta or breadsticks."

"I'm not," I say. "I think your cartoons are great. I *do* think you should start working on portraits, though, especially since you're leaving for fine art school soon, but that's just me."

Graham looks at me, a flicker of annoyance sweeping across his face. "I told you, portraits aren't really my thing."

"I know," I say, looking down at the half-eaten pizza between us. I know better than to bring this up, the idea of drawing portraits, even realistic caricatures, always putting him in a foul mood. "I just think you'd be good at them, that's all."

"Where's your mom at tonight?" Graham asks, quickly changing the subject. "Is she working?"

"No, she's at her night classes," I say, taking a bite of my pizza. "She's almost done, though. I think she'll take her realtor's exam in a month or two."

Graham takes an enormous bite of pizza, shaking his head as he chews, his mouth overflowing with food. "I'm jealous," he says, bits of pizza crust flying from his lips. "I can't wait to go to college, start my art classes. Get away from this town and all of its narrow-minded people."

I nod, looking down at the pizza box, his checkerboard reminding me how much I'll miss his quiet weirdness, his peculiar personality. "I still can't believe you're graduating early," I say, swallowing my feelings. "Aren't you nervous to go to LA by yourself?"

"No, not at all," he says. "This town is too small, I'm over it."

"Does that have anything to do with Blake?" I ask, watching him to gauge his reaction. He won't admit it, but I'm pretty sure Blake has roughed him up a couple times in the past year, even giving him a black eye once. Rachel told me that they were friends in kindergarten, that their parents would get together on the weekends back before her dad left town."He doesn't seem to make your life any easier."

"Maybe," he says, our eyes meeting for a second before he looks away. "But he's just the tip of the iceberg. This place is just..." He goes silent, twirling a piece of leftover pizza crust between his fingers. "Sometimes it just feels like I can't breathe here."

I stare at him, wondering why he hates this town so much, what it would feel like to comfort him, to hold him. "I don't feel that way," I say. "I mean, I want to get out of here too, but... I don't know. This place is simple, straightforward. Not a lot of surprises in a place like this."

"You'll leave when you're ready," Graham says, standing up from the table. He puts the leftover pizza in the fridge for my mom, then sits back down, the metal chair scraping against the floor beneath him. "Okay, ready to get to work?

We start pulling out our art supplies, carefully maneuvering around each other as we fill the tiny table. Graham grabs his sketchbook and pencils and I pull out our old, used laptop, the ancient device barely whirling to life, its power cable connected to a 12-foot-long extension cord that snakes through the entire apartment. We spend the next few hours just goofing around, him doodling in his notebook while I edit pictures in PhotoShop, the two of us chatting and laughing, critiquing each other's work. It's more about experimenting than anything else, enjoying the process and each other's company more than the final product. Around eleven o'clock, Graham packs up, grabbing the empty pizza box off of the counter. "Okay, I'm gonna head out," he says. "See you tomorrow?"

"I'm working at the diner tomorrow," I say, powering down the laptop. "But I'm free on Thursday."

His smile falters a bit but he nods, adjusting the bag on his shoulder. Even on nights when I'm busy, Graham still draws downstairs at Buttercrust, tucking himself away in the dining room till late into the evening, sometimes till close. He's never explained why he doesn't just draw at home, his room devoid of the supplies and sketches that he carries around in his bag. "Sounds good," Graham says, opening the door to leave.

As he starts to close it, I call out, "Hey! You never answered the question: if you won the lottery, what would you buy?"

Graham gives me a half-smile, his golden eyes impossibly sad. "There are some things money can't buy, Avery," he says, his answer hanging in the space between us, an incredibly painful truth to his words that I don't understand. I'm about to press him further but before I can, Graham says goodnight and quietly closes the door.

CHAPTER 13

"Come on, Avery. Time to get up."

Fluorescent lights flicker overhead as I peel back the hood of my sweatshirt, the interior of the airplane slowly coming into focus. Half of the passengers are standing, shuffling about grabbing bags and backpacks, preparing to deboard. Rachel is busy gathering her things as well, slipping her tablet and headphones into her bag.

I sit up a bit, groaning miserably, the slightest movement sending my vision into a tailspin. Leaning against the arm rest, I cover my eyes, a wave of nausea and the throbbing in my head a distinct reminder of how much I drank. After we boarded the plane, I had ordered a glass of champagne; then another, then another. I had told Rachel it was to celebrate, to continue kicking off our "epic girls' trip", but it was really just my reaction to our impending reunion with Graham.

I peek over at Rachel, who's clearly amused by my inebriated state. I can only imagine that I look as good as I feel. "We're here?" I ask, my words muddled and slow.

"Yep, we're here," Rachel says. "So much for enjoying business class, you passed out within the first hour."

"I was tired," I murmur as I take a deep breath. My stomach gurgles, sweat collecting on my brow as guacamole and alcohol churn freely in my belly. I lean forward, holding my stomach, doing my best to stifle a very unpleasant belch. "I didn't sleep much last night."

"Sorry, Avery," Rachel says, "but that was not from a bad night's sleep. That was the three tequila shots we took at the bar, and the bottle of champagne you consumed on takeoff."

I nod, unwilling to argue. After a couple more deep breaths, I carefully work myself into a fully-upright position, surveying the area around us as I lean back against my seat. Passengers are moving toward the exit now, most of our area already empty. Rising slowly, I pull my backpack out from under the seat in front of me as Rachel grabs our carry-ons from the storage bins above. She hands me my bag as I wobble into the aisle, holding up the line of people behind us. "Can we stop by the bathroom?" I ask, leaning on the handle of my suitcase for support. "I need to pee, or vomit... whichever one comes first."

Rachel chuckles, moving toward the exit. I follow, trudging off the airplane and up the boarding ramp, my steps heavy and unstable. As we exit the jetway, I scan our terminal for the nearest restroom, spotting one about fifty yards away. We walk toward it, my speed increasing as a wave of nausea overcomes me, my stomach vibrating and clenching as I lumber toward the bathroom.

The second that we're inside, I abandon my suitcase and race into the nearest open stall, slamming the door behind me. For a moment I stand there, swaying on my feet, breathing deep as I wait for my body to settle. The smell of disinfectant and women's perfume hangs in the air, a combination I somehow find comforting. When I think that I'm okay, that I won't throw up, I gingerly set my backpack on the ledge behind the toilet and sit down to pee.

"I got us a rental car," Rachel calls out from a few stalls over, her voice muffled by the metal walls separating us. I hear the flush of a toilet, then the rotating wheels of our suitcases as she walks past me toward the sink. "We'll be on our way to the hotel in no time."

I sigh, the idea of getting into a car right now less than ideal. "You're driving," I croak, bracing myself on the toilet paper dispenser as I climb to my feet.

I exit the stall and join Rachel at the sink, scrutinizing my appearance in the mirror as I wash my hands. My hair is a mess, a pile of curly, red frizz sticking out in all directions. Eyeliner and mascara are smudged around my eyes, and my red lipstick is all but gone. I swipe at the wandering makeup, smoothing away the black creases, my disheveled appearance a reminder of why I rarely drink anymore. "I look like a rag doll that went through the dryer one too many times," I grumble.

"Raggedy Ann," Rachel says, giving me a wink. I remember that Graham is the one who came up with that term of endearment and I shudder, my stomach twisting all over again. "Miami humidity and too much alcohol will do that to you."

I rummage through my purse, then lean over the sink to apply a fresh layer of lipstick. "Let's get some lunch," I say. "Then you can find a lawn chair to dump me into for the rest of the day."

"Lunch, absolutely," Rachel replies. "But you are not going back to sleep. Our adventure begins tonight and we are *gonna have fun*! I'll load you up with coffee and Red Bull, whatever it takes."

"Let's just get to the hotel first," I say, the fresh lipstick doing wonders for my appearance. "Then you can mainline coffee into my veins."

We make our way through the airport and before I know it, we're out in the sticky Miami heat. After picking up our car keys, we locate the rental and I pour myself into the passenger seat as Rachel secures our bags in the back. She hops into the driver's side and thrust the key into the ignition, the sleek MINI convertible humming to life. "Freeway or scenic route?" Rachel asks, glancing at me as she plugs our hotel's address into the GPS. I give her a shrug and she grins playfully, pressing a button above our heads, the windows and roof retracting in one, smooth motion. "Scenic route," she says, her eyes sparkling with excitement as she turns up the music, modern pop blasting loudly through the speakers.

We pull out of the parking garage, bright sunshine glinting off the surrounding buildings as we make our way down the street. Salty air whips through my hair, tickling my skin as I hold my arm out the window, my hand floating on the breeze. Even with my sunglasses on, everything looks more vivid here, more alive, the bustling metropolis a sharp contrast to the small town we just came from. I feel like I'm waking up, this unfamiliar environment breathing new life into me, the sunshine and crisp, ocean air rejuvenating my soul.

We continue driving east, weaving our way down boulevards and around buildings until we finally see the ocean. I sit up, mesmerized by the vastness of the water, the sparkle of daylight as it dances along the waves. "It's beautiful," I say, my voice barely audible above the wind.

"It is," Rachel says, nodding. "And we get a whole weekend to enjoy it, just you and me."

As I watch the light play across the water, I think back to that day with Graham, rays of sunshine pouring into the canyon from high above us, the vibrant, multicolored walls protecting us from the rain. I think about his peppery skin, the feel of his strong hands, ancient memories made in a beautiful place, just like this. I have no idea how I'm going to face him, what I'm going to say, what I *can* say after what I did. All of the sudden, my phone alarm goes off and the memory is gone, my guilt vanishing with it as I snap back into reality. "Of course," I say, frowning at my phone. "Time to post on social media."

Rachel turns the music down as I rummage through my phone. One-by-one, I go through my client list, checking each automated post that I have listed on my schedule. As I'm checking one of Cynthia's pages, I glance over at Rachel. "When does Graham get here?" I ask, trying to sound casual.

"Oh, he's already here," she says, stopping at a stoplight. "He's in charge of one of the booths, so they've been here prepping the last day or so."

"He's running a whole booth?" I ask, trying not to sound as shocked as I am.

"Yeah," she says. "He's moved up pretty fast at this company. I never thought endlessly drawing cartoons would lead him anywhere, but apparently his artistic eye is an 'in-demand skill.'"

I think back to Graham's drawings, his comic strips on the boxes at Buttercrust, his notebooks full of doodles and sketches. Our love of art was the thing that bonded us, his obsession for drawing as pervasive as my love of photography. When I think about it that way, I'm actually not that surprised that he's found success in his chosen field. "Well, whatever he's doing, it must be impressing someone," I reply.

"I guess," Rachel says, shrugging. She turns right onto another road, palm trees lining each side of the narrow street. "Anyway, we have an entire day to ourselves before we have to deal with him. So, let's get checked in, get us some lunch, sit by the pool... whatever sounds the most enticing. Give ourselves a chill day before shit gets crazy."

Shit's definitely going to get crazy, I think, trying to picture the look on Graham's face when I see him again. I have no idea how I should act around him, if he's going to be happy to see me or not.

We drive another ten minutes, then veer left toward the ocean. As we approach the coast, a massive hotel appears before us, its clear glass structure jutting up into the sky. Sprawling gardens flank either side of the car as we approach, the entire property a lush oasis of flowers and greenery. Rachel drives the rental car into the attached parking structure, zipping through the different levels until she finds a spot near the elevator. She quickly kills the engine and turns toward me. "Okay, Avery, let's get you a gallon-sized coffee and the best pool chairs money can buy."

I laugh at her and unbuckle my seatbelt. "Extra points if you can score us a cabana," I tease.

We get out of the car and collect our bags, then make our way inside the hotel. We're walking toward the lobby when I stop abruptly, noticing the convention center off to the side, its doors wide open as vendors wheel equipment in and out. It's massive, with lights and stages and booths as far as I can see. Panic bubbles up inside of me but also a jolt of excitement, the grandeur of the conference truly sinking in. I watch as people move around inside, wondering if Graham is in there, too.

Rachel comes up beside, putting her arm around my shoulder. She nudges me a bit, her blonde hair brushing against my skin, both of us swaying together as we observe the busy vendors. "Are you ready for this?" she asks.

"I don't know," I admit. I take a deep breath, holding it in to calm my racing heart.

"You're here, Avery; you made it," she says, smiling at me "Now all you have to do is enjoy it. I'll be with you every step of the way, okay? If you need to bail, just say the word and we're out of here."

I smile back at her, a lump rising in my throat as I nod.

"Ok, let's go," she says. "Maybe I can flirt with the receptionist and get us an upgrade."

CHAPTER 14

AFTER CHECKING INTO OUR hotel room and doing a quick outfit change, Rachel and I head downstairs to soak up the afternoon sun. We make our way toward the hotel's main restaurant, its attached bar and infinity pool featured amenities of the hotel. We choose a table outside as close to the ocean as possible, the salty sea breeze caressing our skin as we order coffees and fresh pastries, the crash of the waves reverberating off the side of the building.

The food settles my stomach, rejuvenating me as I stare out at the water, my wide-brimmed hat and dark sunglasses protecting me from the sun. Seagulls fly overhead, diving at patrons on the beach, searching for leftover food scraps. It's peaceful and beautiful, the stress of our cross-country trip dissolving into the gentle murmur of the sea. "I could get used to this," I say, taking a generous sip of my coffee.

"Me too," Rachel says, propping her bare feet up on an empty chair. She scans the patio, observing the other guests, a mix of well-dressed hotel patrons and scantily-clad pool dwellers. "It would be hard to move away from home, though," she says, her gaze returning to me. "We're too tied down to leave, at this point."

Her statement catches me off guard, settling over my heart, the thrill of the Florida coast losing a bit of its luster. "Yeah, leaving home is definitely not an option," I say, tearing my eyes away from the water. I pull out my phone and take a picture of the beach, texting it to my mother. *Just landed, sitting by the ocean. Everything good there?*

She responds almost immediately, the text message progress bubble flashing at the bottom of the screen. *All good, having a movie marathon with Susie and Hank. Hank insisted on watching Miss Congeniality.*

I laugh, imagining the three of them lounging on the couch together, the coffee table covered with take-out boxes and snacks. *Love you*, I reply, then I silence my phone and set it on the table.

"So," Rachel says, staring at me through her translucent sunglasses, her pink lips curving into a perfect smile. "I've got an idea for tonight."

I study her, her reserved enthusiasm giving me pause. "Does it involve tequila shots?" I ask.

"Not if you don't want any," she replies, her face calm as she sips her coffee.

"I don't," I assure her, my tolerance for alcohol already maxed out for the day.

"We'll play it by ear," she says, dismissing my comment as she sets down her drink. "Apparently there's a cute little salsa club just a short walk down the beach. The receptionist told me they're famous for their fish tacos." Rachel starts swaying back and forth, dramatically shimmying her shoulders. "How about we pop over there, have some dinner, and dirty dance with sexy, sweaty locals? It's also ladies' night, so if we *do* want a drink, it's 'buy one, get one free!'"

I groan, propping my arm on the edge of the table, my cheek resting against my palm. "I'm not sure I can handle that, Rach. I'm finally sobering up, and I have a bunch of work to do today."

"Oh, you can do it," Rachel says, shaking her head as she leans back in her chair. "You've got, like, six hours to finish everything, plenty of time! Then we can go get you drunk again."

I laugh, shaking my head before giving her a serious look. "The conference starts at 10 AM tomorrow. We can go out for a bit, but I'm not getting wasted."

"Fine, we won't get 'wasted,'" she says, rolling her eyes. "A couple drinks, tops. Just enough liquor to get you out on the dance floor."

***

After a few hours of relaxing by the pool, me working on my laptop while Rachel reads trashy tabloid magazines, we go upstairs and get ourselves ready for dinner. Rachel decides to choose my outfit, a short, blue-green sequin dress that I can barely breathe in paired with strappy black heels. Rachel had bought me the dress before we left, insisting it was all part of the "new me". I figured she just wanted me to wear something that matched her own risqué nightlife attire.

As I'm standing in the bathroom, curling the last few strands of my hair, I call out to Rachel. "Did you invite Graham tonight?" I ask, wanting to mentally prepare myself in case she did.

"No," she says, her voice slightly muffled from the other room. "We'll meet up with him tomorrow. He's networking with some of the other sponsors tonight."

"Oh, okay," I say, combing my fingers through my hair. As nervous as I am to see him again, I'd rather just get it over with, rip off the "awkward reunion" Band-Aid. Trying to navigate our complicated history in the middle of a professional conference isn't exactly my ideal situation.

Rachel steps into the doorway, her curvy figure prominent in a sexy two-piece, floral-print dress. She works a huge pair of sparkly hoops into her ears, her blonde hair piled high on her head. "What do you think?" she asks, giving a little twirl. "Sexy enough to reel in the locals?"

"Definitely sexy enough," I say, admiring her gorgeous silhouette. Her hands are covered in cheap, stackable rings, her ring finger currently bare. "Better not text Daniel any photos tonight, he might get jealous."

She waves a hand as she walks into the bathroom, inspecting herself in the mirror. "He has no reason to be jealous. Besides, I can't go out in Miami without a little pizazz. Come on, let's get this show on the road."

We make our way downstairs and walk out into the balmy night, the heat of the day pulsating through my heels as we hit the sidewalk. We walk toward the ocean then turn right on the boardwalk, making our way down the beach. There are people everywhere, our presence a blur in a sea of faces. We pass groups of people sitting around bonfires, hotel bars filled with music and laughter, vendors selling souvenirs and boogie boards. The stream of people is oddly comforting, my need to blend in seemingly unnecessary as we naturally dissolve into the crowd.

After walking five or six blocks, Rachel looks up from her phone's GPS and beams. "We're here!" she says, turning toward a two-story, hut-style bar. It's a couple hundred yards from the water, its large balcony outlined with tiki torches, Latin music drifting out of the open doors. I examine the building, its shingles cracked and warped from the unrelenting sun, its paint chipped and faded from the salty air. I give Rachel a look, unsure about her latest discovery. "Are you sure you want to go here?" I ask. "Seems kind of run down."

"I'm sure," she says, hooking her arm through mine. "It'll be a blast, you'll see."

We ascend the uneven balcony stairs and walk inside. A woman in a tight pink pleather dress greets us at the host stand. "How many?" she asks, tapping her long nails on a stack of menus.

"Two please," I say. She grabs a few menus and leads us inside, seating us at a high top in the corner. There's a large, open balcony above us and a small salsa band playing in the adjacent corner. Most of the main floor is covered in low folding tables, but there's a small area where people are dancing, their moves tight and coordinated. We slide into our seats and a young woman rushes over, setting down a couple of lemon waters.

"Two margaritas," Rachel says, not waiting for introductions or asking for my order. "And two orders of fish tacos. A large chips and guac, and a side of salsa you could drown in."

Our server nods and walks away, unbothered by her abrupt order. I look over at the dance floor, watching a couple as they lean

into one another, their bodies spinning and twirling to the beat.
"Wow, they're so good!" I say as I take a sip of my water.

"Yeah, this place is really popular," Rachel says. "It's quite the hot spot for dancing, apparently."

"Doesn't look like it's that popular," I say, glancing at the empty tables.

"Don't worry," Rachel says. "Once the sun goes down, this place will fill up. We'll have plenty of hot locals to choose from then."

Our food arrives, the crispy, hot fish steaming on our plates. We dive in, laughing and drinking, watching the sunset sink below the horizon as the nighttime crowd starts pouring in. The inside lights come on, the tattered walls glowing red and yellow, hundreds of string lights dangling from the railing above us. I gaze up at the warm lights, feeling giggly and tipsy, the chilled drinks and warm bar a perfect combination. I'm relaxed, happy, finally feeling like I'm on a real vacation.

As we sip on our latest round of cocktails, the servers begin folding up the shorter tables and chairs, placing them against the far wall. Within minutes, a majority of the main dining area is cleared off, revealing a large dance floor.

"Looks like it's time to salsa," Rachel says, rocking back and forth on her chair. She spots a group of guys eyeing us, and she salutes them with a wink before sipping on her drink.

Our server comes over, setting down our check. "The dancing should start any minute," she says. "If you want more food, you can move out onto the patio. Otherwise, it's 'drinks only' inside, and you'll have to start a tab at the bar."

"Of course," I say, glancing at the bill before handing her some cash. "Go ahead and close us out. And keep the change."

"Thanks," she says, dropping the money into her apron. She reaches into another pocket, pulling out a handful of black packets. "They're on the house," she says, setting them on the table. "Have fun, you two - enjoy ladies night!" She scurries away without another word, disappearing quickly into the building crowd.

I pick up a packet, turning it over in my hands. "What is it?" I ask.

Just then, the house lights go out, the entire building plunging into darkness. I start to panic, grabbing for Rachel in the dark, when suddenly the room is glowing, the ceiling and dance floor a hazy purple. The walls are littered with graffiti, UV paint splattered across every surface, and the band is decked out in glowing attire. I look at Rachel and she's grinning ear to ear, her white floral outfit basically turning her into a fluorescent light bulb.

"Black light salsa dancing!" she squeals, reaching for one of the packets. She opens it, pulling out a long, clear stick that she promptly snaps in the middle. She shakes it, the clear liquid inside turning a lava-lamp pink as she secures it around my wrist.

The music swells and people start pouring onto the dance floor, their shirts and shoes and bracelets glowing under the lights. There are bodies everywhere, people spinning and twirling, their faces obscured by glowing body paint and LED glasses. I gaze up toward the second floor at the couples on the balcony, their dark silhouettes bobbing and swaying against the railing. Light scatters across the room, the chandelier above us a dazzling spectacle of blue and pink, making the whole room sparkle. I watch in awe as bubbles start floating down from above, disappearing into the crowd as they sink toward the floor.

I am transfixed, my skin tingling as I watch the vivacious crowd. I turn toward Rachel, laughter bursting out of me. "So much for a tame night!" I yell.

"I know," she says, her voice barely audible over the loud music. She rips open another packet, slipping a glowing blue tube around her neck. "I saw the pictures online, I figured it would be a good time!"

We open the rest of the packets as we finish our drinks, adorning our arms in glowing bracelets. By the time we finish, the dance floor is packed with people. "You ready to dance?" Rachel asks.

"Hell yeah," I say. I slip off my chair and grab her hand as I follow her into the crowd, the dance floor already a sweaty mess of bodies. We sway and spin each other, our movements a blur of hands and heat and neon lights. I lose myself in the crowd, a face in a sea of strangers, and it feels good to be this anonymous, this free. I feel weightless, my body relaxed and loose as I swing my hips, releasing myself fully to the music.

After a couple of songs, I am dripping in sweat, my arms hot and slick as heat radiates from my body. "I need to go to the bathroom," I shout at Rachel.

She nods as she's quickly snatched up by a man with glowing white hair. "I'll be right here," she says before turning around to face him. She pushes into him, their bodies flush, his hand caressing the skin on her lower back. I watch for a moment as they begin to dance, their movements in sync, Rachel relishing the flirtatious attention.

I push through the crowd toward the bar, weaving through an endless throng of bodies. I'm almost off the dance floor when someone grabs my hand and yanks me toward him. Stumbling backward, I crash into him, clumsily stepping on his foot. "I'm sorry, I need to.."

But the body I fall into is warm, his scent a familiar blend of cinnamon and zesty spices. His white, striped shirt is glowing under the lights, and he's wearing a pair of neon green sunglasses. He flips them onto his head and time stops, air suspending in my lungs. The man before me is none other than Graham.

CHAPTER 15

Ten years old, two years before "The Incident"

LAUGHTER SWIRLS AROUND ME as we sprint toward my mother's car, my friends and I waving at her as she comes into view in the school's pickup lane. Her car windows are covered in blue and green paint, the words *Happy Birthday Anna!* and *Bon Voyage 9!* in bold, swirling letters, the car blasting "Kokomo" by The Beach Boys. My mother is standing outside the car wearing a tropical sundress, an armful of lei necklaces in her hands. "Alright girls, let me see your tickets!" she cries, each of my friends holding up a postcard party invitation, their official "ticket" to my tenth birthday party. My mom gives each girl a necklace before turning toward me, her smile wide as she slips a huge multi-colored lei around my neck.

"Happy birthday Annabelle," she says, setting a matching flower crown on my head before kissing me on the cheek. "Alright ladies, let's do this thing!" she says, her dress swirling around her ankles as she dances to the music, all of us boogieing on the sidewalk, excited for the night ahead. My mother leads us toward the back of the car, the trunk already open for all of our backpacks and overnight bags. "Where's your bag, Vicky?" my mom asks, looking down at the single backpack in her hand.

Vicky squirms a bit, looking embarrassed. "My mom forgot to pack mine, she hasn't done laundry yet. I brought my toothbrush, though."

My mom smiles at her, smoothing her hair. This isn't the first time we've had a sleepover where she needed to borrow clothes. "That's okay, we have plenty of pajamas to go around." She shuts the truck, ushering us toward the car as people begin to honk. "Okay girls, everybody in! Anna, you sit in the front. The rest of you, there's a little care package on each of your seats, so don't sit on them!"

We climb into my mother's sedan, each of us picking up a small, white box as we slide inside and buckle our seatbelts. My mother hops into the driver's seat, the whole car rocking as she slams the door. Turning to face my friends, my mother gestures toward the white boxes, giving them her best flight attendant impersonation. "Courtesy of Anna's 'Around The World' birthday experience, please enjoy the in-flight snacks on the way to our destination." She grins, pleased with her little skit as she turns around to start the car.

The girls squeal, opening their boxes, each one containing a cupcake, a few pieces of candy, and some popcorn. "Awesome, I'm starving," Kate says, grabbing a handful of popcorn and shoving it in her mouth.

"Don't worry, there's plenty more at the house," my mom says, shaking her head. She turns toward me, setting a glittery, blue bag in my lap. "Open it," she says, her eyes flashing as she waits with anticipation. I pull out the white tissue paper, revealing four disposable cameras and a beautiful handmade photo album, my name on the front in little, tiled letters. "You're double digits now, baby," my mother says, watching me as I run my hand over the scrapbook, my fingers tracing bits of lace and buttons. "It's for your adventures as you go through school, for your travels someday. To document all the wonderful memories ahead of you." She grabs one of the cameras out of the bag, tightening the dial as she points it at my friends. "Say 'Happy Birthday, Anna!'" she cries, their faces smudged with frosting and popcorn as she snaps a picture. She then turns the camera toward me, snapping one more photo before tossing the camera back in the bag. "Okay, okay, let's get this show on the road!" she says, the honking behind her overshadowing the festive music. She takes off for home, the four of us snacking on our treats as she drives, all of us swaying to the music.

***

We sprint into the house, kicking off our shoes and throwing our school bags down on the floor. My mother leads us toward the basement stairs, a location that's been off-limits for days. "Your luxury birthday experience awaits," she says, smiling proudly as she opens the door. The four of us run downstairs, shrieking as we lay eyes on the elaborate set-up my parents created.

The basement has been cleared out to look like a first-class airplane cabin, the couch moved back to make room for four lounger air mattresses, each of them pointed toward the TV project screen on the far wall. The loungers are piled high with pillows and blankets, a tray of "complimentary snacks" placed next to each one. There's a separate table in the back featuring drinks and board games, as well as a basket of age-appropriate Blu-ray movies. Paper streamers hang from the walls and ceiling, matching the blue and green paint from my mother's car windows.

"Alright, girls, this is your night," my mother says, gesturing toward the excessive room. "Your father will be home around six with dinner. Until then, let's have some fun."

My friends and I sprint toward the loungers, each of us claiming one as our own. We spend the first hour or two watching a movie together, snacking on candy and chips as my mother comes around to each of us, offering a special "pampering service." She paints our toenails and gives us hand massages, the four of us giggling at each other as we wear animal sheet masks on our faces. After the movie, we grab a couple board games, a pile of blankets beneath us as we spread out on the floor.

We're just starting a game of Monopoly when my father descends the stairs, carrying several giant bags of food. "Well hello, ladies!" he says, giving us a warm welcome. "Is everyone having a good time?"

"We're doing great," my mom says, finishing up a French braid on one of the girls before standing up to greet my dad. "How are you?"

"Oh, I'm good," he says, setting the food and a small stack of mail on the table. "I got the whole spread, exactly what you asked." My parents start laying out dinner, a smorgasbord of dishes from 'across the globe', even though it all came from the same restaurant chain. "Okay girls, we've got some Chinese food, some mini burgers, a cheese pizza, and some fish and chips," my dad says, admiring his contribution. "There's a little bit of everything, so enjoy."

We eat dinner together, the six of us devouring the assortment of dishes in no time at all. Afterwards, my father disappears upstairs, the lights overhead dimming as he returns with a two-tiered cake, a lit "10" candle sticking out the top. The bottom of the cake is shaped like a suitcase while the top mimics a map of the world, my name written across the side. "Wow, that's so cool," my friend Tara says, walking around it to get a better look.

"It is," my father replies, smiling at my mom. He carefully leans over, giving her a kiss. "Just a little preview of my wife's amazing work before she opens up her own shop."

"All in due time," my mother says, winking at him. As she rearranges the table to make room for the cake, she bumps the pile of mail, the entire stack falling to the floor. She bends down to pick it up, her face going pale as she holds up a letter, its envelope crinkled and dirty. My dad, noticing her change in demeanor, steps in beside her, frowning at the letter, the two of them seeming genuinely concerned.

"Mom, are you okay?" I ask, shadows from the candlelight dancing over her face.

She shakes her head, her attention coming back to me. "I'm good, sweetie. It's just a bill." She folds the envelope in half, tucking it in her back pocket. "Okay, Anna, make a wish," my mother says, her face lit from the candlelight of the cake she made especially for me.

Looking at my parents and my friends, I realize that I don't need a wish. I'm happy, my life is just what I want it to be. I run and grab one of my disposable cameras that's been floating around the room, taking a quick picture of my cake, my parents' faces glowing behind it as I blow out my candles.

CHAPTER 16

"Hi, Avery", Graham says, his demeanor calm and collected as people dance wildly around us. He's so close to me that I can see a hint of stubble across his chin, feel the heat of his body as he looms over me, his hand still clutching mine. I suddenly feel too hot, the room muggy and stifling as bile rushes up into my throat. I heave but catch myself, then I rip my hand from his and run for the patio. I break through several groups of people and hurl myself at the railing, ocean waves crashing in the distance as I vomit violently. I wretch and heave, our drinks and tacos splattering across the sand.

I lean against the rough wood of the railing, breathing in the cool, salty air as I try to compose myself. I hear a laugh coming from behind me, my skin prickling at the deep tone of his voice. "Not the reaction I was aiming for," Graham says, his footsteps thumping against the patio as he walks over to check on me.

"Sorry," I say, wiping at my mouth. I turn around slowly, half expecting him to look disgusted, but he doesn't. He's standing a few feet away, his silhouette backlit by the indoor lights, his hands firmly in his pockets. I shift uncomfortably, unsure what else to say. "It was really hot in there. Plus, it's ladies' night... I think Rachel ordered us one too many margaritas."

"That sounds like her," Graham says. He's silent for a moment, his eyes studying my face before wandering down toward the contours of my dress. I'm glad it's dark out here because I can feel myself blushing, the heat rising in my cheeks as my body responds to his scrutiny. "You look different," he says, his statement curious, as though he's asking a question. "If Rachel hadn't sent me that picture earlier, I wouldn't have believed it was you."

"Yeah, she did quite the makeover on me," I say, tugging at the hem of my dress.

"She did," he agrees, falling silent once again. He looks away and I follow his gaze, the two of us staring out at the ocean, the sounds of the tide filling the void. This isn't exactly the reunion I expected, but it isn't a bad experience, either. "Looked like you were having fun in there," he says, nodding toward the restaurant, the music still blaring over the bustling crowd.

"I've always enjoyed dancing," I say, giving him an awkward shrug.

He nods, a knowing smile playing across his lips. "Yeah, I remember."

For a moment I just look at him, the man before me a far cry from the boy I once knew. His body has changed, his build thicker and more sturdy, his boyish features more subdued. Even in the dark, I can make out his strong jaw, the broad set of his shoulders. He seems relaxed, confident, more self-assured than I've ever seen him. I, on the other hand, not only don't look like myself, I am also a vomiting, nervous wreck.

Graham notices me watching him and he smiles, his golden eyes sparkling. "It's been a long time," he says quietly.

"Yeah," I agree, struggling not to look at his mouth when he speaks. "A couple years now."

"Five, to be exact." His words punch me in the gut, his statement deliberate and packed with thinly-veiled meaning. I feel like I'm going to be sick all over again, my stomach churning as Graham stares at me, his honey-colored irises glowing in the light from the tiki torches.

I cross my arms over my chest, desperate to change the subject. "I didn't know you'd be here," I say, my words coming out in a rush. "At the conference, I mean. Rachel told me right before we hopped on the plane."

"I didn't either," he replies softly. Now he's the one who looks uncomfortable, his head dipping a little as he shuffles between his feet. "I just got a promotion, a pretty good one, actually. They asked me to run one of our teams a few days ago, it was all very last minute."

"So what are you doing here?" I ask, gesturing to the bar. "Rachel said you were working tonight."

"We were," Graham says. "We finished setting up our booth early. Some of the veteran employees have been here before, so we walked down after dinner to check it out."

As soon as he says it, two guys decked out in glow sticks stroll onto the patio, one of them slapping a hand on Graham's shoulder. His blond hair has been sprayed neon pink, and there's a dusting of body glitter in his beard. "Wow, Graham, who's the goddess?" he asks as he unabashedly admires my dress.

"Tim, this is Avery," Graham says, nodding toward me. "She's a long-time friend of my sister."

Tim takes my hand and kisses it before performing a slight bow. "Hello, Avery, I'm Timothy—Tim for short. This is Connor, my shy-but-brilliant work husband." I glance toward his friend, who smiles and gives me a little wave, his garish flamingo shirt and bright orange shorts both radiant in the moonlight. He sips happily on his cocktail as Tim steps in closer, a strong scent of liquor hanging on his breath. "Are you one of the models this year?" he asks, his odd question apparently genuine.

"No," I laugh, taking a step back. "I'm a contestant, actually—a finalist for 'Photo of the Year.'" I glance at Graham and I see his expression shift, his jaw twitch. It's obvious that he's seen my entry photo, the look on his face indicating that he remembers that moment as much as I do.

"Oh, beautiful *and* talented," Tim says, throwing his hands on his hips. "I might just be in love!"

I see movement behind the boys as Rachel comes rushing out onto the patio, her sexy dance partner in tow. "Avery, where have you been? I've been looking all over for you!" She grabs me, pulling me in for a hug, but her attention veers off course when she catches sight of her brother. "Graham! What are you doing here?" she cries, releasing me to latch onto him.

"Enjoying the calm before the storm," he says, pulling away from her. He frowns at her male companion for a moment before turning his attention back to her. "Our company is expecting a huge crowd this year, so we thought we'd enjoy a night out before things get crazy. What are you doing here?"

"Just having some fun with my girl," Rachel says, throwing an arm around my shoulder. "It's not every day I drag her ass out of town, I have to make the most of it!"

"Indeed," he says, gesturing toward the open dance floor. "Shall we go back inside, then?"

"Hell yes!" Tim cries, grabbing Connor's arm and running for the door, his neon hair glowing under the lights as soon as they step inside. Rachel releases me and struts across the patio, beelining for the dance floor with her eager partner in tow. I stand there, watching her walk away, acutely aware of Graham's presence as he steps in close to me. I look up at him, my heart fluttering as he smiles and extends his hand.

"Care for a dance?" he asks, his warm eyes melting through me. "For old time's sake?'

I look at his hand, then back at him, wondering if this is a good idea. So far he's been friendly, no traces of anger or resentment about the past, but a part of me is still afraid to dance with him, to touch him. Sensing my hesitation, he reaches out himself, his expression warm and reassuring as he slides his hand into mine. He pulls me forward into the club, his hand an anchor as we float back into a dazzling sea of people.

At first I'm nervous, my movements mechanical and jerky. He tries spinning me a few times, laughing when I stumble and step on his foot. But then he pulls me in closer, my body flush against his, and everything between us shifts. We lock onto one another, every move I make mimicked by him, the air around us becoming unbearably hot. He isn't laughing and I'm not thinking, both of us lost in the rhythm of each other's bodies.

We are melded together, our faces tilting dangerously close to one another, when a horn blares and the music dies. "We're taking a short break," the salsa band declares, raising a hand to the crowd. "Enjoy the house music, we'll be back in ten minutes!"

Graham and I break apart, our chests heaving, his shirt damp and clinging to his body. Wet strands of hair stick to my face, and without warning, Graham reaches up, brushing them aside. His fingertips scrape along my skin and I shiver, the gesture sensual and familiar. I take another step back, increasing my distance from him, his hands bringing back memories I can't handle right now.

Rachel runs over to us, her blonde curls now loose around her shoulders. "My feet are killing me and this guy is getting a little too handsy," she says, grabbing my arm. "You ready to head back?"

I look at Graham for a split second before nodding at Rachel. "Yeah, I'm ready to go," I say.

"See you tomorrow, bro," Rachel says, running over to give him a peck on the cheek. "Don't stay out too late, you have a big day tomorrow!"

"I won't," he says. He hugs her then looks toward me, giving me a small nod. "Goodnight, Avery."

"Goodnight," I say quietly. I hold his gaze for a moment, an air of longing suspended between us. Then I turn and follow Rachel toward the door.

***

When we get back to the hotel, I check my phone. There's a text from my mom, letting me know all is well, and another email from Cynthia, this one about changing some of her posts' captions. I text my mom goodnight, then decide to wake up early to address Cynthia's issues. I doubt I'd be able to do a very good job right now, anyway, considering I'm tired and slightly tipsy.

I'm about to put my phone away when I get a message through my business social media page. It's Graham. *Thought I'd message you on here, not sure I have your number. We're at Booth 402 if you want to stop by tomorrow. It's to the left of the main stage, can't miss it.*

I think for a moment, then text him back. *Thanks, we'll be sure to stop by. Not sure what time, depends when I can coax Rachel out of bed.*

Good luck with that, he replies, adding on a winky face. A few minutes go by, then he messages again. *It was nice to see you tonight.*

I blush, chills running through me at the thought of his hands on my body. *You too,* I reply. *Thank you for the dance.*

Anytime, he texts back.

We're both silent for a beat, so I send one final text to end the conversation. *Goodnight Graham, see you tomorrow.*

Goodnight, Avery, he replies, promptly logging off of the app.

I stare at the messages for a moment, wondering where he's at, if he made it back to the hotel. Pushing my curiosity aside, I plug my phone in and go get ready for bed.

CHAPTER 17

It's just past 10 AM when Rachel and I walk into the lobby the following morning, a line of attendees already snaking its way toward the convention center doors. I'm on high alert, scanning the bustling crowd, nervously adjusting my hair and fussing with my dress. I'd risen well before my alarm clock, anxiety racing through me as I rewrote captions for Cynthia, the looming competition making it hard to focus. By the time Rachel got up, coaxed out of bed by the smell of pancakes and fresh coffee, I was already dressed and ready for the day.

I hadn't slept much, the rush of seeing Graham and the uncertainty of this conference keeping me awake. Every time I started to doze off, I would feel the grip of Graham's hands on my waist, smell the spicy aroma of his skin. I jolted awake several times before eventually falling asleep, my dreams a kaleidoscope of neon lights, shifting bodies, and the sensation of heat.

We linger near the elevators for a moment, observing the massive crowd. "Wow, there's a lot more photography nerds here than I expected," Rachel says.

"A lot more," I say, anxiously scanning their faces. I'd watched the conference online many times, but I hadn't anticipated this many people.

Rachel clocks my nervous expression, putting her arm around me. "Don't worry," she says. "We gave you a *full* makeover—you're a whole new person. Between the hair, contacts, and excessive use of makeup, you really don't look like you."

"Promise?" I ask, glancing over at her for reassurance.

She bumps me with her hip, both of us swaying sideways together. "I promise," she says. "Like I said, if anything goes wrong and you need to leave, we bolt and never look back."

"Okay," I say, shaking off my nerves and standing up straight. "Come on." I walk us toward the front of the line where several employees are scanning badges. A woman looks up from her clipboard at me, her smile as bright and cheerful as her crisp, yellow blazer. "Hi, my name is Avery Walters," I say. "I'm a contest finalist, I think we're supposed to pick up our badges here?"

"Oh, of course," the woman says. "Can I see some ID?" I show her my driver's license as she scans a sheet of paper, verifying my name. Then she rummages through a large, plastic bin of yellow envelopes, eventually handing me one with my name on it. "These are your badges for the entire conference, they'll give you an all-access pass to the daytime and evening events," she says. "You're good to go, ladies, have a wonderful time!"

"Thank you," I say, handing a badge and matching lanyard to Rachel. We slip them over our heads, securing them into place, then shuffle past security and walk into the convention center.

The moment we step inside, I'm completely awestruck. There are booths everywhere, brands I love promoting cutting-edge camera equipment and innovative editing software. I look around at the companies I don't know, their impressive displays of backdrops, bags, lenses, tripods, anything you could possibly need to take amazing photographs. I feel like a kid in a candy store, every booth exciting and interesting, my nerves and fear washing away as I'm caught up in the moment. I never imagined that the first conference I would attend, let alone compete in, would be as massive and impressive as this.

I grab a program off of a side table and open it to the convention center map, looking to see where the individual vendors are. "There's Graham's booth," Rachel says, pointing toward the middle. I look and sure enough, it's to the left of the main stage, smack in the middle of everything.

I flip to the next page, scanning the list of speakers. "Oh wow!" I cry. "There's a panel by Anthony Freeman! We *have* to go to that, he's an absolute legend."

"Sure," Rachel says, shrugging her shoulders. "This is your event, Avery. You just tell me where to go and we'll go."

We make our way down one of the outermost walkways, stopping at several booths. I test out a couple of DSLR camera lenses, learn about the newest upgrades to Photoshop and Lightroom, I even buy myself a new camera bag. We wander around for a bit, Rachel trailing behind me as I skip from booth to booth, each new discovery more exciting than the last. After a while, I'm not sure who's having more fun; me, the photography enthusiast, or Rachel, the casual observer.

Eventually we drift toward the middle of the room and spot the main stage. It's massive, with huge projection screens hovering over the crowd and row after row of chairs lined up in front of it. Most of the seats are already full of people, waiting for the next panel.

"Let's go say hi to Graham," Rachel says, pulling me toward his booth.

We make our way around the masses and head toward Graham's booth. I recognize the company, penLite, an innovative tablet and software well-known for its digital drawing applications. I spot him talking to a customer near the back of the booth, and in the clear light of day I can see how painfully handsome he is. He's wearing a crisp button-up shirt and dress slacks, his hair clean and neatly tousled. He sees us walking over and gives us a nod, his eyes lingering on me for a second before returning to his customer.

We meander around the booth, playing with the demo tablets until he walks over. I feel myself tense up a bit as he approaches, his strong build and striking eyes much more intimidating in the daylight. "There you are," he says, giving us a generous smile. "You made it."

"We did," I say, his cheerful grin catching me off guard. It's a smile I've seen a thousand times, a simple gesture that brings back a flood of memories. I blink a couple times before returning the favor, doing my best to appear normal.

"Hey bro," Rachel says, giving him a hug. He pulls away then looks at me, and after a moment of hesitation, I step closer and give him a tentative squeeze. He smells impossibly fresh, his shirt giving off a slight floral scent, and I try hard not to notice the taut muscles beneath his shirt.

"It took us a minute to get over here," I say, pulling away from him. "I was a bit overzealous as we walked around—there are so many cool vendors!"

"She was a bit excited," Rachel says, chuckling. "Geeking out over just about everything, basically creaming in her pants."

I nearly faint at Rachel's remark, flushing scarlet red as I nudge her with my elbow. Graham laughs but he makes a point not to look at me. "That's understandable, there are a lot of great companies here. It's a very popular conference for photographers and other digital designers."

"Absolutely," I agree, looking around at the booth as I get myself under control.

"Well, you made it just in time," Graham says. "Are you ready?"

"Ready for what?" I ask, looking up at him.

Graham's brow furrows slightly as he gives me a skeptical look. "The panel, the one for the contest? You go on in ten minutes."

"What?" I say, looking over at the stage. The seats are all full now and there's a huge crowd gathering around the edges. I turn back to Graham, my face frozen in disbelief. "I'm a part of that panel?"

"Yeah," he says, looking concerned. "It's in the program, you didn't know?"

"I completely forgot about it," I say as I feel myself begin to panic. I look at Rachel, incoherent words sputtering out of me. "Wh-wh-what do I do? Should I skip it? Will that hurt my chances to win?"

"You've got this, Avery," she says, grabbing me by the shoulders. "Just take a deep breath for me, okay?" Rachel squares up to me as I breathe in and out, each of us inhaling and exhaling in unison. We do this together for about a minute, but it doesn't seem to help much.

Graham grabs a nearby program and flips through it, shaking his head. "It's really quick, Avery. It's basically just an introduction of your work. You may be asked a question or two, but there's nine other contestants to get through. You'll be fine."

My chest feels tight and I can tell that I'm already sweating. I look at the stage, at the enormous crowd gathered around it. I think about all those people looking at me, my face plastered across the huge television screens, our panel being broadcast to the world. Every fiber in my being is screaming for me to run.

Rachel shakes me, bringing me back to the present. "*You've got this*," she says, emphasizing every syllable. "You are Avery Walters, you were born to do this. Everything will be okay."

I look at her, terrified, but then I think about the prize money, about my mother's treatments. "Okay," I say, nodding my head over and over again. "Okay."

"Let's get you over there," Rachel says, taking me by the arm. Before we go, she looks back over her shoulder at Graham. "We'll swing by afterwards, we can all go grab lunch together."

"Okay, sure," he says, clearly still concerned about the situation. He looks at me, his gaze steady, his eyes a brilliant amber. "You've got this, Avery. You can do it."

Rachel pulls me away, guiding me toward the stage. I look back at Graham and he gives me a reassuring smile, holding up his hands in a silly thumbs up gesture . I half-heartedly smile back as we disappear into the crowd.

CHAPTER 18

We make our way to the left side of the stage where a small area is roped off, the red velvet stanchions separating the contestants from the rest of the crowd . A short woman sporting a blunt bob haircut and wearing exceptionally tall heels is standing near the entrance, holding a clipboard. As we get closer, I recognize several of the other finalists standing behind her, most of them mingling as they prepare to go on stage. A few of them glance at me as we approach, sizing me up, their critical gazes increasing my sense of panic.

Rachel drags me over to the woman wielding the clipboard and shoves me toward her. "This is my friend, Avery Walters. She's a finalist. Are we in the right place?"

"Oh yes," the woman exclaims, her hair swaying in unison as she nods her head. The badge around her neck indicates that her name is Barbara. "I'm so glad you made it, we're just about to take the stage"

"Perfect," Rachel says. She turns me around, locking eyes with me as she takes my hands. "You're gonna do great, okay? It'll be super quick." She looks at the audience, pointing toward the right side of the crowd before turning back to me. "I'll be right over there, standing next to that speaker. Just look at me if you get nervous."

"Okay," I say, my voice small and squeaky. She takes a deep breath and I mimic her, both of us releasing it at the same time. As we do, music starts playing and a voice comes through the overhead speakers. "Ladies and gentlemen, please welcome our 'Photo of the Year' finalists!

The finalists begin filing onto the stage one-by-one. I peel away from Rachel and step forward into the line-up, shoulders back, trying to appear composed. My heart beats wildly against my chest as I ascend the stairs, my thoughts drowned out by the roar of the crowd as I take my place among the other photographers.

I smile weakly, wondering who is in the audience, if anyone out there recognizes me. I look to the right and Rachel is standing with a large group of observers, her lanky silhouette in plain view, her smile wide with pride. I smile back at her, thankful for a friendly face. As the cheering dies down, we take our seats in a semi-circle of plush, green chairs, me crossing my ankles in an attempt to not fidget. After a few moments, our host, legendary wildlife photographer David Hermann, strides onto the stage, the crowd cheering loudly as he begins his introductions.

"Hello, everyone!" he says, his voice booming through the nearby speakers. "It's such an honor to be here today and to introduce you to our incredible finalists! A quick reminder of how everything works: each contestant's entry will be reviewed and voted on by our esteemed panel of judges. This happens tomorrow and will account for forty percent of their final score. The other sixty percent will be based on a popular vote, which starts *right now*! That gives each of you two days to vote for your favorite entries!"

The crowd erupts in applause, cameras flashing all around us, each burst of light blinding me. I keep smiling, glancing repeatedly at Rachel for reassurance as David continues. "Online voting will end at midnight tomorrow night, and the top three contestants will be announced at noon on Sunday. Now, it's time to meet our finalists!"

One by one our names are called, each person joining David in the middle of the stage to discuss his or her work. There's a lot of laughing, schmoozing, smiling, whatever needs to be done to gain the favor of the audience. His questions are innocent enough: details about what inspired your entry, what camera or editing software was used, what you were thinking about as you took the shot. Each time an interview ends, I hold my breath, wringing my sweaty palms in my lap as I wait for him to call my name.

After chatting with a rather disheveled contestant sporting a scraggly beard and large, circular glasses, David beams at the crowd and reads the next name on his list. "Avery Walters!" he says, his wide, crooked smile turning toward me.

I stand up slowly, my arms and legs like Jell-O as I walk toward the middle of the stage. I reach out to shake his hand, my smile awkward and forced, my whole body trembling as he hands me a microphone. I take it, praying I don't drop it as we sit down, facing one another.

"Avery, thank you so much for being here," he says, his demeanor warm and welcoming.

"Thank you for having me," I say, trying to act naturally. I look out at the audience, at the cameras pointed at me, the vulnerability of the moment completely overwhelming. Holding tight to the microphone, I refocus on David, zeroing in on his features in an effort to get me through this interview.

"Can you give us a little background on yourself?" he asks, leaning forward in his chair. I notice his fresh haircut, the freckles along his nose and cheeks from years spent outside. "What got you interested in photography?"

"Nothing in particular," I say, my words mostly steady as I tighten my grip on the microphone. "I just wanted to capture things, hold onto memories. Eventually I got better at it, upgraded my equipment, learned more about editing, lighting, things like that." David nods along, waiting for more, so I continue. "By the time I finished high school, I'd decided that photography would be my career. Over time, I've come to specialize in product and event photography, which led to some social media management, as well."

"So that's what most of your work consists of today, then? Product photography and events?" he asks.

"Yes," I say, flashing the audience a smile. The whole point of doing this is to place in the top five, and if I want to win, I need to loosen up, be more likable.

"That's amazing!" he says, playing it up for the crowd. "I find that pretty fascinating because the shot you sent us is *far* from product photography."

"Yes," I admit, chuckling a little, partly because it's true but also because I wasn't the one who sent it in. "It is a bit different."

"It is, it's incredible!" he exclaims. "Every time I see it, it truly takes my breath away." He looks up at the giant screen behind us, my photograph blown up for everyone to see. The audience begins to clap and cheer, their enthusiasm making me feel a little more comfortable.

"It really was a beautiful location," I say, admiring the picture as the applause dies down. "The light that day was magnificent, I feel lucky I was able to capture it."

"Well, I think you might need to add 'nature photographer' to your resume, because this is just simply exquisite," David says, his eyes still on the screen.

Considering his area of expertise, I hope he actually means that and isn't just feeding me empty compliments for the sake of the contest. "Maybe," I say, giving a slight shrug. "We'll see what happens."

"What kind of equipment did you use to capture this?" he asks, looking back at me.

I think back to that weekend, me running around the scorching desert with two cameras hanging from my neck. "I used a DSLR for test shots, but for this I used an old Hasselblad with Kodak Ektachrome film. I developed the photos myself, then I scanned them and did all the editing and color adjustments in Lightroom and Photoshop."

"The colors are what's really fascinating," he says thoughtfully, "truly a masterpiece in temperature and vibrancy. Is it a true reflection of what you saw that day, or are the final images something different entirely?"

"I worked on them a lot," I say quietly, my mind combing through the hours I spent at my computer, examining every detail. "They're still very true to the originals, but I did experiment quite a bit with the color elements. It was just such an amazing place, I really wanted the pictures I took to embody that."

"So this image, your submission, is more a visual reflection of the *emotional* memory of this location? Am I understanding that correctly?" David looks up, his smoky blue-gray eyes examining the screen once more before returning to me.

"Yes," I say, my voice weak, soft, like I'm telling him a secret.

"And what was so special about this place?" he asks.

"It was.." I hesitate, glancing over at Rachel. She's watching me intently, nodding for me to continue. My eyes shift away from her, scanning the unfamiliar faces of the crowd until they suddenly fall on Graham. I can see him standing next to his booth, his posture rigid, his jaw tight as his eyes bore into mine. He's staring at me, waiting like everyone else for my answer.

"Ours," I say, my focus entirely on him, my voice barely a whisper. My mind sinks into the past and I can feel him kissing me, his hands in my hair, our bodies twisting around one another in the dark...

"Excuse me?"

I snap out of the memory, sputtering as I return my attention to David. "It was our.. first big road trip across the country, fresh out of high school. It was a very significant moment in my life and these pictures reflect that."

"Of course," Frank says in an empathetic tone. "Getting a taste of freedom, independence."

I smile but the words sting, knowing what happened next. "Yes, exactly."

"Well, thank you, Avery—it's been a pleasure meeting you and discussing your incredible work! With that, I shake his hand and stand up, walking back to my seat. I look at Rachel, who gives me a thumbs up as she cheers enthusiastically along with the crowd. I search for Graham next but he's no longer watching, his attention returning to the customers at his booth. He looks calm, normal, his demeanor completely unphased, as if nothing ever happened.

CHAPTER 19

Fifteen years old, three years after "The Incident"

People swirl around us as we walk out of the movie theater, the small town bustling with locals and tourists. Swarms of music enthusiasts wander down the street as they partake in this year's winter music festival, the rhythmic sounds of drums and bass guitar pouring out of nearby venues. I walk alongside Graham, pulling my wool hat down over my ears, our breath coming out in cloudy bursts in the cold weather.

"What'd you guys think of the movie?" Graham asks, glancing around the group. He'd driven us over to Glenwood Springs for the day, borrowing Maggie's car at Rachel's request to go antiquing. In reality, she just wanted to get out of town so she could hang out with her boyfriend, Robbie, the two of them currently walking in front of us, Robbie blatantly grabbing her ass.

"It was cool," Rachel says, giving a little shrug. Not that she'd know, since she and Robbie spent the whole second half making out. Graham and I tried throwing popcorn at them to get them to stop, but it was no use.

"Well, where to next?" Graham asks, doing his best to ignore Robbie's hand placement. "Do you want to check out a couple of shops, get a bite to eat?"

"I wouldn't mind checking out the festival," Robbie calls over his shoulder, sticking his hand into the waist of Rachel's jeans. He winks at her and I cringe, knowing they just want another dark place to sit and make out.

Graham frowns, turning toward me. "How about you, Avery? Anything you want to do?"

I stare at him, my mind drifting toward things I shouldn't think about, moments in a dark movie theater that I wish the two of us could share. Pulling myself out of the fantasy, I look up at the sky, focusing on the twinkling lights overhead as they sway back and forth in the wind. "I kinda want to just walk around, maybe check out the Christmas lights near the park," I say. "They'll only be up for another week or so."

Rachel turns around abruptly, the four of us motionless on the sidewalk as couples and families maneuver around us. "I *cannot* do the park right now, it's too cold," Rachel says, squirming in her thin pleather leggings. "How about Robbie and I go check out the festival while you two go see the lights? We can meet up with you in an hour or so." She smiles sweetly at Graham and me, an expectant look on her face as she practically begs us for permission to venture off alone.

"Ten o'clock," Graham says, "outside the Crescent Park Hotel. Not a second later or Mom is gonna have my hide."

"Thanks bro," Rachel says, running up to give him a hug. She and Robbie scamper away, leaving Graham and I alone on the cold, crowded street. I burrow into my coat, feeling a bit nervous to be alone with him. It's become more difficult to be around him when it's just the two of us, which is still fairly often.

"I hope you don't mind," Graham says, glancing down at me with a sour look on his face. "If I had to watch him grope her for the next hour, I may have had to punch him."

I chuckle, trying not to blush. "Not a fan of Robbie, I take it?"

"He's okay," he says, shrugging. I know he's just being protective of Rachel, his big brother instincts getting stronger the older that she gets. "He seems like a nice enough guy. I just don't want a front-row seat to the show."

I laugh, shaking my head, the sight of Rachel kissing boys not exactly comfortable for me, either. "Neither do I. If that's all they plan to do tonight, we'll probably have more fun without them."

Graham smiles, the Christmas lights above us shimmering in his eyes. "I think so, too. So, where to next?"

Graham and I zigzag through downtown, popping in and out of shops, laughing at the ridiculous things people sell, like handmade pig ornaments and ceramic baby sculptures. A chill falls over the town and people slowly begin to scatter, hurrying toward their vehicles, their families in tow. Graham and I pop into a small cafe, ordering hot chocolates to keep our hands warm before heading back out into the cold. Christmas lights sparkling around us as we veer into the town square, the two of us walking in silence as a light snow starts to fall on our shoulders.

Graham holds my cup as I take a couple of pictures, my hands barely warm enough to adjust my camera settings. "So, did you decide when you're leaving for college?" I ask, glancing sidelong at him before snapping a photo of an ice sculpture, the incredible display in the shape of a giant cowboy boot.

Graham looks around the square, his cheeks red from the cold. "Not yet," he says. "Trying to decide if I want to stay for the summer or not."

I pull the camera away from my face, my brow scrunching together as I turn to look at Graham. "You're graduating early and plan to move halfway across the country for college, just to get away from this place. Now you're considering staying for the summer? Why?"

Graham stares at me, shadows moving over his face as Christmas lights flicker around us, his warm breath rising and dissipating into the frigid air. I can see his mind working and I'm curious to know what he's thinking, the square silent except for the soft whisper of fresh snow. "I have my reasons," he says, holding out my hot chocolate.

I cap the lens of my camera and take the hot chocolate from him, my fingers grazing his gloved hand as I accept it. My heart pitter-patters in my chest, my feelings attempting to rise to the surface as I take a big swig of my drink. "Summer is probably a lot more fun on the West Coast," I say, hiding my now scarlet-red cheeks behind the cardboard cup. "A summer on the beach definitely beats our local swimming hole." Graham nods but doesn't say anything, the two of us moving away from the square and into the nearby park.

We wander through the illuminated trees, passing unique Christmas displays created by families and local businesses, both of us bracing against the cold as we trudge along the frozen ground. As we exit the park, I notice a makeshift ice rink across the street, its overhead lights turned off, the rental booth for ice skates locked up for the night.

Graham follows my gaze, acknowledging the empty rink. “Want to take a turn around the ice?” he says, looking down at me with a playful smirk.

I frown, his proposition making no sense. “We can’t,” I say, gesturing toward the boarded-up rental booth. “The skates are all locked up.”

“Where there’s a will, there’s a way,” he says, turning around in circles. He pulls me across the street toward the rink, snow flying as he pops the lids off of two plastic trash cans. I look over my shoulder, afraid someone will see us and call the cops or something. “We can use these,” he says, handing me one of the lids. “Or just slide around in our boots, whatever works better. I do consider myself an excellent ice waddler.”

I laugh, nervously looking around at the empty street. “Do we even have time?”

Graham shrugs. “Probably not, but it doesn’t matter. Rachel and Robbie are going to be late anyway.”

We chuck our empty cups into the trash before walking over to the deserted rink, glancing around as we climb over the fence. The ice feels cold and slippery beneath my feet, my chances of falling more than probable since my winter boots have virtually no tread left. I look down at my camera, the expensive equipment still hanging around my neck. “Think it will be okay out here?” I ask.

Graham takes his scarf off, his bold scent hanging in the air as he wraps it around my camera, a layer of extra padding in case it falls. Then he tucks the camera back in its sleeve and removes it from my neck altogether, hanging it on a nearby fence post. “Just in case,” he says, giving me a quick wink, my heart fluttering again, in spite of myself. Leaning over to pick up one of the plastic lids, he grins as he pushes away from the fence, lunging face first onto the ice. The lid glides over the frozen water, spinning him in lopsided circles until he eventually comes to a complete stop.

We slide across the ice together, twirling and bumping into one another, neither of us particularly graceful on the plastic lids. At one point, Graham tries to slingshot me across the rink using his belt, the lid wobbling terribly until I tumble out of it, cackling uncontrollably on the icy surface. We try sliding around on our own, Graham awkwardly striding across the rink in his heavy boots, attempting to show off but mostly falling down for sport. We laugh and laugh, each of us acting like idiots as we drift back and forth under the falling snow.

Grabbing my camera off the fence post, I carefully turn to face the rink, holding it close to my body as I adjust the settings. "Okay, go!" I cry out, pointing the camera in Graham's direction. He runs and dives onto the ice, flying toward me through the snow, his expression so goofy and wholesome that I'm full-on grinning behind the camera. I take a quick burst of shots, Graham's scarf draped loosely over my shoulder, his scent lingering on my camera as I snap his picture.

I carefully tuck my camera away as Graham slides up to me, his cheeks pink from the cold. "Kind of surprised no one's kicked us off the ice by now," Graham says, grabbing my hand as I help him off the ground.

I laugh, struggling to keep my balance as he rises to his feet. "Well, I'm impressed. I didn't think those lids would work, but we pulled it off," I say, smiling at him.

Graham grins, panting as he hunches over in front of me, his hat covered in a layer of fresh snow. "I'm going to miss you, you know," he says, his smile fading as he stands up straight. "You're the one good thing about this place, besides my mom and my pain-in-the-ass sister."

I look away, my cheeks growing warm as I shake my head. "You're gonna have a whole new life out there, Graham, it's gonna be great. You won't even have time to miss me."

"Time has nothing to do with it," Graham says, stepping a little closer. His hand comes up, brushing the snow out of my hair, the look in his eyes sucking all the air out of my lungs. I'm frozen, my breathing ragged as he stares at me, his eyes flickering down to my chapped lips. Excitement and terror rips through me like wildfire, my desire for him beautiful and excruciating all at the same time. My mind flashes to my parents, their happy faces before everything fell apart, and all of the sudden I'm unsure, doubt coursing through my veins as he leans down to kiss me.

I instinctually pull away but, in doing so, I throw myself off balance, tumbling backwards onto the ice. I reach out, accidentally taking Graham down with me, the two of us landing with a hard thud. "Ow," I groan, grabbing my head where it bounced off the ice, my hat luckily softening the blow.

Graham, having partially fallen on top of me, rolls onto his side, sitting up quickly to make sure that I'm alright. "Okay, I think it's time to go," he says, averting his eyes as he slowly climbs to his feet. He pulls me up, a weird tension growing between us as he helps me over the fence, both of us somewhat mortified by what just happened. We hobble away from the rink in silence, neither of us saying a word, our previous playfulness and dignity no longer intact.

CHAPTER 20

One-by-one, we walk off the stage, my heart returning to a normal rhythm as I slowly descend the stairs. As soon as I hit the ground, Rachel seizes me, wrapping her arms around my neck, her soft, flowery scent settling over us as she squeezes me tight. "That was so good!" she says, her voice booming. "You were the best one up there!"

I laugh and clear my throat, nodding toward the other contestants surrounding us.

"Oh, they'll get over it," she says, dismissing my concern. "I'm so proud of you! You got up there and you absolutely crushed it—people have to vote for you."

"We'll see," I say, trying not to get my hopes up. "Hopefully some of my online followers will see the panel, cast a few votes."

"Ms. Walters?" I turn to find Barbara, the woman with the clipboard, standing behind me, her posture impeccable in her stiletto heels. I look past her to the other contestants, who are moving in clusters toward the lobby. Her red lips curve into a smile as she gestures toward them. "Would you like to join us for our finalists' luncheon?" she asks.

"Oh," I say, glancing toward Rachel. "I didn't realize there was a luncheon. Can my friend come, too? She's my travel companion."

"Of course," Barbara says, pointing toward Rachel's badge. "She has an all-access pass, so she can attend any of our VIP events. Same as you."

"I like that," Rachel says, adjusting her badge for maximum visibility. The woman starts leading us toward the exit but Rachel stops her, looking back at Graham's booth. "Give me one second, I need to let my brother know where we're going." Rachel scurries away and I watch as she chats with Graham, pointing repeatedly in my direction. They speak for about thirty seconds, then she gives him a quick kiss on the cheek and hurries back toward me. As he watches her walk away, Graham's gaze catches mine, sadness briefly flashing across his face. I don't know if what I did, what I just said, hurt him or not. He nods stiffly, then turns to help another customer.

"He's good," Rachel says, smoothing her hair back down as she approaches. "He'll have lunch with his team. I told him we'd just text him afterward."

"Okay," I say, a mixture of disappointment and relief flowing through me. I'm glad we don't have to sit together through an entire meal making small talk, but a part of me wanted to catch up a bit, find out how he's been. It seems like a lot has changed for him in the last five years.

"Okay, are you ladies ready to go?" Barbara asks, clearly anxious to catch up with the group.

"Yep, we're good," Rachel says, linking her arm through mine as we set off toward the lobby.

Barbara leads us out of the convention center toward the main entrance of the hotel. As we get close to the front desk, she takes a left, guiding us down a short hallway to a set of double doors.

She pushes them open, revealing a small, modern parlor, its far wall open to a private patio overlooking the beach. There's a self-serve buffet on our left, as well as a bartender serving champagne and cocktails. Most of the other contestants are already seated, chatting amongst themselves as they eat their food, a light ocean breeze drifting in from outside.

"Have fun, ladies," Barbara says, smiling at us before retreating through the double doors.

"This is beautiful," Rachel says, spinning around survey the room. It's a charming space, the beige walls and plush blue chairs mimicking the scenery outside. "Way better than the sandwich vendors I scoped out this morning."

I laugh, feeling myself relax a little bit, the sight of the ocean and the smell of brine rejuvenating me. By all accounts, the worst of the contest is over; no more interviews, just the judges' panel and the final announcement on Sunday. I feel like I can breathe again, like I might actually enjoy the rest of the trip, a fun weekend away with my best friend. "Let's eat," I say to Rachel, leading the way toward the buffet, my body in need of energy after such a stressful morning.

We grab a couple plates and load up on fresh seafood: shrimp scampi, baked sea scallops, a cluster of king crab legs. I take Rachel's plate while she grabs us some drinks, walking out onto the patio. It's such a beautiful, calm day, locals and tourists scattered across the sand, their bodies slick with oils and lotions. I spot an open table with a large blue-and-white umbrella and take a seat, angling myself so that I'm facing the ocean.

"We need to get some beach time in," Rachel says, walking up behind me. She sets a fruity cocktail down in front of me, a pink umbrella and a variety of tropical fruit floating off to one side.

"We do," I agree. "Maybe we can find some time on Sunday morning before we leave."

"We'd better," Rachel says, setting a napkin on her chair to protect her cream-colored palazzo pants. "I am not going back home without a hint of a tan line."

"What is this?" I ask, pointing to the drink she brought me.

"Not sure, I didn't ask," Rachel says as she sits down and takes a generous sip. She smiles then looks at the drink, nodding in approval. "It's tasty and it's free, that's all I need to know."

I laugh, shaking my head as I dig into my lunch, the smell of seafood intoxicating. I take a bite of the scampi, the shrimp buttery and hot and well seasoned with garlic. I eat faster, sampling all the tasty entrees as my hunger gets the best of me. I'm just biting into a flaky biscuit when a young couple walks onto the patio, looking around the crowded space before approaching our table.

"May we join you?" the man asks, gesturing toward our two empty chairs. "It's a full house out here, not many seats left." I recognize him as one of the other finalists, his flashy smile and sandy blond hair hard to forget. He's slender, a bit taller than Rachel, sporting khaki pants and a red shirt that fits snugly around his toned biceps.

"Sure," Rachel says, gesturing toward the chairs with her drink in hand. "Take a seat."

I nod my head in approval, quickly chewing my food as I give him a sheepish smile. I glance at his companion, a petite woman with long, brown hair, her body decorated with tattoos and various piercings. I stare at her for a moment, studying her face, certain that I've seen her in his bio pictures. She stares back at me, visibly frowning as her eyes drift over me, and I'm not sure if she's as friendly as he seems to be.

The two of them sit down and the man immediately leans toward me, extending his hand. "I'm Cooper, I'm one of the finalists. I submitted that photo of the deranged goose."

"Avery," I say, wiping my hands on my napkin before returning the gesture. "I really liked that one, you have some great action shots."

"Thanks," Cooper says, clearly enjoying the compliment. "Wildlife photography can be tricky. You never know what animals are going to do or how long it may take to capture something special."

"That's so true," Rachel says, pointing her fork in his direction. He smiles at her before turning back toward me, his attention perhaps a tad too earnest.

"I have to admit," he says, "I've been dying to meet you. I've followed your work for years and was blown away by your submission. Your stuff is really good."

"Thank you," I say, a bit embarrassed by his blatant flattery.

"Didn't expect you to be so young, though," Cooper says, taking a sip of his drink. He looks at me, his eyes raking over my body in a very obvious way. "Were you down at the salsa bar last night?" he asks, his question completely out of the blue.

Rachel and I look at each other. "Yeah, we were," I say cautiously. I don't know if this guy is a threat or just overly forward, but he's coming on rather strong. "For a little while, anyway."

"I thought so," he says, nodding his head. "I saw you out on the dance floor. If I'd known who you were earlier, I would have come over, introduced myself." He gives me another dazzling smile, every signal indicating that he's flirting with me.

I glance toward his companion as she sits awkwardly beside him, eating small bites of fish. She hasn't said anything yet but she doesn't seem very happy about this exchange. She studies me, her deep brown eyes watching me carefully as she slowly chews her food.

"Oh," Cooper cries. "I'm so sorry, this is my colleague, Vicky. We work together in Chicago, she's my second shooter."

That name, her face, all the pieces finally clicking together in my mind. I start to panic, and it takes everything in me not to recoil in terror. *Victoria*, I think, forcing myself to smile at her. Victoria, who lived four blocks away from me. Victoria, who likes hot dogs with peanut butter. Victoria, who had a purple bike and loved science fiction and knows exactly who my father is.

"Nice to meet you, Vicky," Rachel says, oblivious to internal hysteria. "How are you enjoying the conference so far?"

"It's okay," Vicky replies, still staring at me as she picks at her food. "It's my first time. Cooper is much more interested in these events than I am."

"I like them," Cooper says, facing me once again. "You always meet such fascinating people."

I attempt to laugh but it comes out a bit awkward and forced. My heart is racing, my arms and legs trembling as I try to maintain my composure. Rachel can tell something is off, her eyes scrutinizing my face as she continues the conversation. "How long have you worked together?" she asks.

"Well, we met in college," Cooper says. "Studied photography and fine art together. I convinced her to stay in the city instead of driving back to Washington, and we've worked together creatively ever since."

"Washington?" I chime in, my voice slightly off-key. I clear my throat, hoping that I'm wrong, that she won't confirm my suspicions. "That's where you're from?"

"Born and raised," Vicky says matter-of-factly. "Little town near Seattle, it's a very boring place."

"I can imagine," I say, swallowing hard, wondering how to get us out of this.

"And where are you from?" Cooper asks, leaning toward me again. "It didn't say in your bio."

Rachel starts to answer. "We're from..."

"Arizona," I say, cutting her off. She stares at me, tilting her head ever so slightly as I continue. "Scottsdale, specifically—very hot and dry. Nice to enjoy some beach weather for a change."

"Definitely," Cooper says, his blue eyes shimmering in the afternoon sun. He grins at me, another dazzling smile, not even remotely aware that I'm lying to him.

"I need to run to the restroom," I say, pulling away from him as I give Rachel a knowing look.

"Me too," she says, smiling politely as she stands. "We'll be right back. Don't drink my cocktail."

Cooper laughs obnoxiously as Victoria half-smiles, taking a long sip of her own drink.

We stand and walk inside, my hand clutching Rachel's arm. The second we're out of sight, I pick up the pace, pulling her along with me as I beeline for the door.

CHAPTER 21

I'M PRACTICALLY JOGGING BY the time we reach the lobby, dragging Rachel along beside me, my mind a spinning vortex of panic. *Victoria, Victoria, how the hell could she possibly be here?!* I spot a bathroom on the far side of the room and rush toward it, desperate to get out of view. Rachel doesn't say anything as she scurries along next to me, our heels clicking in unison against the tile floor. She knows something is wrong, and like she promised, she doesn't ask questions. Within seconds, we cross the open lobby and dash into the bathroom.

As soon as we're inside, I quickly check the stalls for other occupants, then go to the entrance and lock it. I fall back against the door, my breathing labored, sweat pooling around the nape of my neck and seeping through my clothes. I don't even care if I look presentable at this point, as long as I'm away from Victoria.

Rachel stands by the sink, watching me closely, waiting for me to talk. After a moment, she goes into a stall to use the toilet, then comes out to wash her hands. She's trying to act very nonchalant, like me dragging her out of the luncheon was a totally normal thing to do. "Well, Cooper seems interesting," she says, drying her hands on a towel. "Hopefully he doesn't ask us anything about

Scottsdale, since we've never been there. Also, I really hope they aren't a couple because he was drooling all over you."

I shake my head, the image of Victoria's dark, piercing eyes burned into my brain. "She knows me," I choke out, the words raspy and hoarse, like I'm scraping them out of my throat. I don't want them to be real, I don't want *her* to be here.

"Well, of course she knows you," Rachel says, turning toward me. "You're a contestant and you were just sharing a meal together."

"No," I say, my eyes locking onto hers. "She *knows* me. We lived in the same neighborhood."

Rachel is silent for a moment, a veil of confusion hovering over her features until it clicks, the truth sinking in. "Wait, what?! How?" Her face morphs into a look of shock and utter disbelief. "I can't believe this... did she recognize you?"

"I don't think so," I say, my fingers digging into my temples. "But this is bad. She is a direct line to my past, to everything my mother and I left behind."

"Shit," Rachel says, looking down at the floor. She walks over and kneels in front of me, her hands resting on my knees. Her hair is perfectly curled, falling gracefully around her shoulders, the lights above us giving her a graceful radiance. "What should we do? Do you want to leave?"

"I don't know," I say, burying my face in my hands. "I'm afraid that would just draw more attention." My heart accelerates again, anxiously tripping over itself as I contemplate what to do. I close my eyes and we sit in silence for a few moments, the sounds of the lobby echoing against the wooden door. I'm about to suggest barricading ourselves into the bathroom when it hits me. "The class!"

I cry, throwing my hands in the air. "We can leave the luncheon to attend the class!"

My sudden movement startles Rachel, nearly knocking her to the ground. She grabs onto the nearby wall, steading herself. "What class?" she asks.

"The class I mentioned earlier, by Anthony Freeman," I say. "It starts in, like, twenty minutes. That can be our excuse to ditch the luncheon and get away from them."

"Oh, that's perfect," Rachel says. "We can leave early without raising any red flags."

"Exactly," I say. The idea brings me some relief, but knowing Vicky/Victoria is here is anything but comforting. I have enough to worry about between checking in on my mom and running into Graham. "If we're going to make it through Sunday, we need to steer clear of her, and Cooper."

"Ok," Rachel says. "We can do that, I think. Might be kinda difficult, he was really into you." Her hand reaches out, straightening the ID badge around my neck, and she frowns. "Man, I really wanted to sit on the patio for awhile, enjoy the VIP treatment."

"I know," I say, "but we can't, or at least I can't. I need to stay away from Victoria at all costs." I feel myself panicking again, my anxiety rising as unwelcome memories rush into my mind. I can hear my parents fighting, angry voices echoing through my walls, the sight of my mother swollen and bleeding. I lean back against the door, tears stinging my eyes as I try to breathe and regain control. My biggest fear, my absolute worst case scenario, is somehow happening right now.

"Calm down, Avery," Rachel says, grabbing my hands and giving them a gentle squeeze. "Just breathe, everything is okay. We'll just pop back in there real quick, tell them we have to go, and that'll be it. We can avoid them like the plague from now on." She stands up, smoothing her pleated pants, a small smile creeping across her face as she shakes her head. "The good thing is, your makeover is working. She clearly has no idea that you're you."

"Yeah," I say, taking in a steadying breath. I feel my body relaxing, the throbbing in my temples dwindling to a dull ache. "I guess your disguise is pretty effective."

"Of course it is," Rachel says, giving me a wink. "We didn't spend all that time and money on it for nothing. Now let's go back out there, say a quick goodbye, and we'll be on our way."

"Ok," I say, scrambling off the floor. I do a quick check in the mirror, my hands shaking as I smooth out my makeup and adjust my skirt. The last thing I want is to return to that patio, but I need to wrap things up with them as clean and tidy as possible. I don't want to just disappear and risk one of them seeking me out. "Okay, let's go," I say, turning toward the door. Rachel unlocks it and we step out together, her arm holding me steady as we cross the bustling lobby.

We walk back into the lounge and straight onto the patio. Cooper and Vicky are sitting in silence; Cooper on his phone, Vicky staring out at the waves. "Hey," I say, causing them both to jump. "We just realized we're late for the Anthony Freeman class at two. Sorry to eat and bolt, but we're gonna have to head out."

"Oh, ok," Cooper says, his dazzling smile faltering as he rises from his chair. "I actually wanted to attend that as well. Mind if I come with you?"

I hesitate, looking at Rachel. She gives me a faint shrug, unsure what to do. "Well, we don't want to cut your lunch short," I say, hoping he will take the hint.

"Not at all," he replies. "I'm done, plenty of food for me." He glances at Vicky, who's already turned her attention back to the ocean. "You want to come, Vicky?"

"Nah, I'm good," she says, watching the waves churn and swell. "I'm going to sit here for a bit, then catch the Photoshop panel at three."

Rachel picks up her cocktail, downs it, then grabs the biscuit off her plate. "Ok, let's go," she says, taking a hefty bite as she moves toward the door.

"After you," Cooper says, ushering me to lead the way. As I turn, he steps in a little too close, the acrid smell of cheap cologne cascading off of him. "I'll text you later," he calls out to Vicky, clearly unbothered about leaving her behind.

We exit the lounge and make our way toward the convention center, every step confirming that this was a bad idea. Cooper is polite enough but arrogant, his attempts at smooth conversation coming off as shallow and self-indulgent. As we pass by the main stage, we run into Graham and his co-workers, the three of them clearly just coming back from lunch.

"Hey girl," Tim says, leaning in to give me a kiss on the cheek. "You were incredible up there, an absolute sensation! We voted for you, like, fifty times already."

"Thanks, that's so sweet," I say. "Hopefully the rest of the crowd did the same thing."

"And who is this?" Connor asks, thoroughly assessing Cooper from head to toe.

"Oh, this is Cooper," I say, gesturing toward him. "He's one of the finalists, too. We all attended the luncheon together."

"Nice to meet you," Cooper says, shaking hands with everyone. Graham shakes his hand then glances at me, acknowledging the lack of space between us. There's a weird tension in the air, a subtle rigidity in Graham's shoulders that no one else seems to notice.

"We're actually in a bit of a hurry," Rachel says. "We're going to the Anthony Freeman class, it starts in a few minutes on the other stage."

"Oh, ok," Tim says, making a sad face. "Well, you guys have fun! We'll just be over here, toiling away in our dingy booth."

"Actually," Graham interjects, "if you guys don't mind, I'd like to attend the class, too."

"Really?" Rachel asks, giving her brother a disbelieving look.

"Yeah," Graham replies, shrugging. "He's a brilliant photographer, I'd love to hear more about his work. Maybe learn some of his composition techniques."

Connor chuckles, shaking his head. "You're not fooling anyone, buddy. You just want to play hooky for the rest of the day."

"Something like that," Graham says, glancing quickly in my direction. "Can you live without me for an hour or so?"

"Sure," Tim says, smiling at him. "Go, have fun! Enjoy learning about lighting and composition and all that technical junk."

"Will do," Graham says, nodding at them as we walk away. The four of us set off again, Rachel leading the way, Graham trailing quietly behind Cooper and me. As Cooper chatters on about his most recent work trip, capturing bears and bobcats in Yosemite National Park, I quickly glance back at Graham. He's watching us, his face impassive but his eyes sharp and focused. He looks back and forth between us before quickly turning away, the muscles in his jaw tense. I spin back around, pretending to engage in Cooper's story as we move deeper into the crowded arena.

We arrive at the secondary stage and find some seats in the back, sliding in silently as an announcer reads off Anthony's many accomplishments. Cooper sits next to me and so does Rachel, leaving Graham to sit on Rachel's other side. Just as we're settling in, Anthony Freeman pops on stage, his arms waving exuberantly over his head as people clap and cheer.

"Hello everyone, it's great to be here!" he cries, his voice thundering through the loudspeakers. After a few moments, the crowd quiets down, and Anthony adjusts his headset as he begins his presentation. "Thank you, thank you everyone. I'm Anthony Freeman, and today I'm here to talk about time. Photography, as a skill, is all about timing. Waiting for the perfect shot, taking it at the right moment for maximum impact, and how that distinct image can transcend time itself. Having the instinct of knowing when you've got it, and if you *do* capture it, where to go from there. This part of our work is what transforms photographers into icons, images into significant moments in history. One shot, if executed correctly, can capture so many things. Culture, the human experience, a collective feeling about the world—and it all begins with time."

I am listening intently, completely mesmerized by Anthony's words, when Cooper leans in, the smell of afternoon cocktails still on his breath. "He's such a legend, I love his work," he says.

"Me too," I agree, keeping my eyes on the stage. I don't like how close he is to me, how comfortable he seems to be encroaching on my personal space.

"Are you two going to the launch party tonight?" he asks.

I fidget in my chair a bit, debating what to say. "I'm not sure, we haven't decided on anything yet."

"Well, if you do go," he says, "me and Victoria will be there. It's not as fun as the salsa club, but it's still a good time." His leg lightly brushes mine, and I do my best not to immediately jerk it away. "You should definitely come."

"Maybe," I say. "I have to get some work done later, I have some needy clients back home. No such thing as a weekend away in the social media game."

"I get it," Cooper says, flashing his wide grin of perfect teeth. I smile back politely, then turn to focus on the lecture. From the corner of my eye, I can see Graham watching us again, his gaze shifting between Cooper and the stage. I ignore them both, casting my eyes forward, determined to focus on the man at the front of the room and not the two sitting beside me.

CHAPTER 22

When the lecture ends, I jump up and scurry toward the front, leaving Rachel, Cooper, and Graham in their seats. There's a small crowd gathering around Anthony and I wait my turn to speak with him, lightly bouncing on my toes in anticipation. I've studied his work for years, watching online demonstrations and reading fan theories about his techniques, the complexity of his images deceptively effortless. For the first time this whole trip, I'm not thinking about my mother or Graham or even Rachel. I'm just excited to be here, happy to be part of a community that I've invested so much of my life into.

The rest of our group saunters forward, the guys hanging back a bit as Rachel comes up beside me. She loops her arm through mine, bumping me with her hip, the familiar gesture calming my nerves. Her stomach rumbles loudly and she makes a face. "I need a proper meal," she says. "Cocktails and a biscuit were not enough." I nod, my own stomach relatively empty.

I move steadily forward as the crowd dissipates, pulling Rachel along with me. I keep thinking about what I'll say to him, how I could even express the influence his work has had on mine, but I decide it's best to keep things simple. Anthony clocks our approach, his smile warm and inviting as I close the distance and extend my hand. "That was a great class," I say, a smile stretching across my entire face. "It's such an honor to meet you, I've followed your work for years."

"Thank you," Anthony says, his handshake strong and steady. "I haven't followed your work for long, but what I've seen has been intriguing."

I freeze, several seconds passing as I try to process his words. "You've seen my work?"

"I'm one of the judges for the contest," he says, a low chuckle rumbling out of him. "I believe I saw you on the stage earlier, am I right?"

"Yes", I say, nodding my head slowly. I don't remember seeing him in the audience, but that's not exactly surprising. All I could really see at the time was Rachel's encouraging smile, Graham's intense expression in the distance. "I was on stage, I spoke near the end."

"I was there as well," Cooper says, leaning in front of me to shake Anthony's hand. His shoulder brushes my arm, his rude interruption just another example of his blatant disregard for my personal space. "Cooper Matthews, nice to meet you."

"Likewise," Anthony says, his dark eyes appraising Cooper as he releases his hand. "It's a pleasure to meet you both, and to have you here sharing your talents. Win or lose, you should be proud you created something different, put it out into the world."

"Well, *I'm* the one who submitted Avery's photo," Rachel says proudly, "but I did it out of love. I've known for years how talented she is, but I knew she wouldn't do it on her own. Someone had to take the wheel."

Anthony nods his head, his expression thoughtful as his eyes fall back on me. "You've got a good friend here. A lot of people are afraid to submit, but the best artists are the ones who take risks. From what I've seen, your images are bold and decisive. You should embrace that mindset when it comes to sharing your work in the future."

Something about his words, the way he presumes to understand my reservations about entering the contest, rubs me the wrong way. As much as I respect him, I can't help but find him a bit irritating. "I'm not afraid to share my work," I say, my words clipped and biting. I feel my cheeks flush as my friends turn to look at me, everyone shocked by my reply.

Anthony's brow lifts, his eyes dancing over my face as he studies my reaction. "Then why didn't you submit the image yourself?" he asks, clearly challenging my statement.

I stare at him, my face burning, everyone waiting intently for my answer. I think about my mother, about all the things I've sacrificed in order to protect her. I think about Graham, our road trip together, the moments we shared both magical and sacred. I can't talk about my past or explain my intimate connection to those photos, so I go for a half-truth instead. "I spend a lot of time tweaking things, experimenting with different styles," I say firmly. "Once I find something I like, I share it, *if* I want to. But I'm not afraid."

Anthony smiles slowly, a peculiar grin playing across his lips. He reaches into his back pocket and pulls out his wallet, handing me a business card. "Well, if you ever want to discuss any of your future projects or simply talk shop, please email me," he says. "It's always good to get a fresh pair of eyes on something, find a new perspective."

"Thanks," I say, taking the card from him. I'm not sure why he's rewarding my hostility, but his expression is somewhere between amused and intrigued. "I will."

"I'll see you at the judges' panel tomorrow," he says, motioning for the next group of people to step forward. We shuffle toward the side of the stage and I glance back at him, a crowd of young teens now gathered around Anthony, hanging on his every word. I look down at the card in my hand, running my fingers over the thick, glossy paper.

"Wow," Cooper says, staring at the smooth cardstock, Anthony's contact information glistening in the light. "I can't believe he gave you his card."

"I can," Rachel says. "She was a complete badass back there! Plus, she's a finalist for this contest on her first submission. Even Photog Yoda knows she's special."

"I guess so," Cooper says as I tuck the card into my purse. He pulls his phone out of his pocket, checking the time. "I have to meet Vicky for a quick chat with a client, then we're going to dinner. But maybe I'll see you later." He holds my gaze for a moment, his pale blue eyes sparkling as his mouth curls into a playful grin. "We'll be there around 8:30 PM, if you're able to make it."

"Okay," I say, giving him a timid smile. He seems like a nice-enough guy, but considering his connections to Victoria, I'd really just like for him to leave.

Cooper smiles once more at Rachel before glancing over at Graham. "It was nice meeting you," he says, extending his hand toward him. Graham nods, silently assessing Cooper as they share a brief handshake. Cooper flashes us one more charming smile, then turns and walks away.

"What a hottie," Rachel says, watching him as he moves through the sparse crowd. Her eyes dart back to mine, a devilish grin spreading across her face. "He totally attended this lecture just to hang out with you."

"I doubt that," I say, glancing sidelong at Graham. He stares at me, the corner of his jaw twitching, but he says nothing. "He came for the lecture, just like the rest of us. He's not here for a date, he's here to schmooze people and win the grand prize."

"If you say so," Rachel says, her wicked smile fading into an amused smirk. Her stomach growls loudly and she clutches her belly, bending forward as though she's in pain . "Okay, time for some food. I'm freaking starving."

"I thought you just went to lunch?" Graham asks, clearly confused.

"It got cut short," Rachel says, wobbling slightly on her heels as she stands up straight again. She glances toward me and a silent understanding passes between us, that the less people who know about Victoria, the better. Rachel knows more about my past than anyone, but that's not saying much. Bringing Graham up to speed at this point would only do more harm than good.

"Well," Graham says, "if you want some great food, I know the perfect place."

"Where?" I ask.

"The roof," he says. "One of the best restaurants in the city is up there, with amazing views of the water. We could probably squeeze in pretty easily since it's the middle of the day."

"We?" I say, giving him a quizzical look. "Don't you have to go back to work?"

Graham shrugs. "Our booth closes in an hour, the guys will be fine on their own. Plus, I think I'm ready for a drink, it's been a long day." He pulls out his phone, his fingers flying over the screen as he sends off a quick text. "There, it's done. Now let's get out of here."

"This place better be good," Rachel says, scowling as her stomach continues to grumble. "If I have to find a third lunch spot today, you two are paying for my meals for the rest of the trip." She turns and strides toward the lobby, her golden hair flowing freely behind her.

"I guess that settles it," Graham says, a small smile spreading across his face. He looks over at me, his golden eyes sparkling as he gestures for me to lead the way. "After you."

We turn to follow Rachel and for a second, his hand grazes my back, his fingers whispering over my skin as he guides me forward. Heat radiates through me, sparks of recognition and desire crackling down my spine, and it takes everything in me not to react. I glance at him, our eyes catching for a fraction of a second before I pull away and hurry to catch up to Rachel.

***

"This bread has become a part of my soul," Rachel says.

Rays of sunlight peak through the gazebo above us, the heat of the day softened by a tangled canopy of vines and fresh flowers. We've been lounging on the roof for about an hour now, a bottle of crisp, white wine in the middle of our table, its ice bucket melting into the linen tablecloth. Half-eaten plates of bruschetta, calamari, and fresh oysters are scattered about, our second basket of French bread almost gone. It's peaceful, the restaurant mostly empty, the light chatter of fellow patrons drowned out by the steady, rumbling rhythm of the ocean below.

"So has this view," I reply, gazing out at the endless sea. Late afternoon light spills across the sky, its orange-pink hue dancing along the clouds, the ocean a deep pool of turquoise blue. For the first time all day, I feel truly relaxed, my body sinking into the overstuffed chair cushions behind me, my mind blissfully blank. "You don't see this everyday."

"If you like this view," Graham says, turning his wine glass in his hand as he looks out at the waves, "you'd love Italy."

I glance over at him, his words sinking in as the enchantment of the ocean view subsides. "Italy?" I ask.

"Yeah," he says. "The Amalfi Coast. It's one of the most beautiful places in the world. It's pure ocean and sunshine, afternoons on the beach drinking wine. It's incredible."

Something clenches inside of me, grief and longing tearing through my chest. We'd talked about going there once, the cities we would visit, the foods we would try together. I'm not sure what hurts worse—that he went without me, or that I haven't gone at all. "I didn't know you'd been there," I say, doing my best to keep a straight face. "Where else have you traveled to?"

"Brazil, Japan, Portugal, Alaska. All sorts of places," Graham says. He mentions it very casually, like traveling half the globe isn't a big deal. "I work hard, but our company is somewhat remote, so I get to play hard, too. I can schedule trips and work for a portion of the time, going out to explore at night or on the weekends," he says.

I try to imagine what that would be like, working and traveling for weeks at a time. My mind jumps to Jillian's offer, the big wedding she's coordinating in Colorado, and my heart squeezes again. "Sounds like a dream," I say, reaching for some calamari as a pang of jealousy ripples through me.

"Remember when I met up with you over in Greece," Rachel says to Graham, "and we almost got arrested because I took a picture of that airport?" She laughs, wine sloshing out of her glass as she rolls back and forth in her chair. I remember when she left for that trip, how careful I was not to ask too many questions. I was afraid if I knew too much about it, I'd be tempted to hop on a plane and go with them.

"That was a military base, which is illegal," Graham says, shaking his head. He smiles at her, his affection for his little sister apparent. "It was a fun time, though. You are quite the travel partner."

"I do my best," Rachel says, raising her glass to salute Graham.

I chuckle, grateful for her silly antics. "So, what's your favorite place you've been to so far?" I ask, turning my attention back to Graham.

His eyes meet mine, his irises practically glowing in the afternoon sun. "Arizona," he says, his voice steady, his answer clear and confident. He gives nothing away, but I know instantly what he's really saying. His answer brings everything back, every memory and detail rushing to the surface. The road trip, the fiery desert canyons, the weight of his body pressing into mine. I hold his gaze for a moment but eventually look away, picking up my wine glass to take a sip.

"Arizona?!" Rachel cries, frowning. "Please, there's nothing there except coyotes and cacti. That is not a place worth remembering."

"If you say so," Graham says, his eyes still on me as he drinks his wine.

Our waiter comes over, clearing away a couple of plates. "Can I get you anything else?" he asks.

"I don't think so," Rachel says, groaning. "While I would love to find a vat of ice cream I can dump myself into, I'm stuffed."

"Me too," I say, setting down my wine glass. "Everything was great, thank you."

"You can put it on my tab," Graham says. "Room 714, Graham Abrahams."

"Oh, you don't have to do that," I say, feeling a bit embarrassed. "I'm the one who cost us our free lunch, it's my treat."

"Don't worry, it's going on the company card," he says. "But if you insist, you can buy me a drink before the weekend's up."

"Well thanks, big brother," Rachel says, her speech a little slow. "I don't know about you two, but I am wiped. Between the jet lag and the wine, I think I need a little power nap."

"I should probably head back too, get some work done," I say. "Cynthia has sent me two emails today, wanting me to make even more changes to her posts for this weekend. I swear, she thinks I only work for her, and she writes off all my best ideas as incompetent."

"Sounds like you need some new clients," Graham says.

"Yeah," I say, my mind drifting to the Colorado job once again. "Maybe."

"I'm going to stay up here for a bit," Graham says, topping off his wine glass and throwing the empty bottle back in the bucket. "Finish the wine, enjoy the view. I'll catch you both later."

We slowly get to our feet and Rachel leans in to give Graham a hug. Not wanting to touch him, I give him a shy wave and we turn to walk away. As Rachel and I near the elevator, I glance back to see if he's watching us, but he's not. He's already turned toward the view, his body relaxed but his expression distant as he looks out toward the sparkling blue water.

CHAPTER 23

Eighteen years old, six years after "The Incident"

Rachel throws the car in park and flings herself out the driver's side door, her hair glowing in the afternoon sunshine as she runs around the vehicle to greet her brother. "Dude, how are you?" she squeals, colliding with Graham so forcefully that he has to step back a bit, laughing as he catches her. Watching them from the open car window, I smile at the heartfelt greeting, a warm flutter of joy pinging around inside of me after not seeing Graham in almost a year. "How was Peru?" Rachel asks, pulling back to get a better look at him.

"Incredible," Graham says as he hoists his single backpack off the sidewalk, the overpacked knapsack straining at the seams. I can tell that he's gotten a lot of sun lately, his long, toned arms a deep shade of golden-brown. "Ten hours each way in coach, plus sleeping in a room the size of a walk-in closet with five other guys—totally worth it." He turns toward the car, recognition and joy spreading across his features as he catches sight of me in the back seat. "Hey Avery, long time no see," he says, his smile widening, his full lips curling over imperfect teeth as his face splits in two.

I grin back at him, my heart tripping over itself as I mirror his enthusiasm. "Not unless you count emails and video calls," I say, trying not to blush. Even with his class schedule and the time difference, we've still managed to stay in touch, mostly through late-night drawing sessions like we did before. Sometimes I'll even grab a pizza on my way home, him howling with jealousy as I wave it at him through the computer screen.

"Avery insisted we come to get you," Rachel says, walking past me to open the trunk. "We've both been on a countdown for your arrival since March."

"Is that so?" Graham teases, tossing his bag in the trunk with a thud before returning to my window. He leans against the car, his peppery scent rolling over me, his shirt visibly wrinkled from hours of being on planes. "You've missed me, huh?"

"Only a little," I say, reminding myself not to lean toward him. Nothing ever happened between us before Graham left for college, but there's a tension there now, an awareness that he was interested in me that I simply can't forget. As hard as I try to keep our relationship friendly, knowing this about him eats at me, a longing I can't explore, a thirst I'm unwilling to quench. "I mean, I kinda had to come. Rachel may have finally passed her driving exam, but she's still a menace on the road."

"I only got a few honks on the way here, thank you very much," Rachel says as she climbs into the driver's seat. Graham hops in beside her and slams the door, bracing himself as Rachel takes off without any warning, a symphony of car horns blaring behind us. Graham gives her a look and she rolls her eyes, changing lanes again as we speed away from the airport, wind and music funneling through the car as we fly out of Bentonville toward Selene.

Rachel chatters on for most of the car ride, talking about her job at the local nursing home and her newest boyfriend, Henry. I listen but I'm mostly watching Graham, covertly examining the subtle ways that he's changed. His hair is a bit longer and lighter, most likely bleached by the sun. His face has become more angular, the edges becoming sharper somehow. The thing I notice the most is the slight whisper of scruff along his jaw, an incredibly attractive detail that's hard to look away from. "So, did you get into any more colleges I don't know about?" Graham asks, suddenly turning around to face me.

I blink, my face blank like a goldfish. Shaking my head, I act like I wasn't listening, like I wasn't just staring at him for the last ten minutes. "I just got two more letters," I say. "One from the Art Institute in Chicago, and one from the Parsons School of Design in New York."

"And?" Graham asks, waiting for my response. His eyes sweep over me for a fraction of a second, perhaps noticing the ways I've changed in the past year as well.

"She got into both of them," Rachel says, grinning at me in the rearview mirror. She comes up on the car in front of us too quickly and swerves into the neighboring lane, the tires screeching as we all shift toward the passenger side. "Sorry!" she cries before speeding up again.

"Holy shit, that's incredible," Graham says, gripping the center console for support. A lock of hair falls in front of his face, gently grazing his cheek, and it makes me wonder what it would be like to touch his greasy, tousled mane. "So which one are you going to choose?"

"Neither," I say, shaking my head. "They're too expensive. I got in but they didn't offer me any of the scholarships I applied for."

"Avery, you can't pass up the Art Institute just because it's expensive," Graham says. "That's insane."

I smile, my official college plans something I've been dying to tell him about. "I can if I get a full ride to UCLA," I say, watching him carefully as the information sinks in.

"You're going to UCLA?" he asks, his eyes searching my face to see if I'm serious.

I nod, biting my lower lip as I grin. "Yep, I'm headed to the West Coast, too. Not the same campus as you, of course, but pretty close."

"Might as well be in another country," Rachel calls over her shoulder. "People don't like to drive in LA, the traffic is awful."

"We'll figure it out," Graham says, reaching back to squeeze my hand, an authentic, blissful smile spreading across his face. My skin prickles, the hair on my arms standing up as he touches me, an electrical current buzzing between us. He releases my hand and turns around, the happy news energizing him. "We need to celebrate! Let's go to the diner, lunch is on me."

***

Graham, Rachel, and I stroll into the diner, the bustling restaurant overflowing with the summer lunch crowd. As we're waiting for a booth to be cleaned, Maggie comes out of the kitchen, arms open wide as she runs over to Graham. "There's my boy," she says, giving him a giant bear hug before kissing him on the cheek. Her hair is pulled back beneath a red bandana, her white apron blotchy from splattered grease. "Look at you, all tanned and handsome! You look so much like..." She pauses, closing her eyes as she absentmindedly waves her hands. "California must be treating you well."

"It is," Graham says, smiling at her. He gestures toward the restaurant, every seat filled with customers. "Congratulations on running this place, that's a pretty big deal."

"It is, and a lot of work," she says, sighing. "Charles wants to gradually move into retirement, and I've been here so long that he felt like it was a good fit." She touches Graham's cheek, smiling up at him. "It's so good to have you home. Come on, let's get some food started for you."

Maggie leads us to our booth, Rachel and I piling into one side while Graham sits on the other. Now that we're face to face, I can really see how much he's changed, his boyish teenage features solidifying into something more masculine and sturdy. There's also a subtle shift to the way he carries himself, a confidence that he didn't have before. "So, how long are you in town for?" I ask.

"Well, that depends," Graham says, looking around the diner, taking in all the familiar faces.

"On what?" Rachel asks. "Planning to run back to LA to hook up with Erin some more?" I glance out the window, the mention of Graham's girlfriend making me extremely uncomfortable. They've been dating for awhile now, getting "hot and heavy," according to Rachel. It's definitely not a topic I would bring up or have any interest in discussing right now.

"No, that's over," Graham says. "I ended it before my trip to Peru, it wasn't going anywhere."

"I'm not surprised," Rachel says, pretending to hurl as she makes a fake gagging sound. "She called you 'graham cracker.' I mean, come on... that's gross." I snicker but don't say anything, not wanting to insert myself in the conversation or comment on Graham's love life.

Graham laughs, bowing his head as his face turns red with embarrassment. "Yeah, well, it just wasn't a good fit." He looks at me, the redness fading away as he returns to my original question. "It mostly depends on when I can get my truck going. A buddy from high school is going to sell me his old Jeep Cherokee, help me fix it up so I can take it back to LA. It's getting harder to live there without a car."

"That shouldn't take too long," I say, failing to hide my disappointment.

Graham studies me, his mouth curling into a small smile. "It also depends on when you're ready to go with me."

"Me?" I say, gaping at him before glancing over at Rachel. She shrugs and I turn back to him, my heart beat steadily increasing as my mind skims over the possibilities. "What do you mean?" I ask.

"Well, if you're planning on attending UCLA, I figure we can drive to California together," he says. "We'll check out the southern states before you go to college, make a little road trip out of it. It's up to you and your mom, of course, but I'm making the journey no matter what and I just thought it could be fun. Better than doing the whole trip alone."

"That's not fair!" Rachel cries, folding her arms over her chest. "I have summer classes for nursing school starting, in like, a month. I can't go."

"It's not a huge deal," Graham says, trying to calm her down. "We're just taking the truck back to LA. But I thought I'd put it out there, it could be an adventure."

Terror and excitement pinball through my abdomen, the thought of spending days, if not weeks, alone with Graham enough to make my head spin. "I don't know, I'll have to ask my mom, see what she says. She's already crying about me leaving and I haven't even left yet."

"She could always meet us there, help you settle into your dorm room," Graham says, shrugging.

I shake my head, unable to tell him that she probably won't take me to college. We aren't on high alert like we used to be, both of us feeling pretty secure in our new life now, but my mother still doesn't travel much. If I have to move across the country without her, I may as well do it with a friend. "I'll talk to her about it," I say, my mind buzzing at the thought of a summer road trip. "But if she's cool with it, I'm in."

Just then, a waitress rushes over, setting down a round of chocolate milkshakes. Graham grabs one, hoisting it into the air. "It's a date," he says, clinking his glass against mine, whipped cream and chocolate fudge smearing across his upper lip as he takes a big drink.

CHAPTER 24

By the time I change my clothes and boot up my laptop, Rachel is out cold. She's face down on the mattress, her mouth hanging open, drool sliding down her chin and soaking into the pillow below her. I grab the other half of the comforter she's laying on, stifling a laugh as I throw the blanket over her sprawling body. Rachel has always had the uncanny ability to pass out in the middle of the day, even with a couple cups of coffee in her. I close the heavy curtains, shielding her from the sun as it shines directly on her face, and get to work.

I spend the next few hours editing photos and fixing the "issues" brought up by Cynthia. As I'm uploading the work for final approval, my phone starts vibrating on the desk beside me, the unexpected buzzing making me jump. Snatching it up, I check the screen, frowning when I realize it's a video call through my online business profile. No one I know contacts me through that account, and the unknown caller sends a shiver of fear down my spine. I lean forward, realizing upon closer inspection that the profile picture is of Tim, Graham's co-worker. I sigh, relief flooding through me as I hit "Accept" and dip into the bathroom. Tim pops up on the screen, the camera so close that I can't even see his whole face.

"Hello?" I say, closing the door behind me so I won't wake up Rachel.

"Girl, where are you?" Tim shouts, his face swirling in and out of view. "This party is insane, you need to come down here!"

Squinting at my phone, I see iridescent blue streamers floating in the air behind him, the sound of string instruments playing in the background. "Is that the conference launch party?" I ask.

"They wish," Connor says, his face pushing past Tim's into the camera. He's holding a bright purple cocktail in his hand, the top of the glass garnished with berries and floating flowers, and he's wearing a sparkly, light blue bowtie. "We crashed a wedding, it's being hosted in one of the ballrooms. It's like 'Under the Sea' meets 'Pride & Prejudice,' you have to come down!"

I laugh, covering my mouth as the sound echoes off the tiled walls. "That sounds amazing, but I have so much work to do. And Rachel passed out a couple hours ago."

"So? Come by yourself!" Tim says, jerking the phone back toward his face. "You're here to have fun, you're on vacation! Unless it's an emergency or you're getting paid overtime, you deserve to take a break and come hang out with us."

I glance away from the screen, chewing on my lip as I consider my options. I don't love the idea of going out without Rachel, but I don't want to spend my whole trip hiding in our hotel room, either. I've already skipped out on tonight's launch party because of Victoria and Cooper, but a private event on the other side of the hotel should be okay. I wouldn't run into anyone currently attending the launch party, and the work I truly needed to finish is uploading right now. Feeling adventurous, I turn back to my phone, grinning into the screen. "Okay," I say, nodding my head. "Give me ten minutes, I'll be right down."

***

I walk out of my room twenty minutes later, my new, gray slip dress clinging to my sides, my hair tucked into a messy updo. I fidget a bit as I walk down the hall, the dress making me feel self-conscious, a sensuous version of myself I don't recognize. I'd loved it when I bought it, Rachel clapping and cheering as I spun in joyous circles around the dressing room, but now I worry that it draws too much attention. Pulling at my shoulder straps, I struggle in vain to better conceal my cleavage as I make my way down the hall.

At the end of the hallway, I press the button for the elevator, adjusting my dress once more in the mirror between the doors. I study my reflection, lightly touching my tousled, red hair, guilt and fear rolling through me in waves. It feels reckless going out like this, throwing caution to the wind just to attend a party. It's no way to protect myself, or my mother. *You need to do this, Avery,* she says, her words echoing through my head as I stare at myself in the mirror. *Do it for yourself, for me.* The elevator dings overhead, dispelling the memory. Taking a deep breath, I step in front of the doors, my brave facade crumbling as soon as they slide open.

Graham is standing alone in the back of the elevator car, his eyes cast downward as he leans casually against the railing. He's wearing a fresh suit, his sky blue shirt unbuttoned at the top, his messy hair damp and slicked to one side. Fresh soap and savory cologne hang in the air, a scent so intoxicating it leaves me breathless. He looks up after a moment, the shock of seeing me evident on his face. Then something shifts and he's alert, focused, his eyes moving slowly down the length of my dress. I swallow, unable to move, his unabashed hunger sending heat straight to my thighs.

"Graham," I say, still frozen in place. "What are you doing here?"

"I could ask you the same thing," he says. His eyes rake over me once again and I feel my face flush, desire spreading like wildfire throughout my body. Something simmers in the air between us and I'm reluctant to step inside, the elevator suddenly feeling very small. After a few seconds, the doors start to close but Graham lunges forward, catching them with his hands, the distance between us shrinking from feet to inches in the matter of seconds.

All of my worries and fears vanish as Graham leans over me, his strong hands pressed against the metal doors. I want to touch him, my fingers aching to trace the contours of his chest, the light stubble along his jaw. He doesn't move, his body solid as his eyes bore into mine, his golden brown irises now dark pools of amber. The elevator alarm starts going off and he slowly backs away from the doors, his magnetic gaze still locked onto mine. Without hesitation, I follow him inside, my body gravitating toward his as the doors close behind us.

Graham resumes his position on the railing while I remain by the doors, silence wrapping around us except for the music coming through the overhead speakers. Our eyes stay fixed on one another but neither of us says anything, and after a beat, the spell that drew me in turns into unease. I shouldn't be doing this, I shouldn't be entertaining ideas about us when I'm leaving in two days. Turning away from him, I press the button for the lobby and the elevator descends, its steady movement bringing me back to reality.

"Going out tonight?" I ask, glancing back at him as I try to casually break the silence.

"Tim texted me, asked if I'd meet him in the lobby," Graham says. He's gripping hard onto the metal railing, the knuckles of his hands turning white. "I think he wants to discuss our sales pitch, make adjustments for tomorrow."

I study Graham for a moment, trying to determine whether or not he's serious. I can tell pretty quickly that he is, that he's unaware of Tim's true agenda. "He messaged me too," I say, my statement clearly surprising him. "I guess he and Connor crashed a wedding somewhere in the hotel. They invited me to come join them."

"Oh," he says, his brow pinching together as he assesses this new information. Neither of us expected to see each other tonight, let alone spend the evening together. Graham taps the heel of his shoe against the floor, adjusts his grip on the railing. "Where's Rachel?" Graham asks, changing the subject.

"Passed out in our room," I say. "Between the bread and the booze, she's out like a light."

Graham smiles, a faint chuckle rolling out of him before we both fall silent again. He glances over at me, fidgeting as he assesses my appearance. "You look nice," he says.

"Thank you," I reply, blushing again. "I figured I should dress up a bit, seeing as it's a wedding."

"Probably a good idea," he says, nodding his head as a gentle smile plays across his lips.

We land in the lobby, and as we exit the elevator, Tim and Connor wave to us from a nearby bench. They're both decked out in swanky party attire, a couple of empty cocktail glasses littering the floor next to them. "There you are," Tim says, rushing forward to greet us. He kisses my cheeks then quickly grabs my hand, twirling me around in a wide circle. "Sweetie, you are gorgeous! And you're both right on time."

"Right on time for what exactly?" Graham asks, sliding his hands in his pockets as he scrutinizes their outfits. His powerful, assertive demeanor is incredibly sexy, and I do my best not to stare. "I thought we were having a quick business meeting."

"Well, less like a 'business meeting,' more like a late-night happy hour," Tim says, grinning. "We stumbled upon a little party here in the hotel. It's pretty epic, *way* better than the launch party, so we decided to invite you both."

"It was my idea," Connor says, jumping in to save his colleague. "If you both came, then there's no third wheel. Plus, it's a really cool reception... you'll understand once we get in there."

Graham and I look at one another, both of us hesitant on whether or not to proceed. Finally Graham smiles, offering me his elbow. "What do you say?" he asks. "Want to crash a party?"

Recognition sweeps through me as I smile up at him, the adventurous boy I knew shining through his eyes. I realize in that moment how much I've missed him, not as a man but as my friend, someone I once shared my life with. I slowly slip my arm through his and nod, anticipation for the evening buzzing through me as I set my feelings aside. If he's willing to overlook our history so we can enjoy a night out together, I can do the same.

"Let's do this," I say, glancing over at the guys. "You lead the way." Tim and Connor cheer wildly before turning on their heels, guiding us toward the far side of the lobby. I cling to Graham's arm, relishing the closeness between us as we follow them across the empty lobby, his warm, peppery scent wrapping around us as we make our way toward the party.

We follow the guys down a long corridor to the far side of the hotel. As we get closer, I can hear music playing, a quartet of string instruments echoing through the halls. We turn the final corner and run into a large, blue curtain, a sign reading "Private Event: Wedding Guests Only" displayed prominently to the side.

"Are you sure we can go in here?" I ask, eyeing the sign.

"Don't worry," Tim says. "They know us already, we told them we'd be back. Besides, you could get in anywhere with that dress you're wearing."

We approach the blue curtain and it draws back automatically, the hallway beyond it now in full view. Waves of colored light ripple along the walls, the entire hallway a shimmering tunnel of iridescent blue. A cascade of sparkling bubbles dangles from the ceiling, wrapped in twinkling LED lights. Crates and barrels flank either side of us as we move through the narrow space, propping up dozens of candles, flowers, seashells, and pearls. Purple mist pools around our feet, the floor swirling around Graham and I as we spin in circles, gawking at the amazing display. If I had any expectations of what this party might look like, I certainly couldn't have imagined this.

As we move down the hallway, we come across some crates covered in personal accessories. Elegant gloves and hair combs, pearl necklaces and faux jewelry, bowties and top hats. I pick up a pair of sheer gloves, the elbow-length fabric covered in small pearls. "Are these for us?" I ask, glancing over at Tim and Connor.

"They sure are," Connor says, switching out his blue bowtie for a soft lavender one. He adds a matching top hat for good measure, adjusting it to sit comfortably on his head. "Pick out a few things and we'll go inside. You'll get the full experience soon enough."

Sliding on the pearl gloves, I pick out a few rings and necklaces before turning back to Graham. The top of his shirt is now buttoned and he's wearing a metallic silver bowtie, a matching glittery handkerchief tucked in his breast pocket. He grins, extending his arm toward me once again, his eyes glowing in the candlelight. I'm not sure what we're walking into but I like seeing him like this, his playful attitude stirring up countless childhood memories.

We approach the end of the hallway, classical music swelling around us as the final curtain pulls back, revealing the main room. I gasp, my mouth hanging open as we walk into the most exquisite ballroom I've ever seen, every surface draped in excessive luxury. Flowers and candles cover every surface, with huge fluorescent water vases scattered throughout the room. Vibrant flowers hang from the ceiling, accompanied by string lights and fine drapery, the entire room a hazy glow of purples and blues. A string quartet plays nearby, performing beneath a huge display of floating glass bubbles, the display dangling over the dance floor in front of us. Even after years of working with Jillian, this is easily one of the most decadent and expensive weddings I've ever seen.

"Wow," I say, taking it all in. The room is so overwhelming it's hard to know where to look.

"I know," Tim says. "These people spent some major cash. We met one of the groomsmen out in the lobby and he invited us in. It says 'private event' but no one seems to care, there's plenty of food and booze to go around."

Tim points to the far side of the room, the space left open for an arrangement of plush chairs and couches. Looking past them, I can see glass doors leading to an outdoor patio, guests mingling under mini lanterns that dance in the breeze. "That's the 'parlor' side of the room," Connor says. "It's almost like a post-dinner tea party with dessert towers and espresso drinks. There's also lawn games throughout the room, as well as on the patio. I would suggest you start over there—you can also grab some cocktails at the bar, if you want to."

"Where are you going?" Graham asks, giving Connor a stern look.

"We had several drinks waiting for you two, we need to hit the men's room," Tim says. "Plus, we want to find the people who invited us in, say a quick hello. We'll meet you over there in twenty, just get yourselves started." With that, Tim and Connor scurry away, hurrying toward the bathrooms at the far corner of the room.

Graham watches them leave, his brow creasing a bit at their sudden departure. I don't think either of us expected to be attending such an extravagant party, let alone navigating our way through it by ourselves. Graham looks over at me, his face twisting into a quirky smile as he shrugs his shoulders. "Well, we're here. Want to grab a cocktail, go check out the rest of the room?" he asks.

I nod, clutching his arm a little tighter, a small quiver of excitement snaking through my chest as I tuck in closer to him. "Yeah, sure."

Graham guides us toward the bar, over which there's an incredible coral reef flower display, and we grab a couple drinks. We slowly meander around the room, checking out the band and the decorations, the decadent ball gowns worn by the bridal party and even some of the guests. Graham moves effortlessly through the room, his posture strong and steady, laughing with ease at the extravagant display. It's refreshing to see him this way, the awkwardness of adolescence melted away to reveal the man beside me. I'm grateful I have the opportunity to experience it, even if it's only for a little while.

We make our way toward the plush sitting area and find an empty couch, a table of assorted pastries and decadent desserts spread out in front of us. Setting my drink down, I grab a pink macaron from a platter and take a small bite, humming softly as the sweet, fluffy pastry melts in my mouth.

"So, what's next?" Graham asks, leaning back into the couch, his glass of bourbon propped up on his leg.

"What do you mean?" I ask, covering my mouth as I continue to chew.

"I mean, what are your plans once all this is over?" he clarifies.

I stare at him, his question seeming somewhat dense. "I go home," I say, taking another bite of the spongy dessert.

"Well, yeah, but what about after that?" he says. "If you win, you could use that money to go to college, travel a bit. Maybe check off some of the places on your bucket list."

I immediately stop chewing, my gut bottoming out as I realize what he's asking me. He thinks that I want the prize money for myself, that I'm doing all this to jumpstart my life after what happened five years ago. I turn away from him, my heart breaking as I shake my head. "I don't think so," I say quietly. "It's complicated... I just need to be home right now."

Graham studies me, frowning as he twists his glass back and forth in his hand. "It wasn't complicated before," he says. "You had dreams, plans. You were set on moving across the country, you had no idea when you'd even be back."

"But things changed," I say, cutting him off. I breathe in, trying to control my emotions, his questions making me anxious. We haven't spoken in over five years, and he's choosing this moment to grill me about a bunch of things he doesn't really understand. "My mom had her accident and she needed me. And honestly, I should have just gone to a local college, stayed near home. We're safer when we're together."

"Safe?" Graham says, tilting his head to the side. "What does that mean? Safe from what?"

I look away, cursing myself for such a foolish slip. This is not the time or place to revisit my past, let alone reveal it to Graham. I glance toward the entrance, and as if on cue, I see none other than Cooper and Victoria walk inside, their expressions of shock and awe mimicking ours from ten minutes ago. "Shit," I say, covering my face as I turn away from them.

Graham surveys the entrance, an amused smirk on his face when looks back at me. "I take it you never messaged him?" he says.

"Not exactly," I reply, continuing to obscure my face. "Do you mind if we get out of here?"

"Sure," he says. He sets his drink down and reaches for his bowtie, yanking it off in one, quick motion before throwing it on the table. Slipping off my gloves, we both stand and move toward the far side of the room, Graham blocking me from view as we make our way toward the patio. I can feel Graham close behind me, his body mimicking my movements as I rush toward the doors, the smell of salt and brine increasing with every step. Wind whips across my face as we step outside, my heart racing as I scan the crowded patio, desperate for a means of escape. Graham snatches a bottle of champagne off a drink cart, his smile wide and mischievous as he takes my hand, pulling me down a set of wooden steps and out onto the beach.

Slipping off my heels as we hit the sand, I run alongside Graham, both of us laughing and shrieking as we stumble across the uneven ground. We move aimlessly in the dark, our bodies bumping into one another, my heart singing as I hold on tight to Graham, his warm hand wrapped firmly around mine. For a moment, it feels like we're teenagers again, our past stripped away, all our worries and responsibilities scattering with the wind as we race through the night, claiming it as our own. We make our way around the back of the hotel and ascend the stairs by the pool, its patio empty and eerily quiet. There's an alcove of couches surrounding a fire pit off to one side, and Graham guides us over there to sit.

I plop down on one of the couches as Graham pops the cork from the champagne bottle, throwing it into the fire. He tilts the bottle toward me, smirking as I grab it and take a generous swig. "Thanks," I say, the liquor crisp and bubbly as it slides down my throat. Everything seems slow and hazy, the night a dreamscape of flickering flames and twinkling stars.

"Sure," he says. I pass it back to him and he takes a long drink, setting it between us as he takes a seat on the couch. "That was quite the mad dash," he says, the sweetness of the champagne lingering on his breath as he leans in close.

"Yeah, sorry to spoil the fun," I say. "I'm not a big fan of Vicky."

"The woman Cooper was with?" Graham asks.

"Yeah," I say. "I met her earlier today, I just got a weird vibe from her."

"I see," Graham says, draping his arm across the couch behind us. "And what about Cooper?"

I glance over at him. "What about Cooper?" I say.

"Do you like him?" he asks. He says it so casually but I can see the anticipation in his eyes, the tension in his jaw as he waits for me to answer.

"I don't know him," I say quietly. "We just met today. He seems nice, but it's hard to really tell."

"It just seemed like he was into you, that's all," Graham says. We both go silent, the crackling of the fire and crashing ocean waves in the distance the only sound between us. I grab the champagne bottle off the couch and take another sip, the liquor warm as it sinks into my belly.

"Did you mean what you said today?" Graham asks, his sudden question making me jump. He's hunched over, staring down at his hands, warm light from the fire playing across his face.

"About what?" I ask.

"About your pictures," he says, his eyes coming back to mine. "Why you worked so hard on them, why they meant so much to you."

My throat goes dry as my heart starts to race, a thunderous beat pulsing through every inch of my body. I stare at him, my mouth hanging open, unsure what to say.

"Because I think about that trip," Graham says, sitting up to face me. "When I saw those pictures, I thought maybe it meant something. And then today..." His golden eyes scan my face, his irises molten pools of caramel from the fire raging beside us.

I look away, fidgeting with the champagne bottle in my hands. "Of course it meant something," I say softly. "It was an amazing trip." I hesitate, my heart screaming for me to be honest about just this one thing. "And I know I left, but… those days we had together, that night… I wanted it to be the beginning of something, not the end." Glancing up at him, I can see that he's gone rigid, his body completely frozen, his expression unreadable.

"I'm sorry," I say, turning away. "I shouldn't have…"

Graham grabs my face, kissing me deeply, leaning in as he pushes us into the couch. His thumb scrapes across my chin, fingers digging into my neck as his other hand skims over my shoulder, the strap of my dress falling away as he reaches down to grab my thigh. We turn toward one another, his breath hot and sticky as he presses his lips against my neck, urgently kissing my bare skin. I gasp as his mouth comes back to mine, our desire insatiable as he pulls me closer, his hand twisting through my hair. I can feel him as his hips press into me and I don't care, I don't care that this will kill me. I am alive, aching with want, burning with a need I didn't know existed. In one electrifying moment, I am back in Arizona, back in that tent with him, exactly where I belong.

My mother flashes into my mind. Her bruised face, her broken ribs, her burnt, twisted leg.

"Graham, I can't…"

His lips find mine once again, his mouth burying my words. His hand caresses my face, gently cradling my cheek, and something inside me breaks, my heart fracturing into splintered, jagged pieces. My chest heaves, silent sobs ricocheting through my ribcage as I push him away, trying to break free. "Graham, stop," I say, forcing the words out of me. I don't want him to stop, I don't want this to end, but I know that it won't end at all if I don't separate us right now.

Graham pulls away, his eyes cast downward as he tries to compose himself. "I'm sorry..."

"It's not you," I say, trying to catch my breath. "I'm going home in two days, I just don't want to..."

"I understand," he says, cutting me off. He sits up, anguish shrouding his features as he stares into the fire, his playful demeanor vanishing. He glances over at me, the same look he had five years ago, an agony so palpable I feel like I might cry. He reaches out, slowly lifting the dress strap back onto my shoulder, his fingers lingering on my skin for an instant before falling away. Then his jaw tenses and he pushes up from the couch, walking a few steps before turning around to face me.

"I better go," Graham says, his words heavy and lifeless. He looks down at me, his eyes distant as he nods his head. "Goodnight, Avery," he says, then he turns and walks away.

CHAPTER 25

Eleven years old, one year before "The Incident"

Glass crunches beneath my sneakers as I round the front of my dad's truck, the distinctive scrapping-popping sound stopping me in my tracks. I look down at the asphalt driveway, a spray of blue-tinted glass scattered on the ground, a few shards of it still stuck in the broken passenger side window. "Dad!" I cry, calling for him as he exits the house.

My dad walks out of the garage, his shoulders slumped with a kind of perpetual weariness, his hair greasy and disheveled, like he hasn't washed it in weeks. He lumbers over to where I'm standing, his hands in his pockets, the faint smell of whiskey lingering on his breath. "Shit," he says, combing a hand over his face, his cheeks stretched and hollow. There are dark circles under his eyes, another night of him restlessly pacing back and forth through our living room, his footsteps echoing on the wood floors as I try to sleep, pretending everything is okay. Stepping forward, he carefully opens the door of the truck, a cascade of glass and loose papers falling at his feet.

"Did they take anything?" I ask, stepping around him to get a better look. The inside of the truck is trashed, debris and papers scattered everywhere, the seats gouged and torn.

"Just the radio," he says, stepping back as he slams the door. He sighs, his eyes bloodshot and distant as he stares absentmindedly at the mess. "Just more vandalism, like before."

Our neighborhood had been experiencing a string of break-ins over the last couple of months, our house one of many that had been repeatedly hit. Sometimes they'd steal things, like when they propped open our garage door and took a bunch of power tools, but usually it was just damaging things, causing a nuisance. My dad's truck tires had already been slashed a few times, our house spray painted along one entire side, my mother's outdoor plants torn to shambles, her yard ornaments and decorative pots smashed. The police were notified, complaints filed after every incident, but so far the events are sporadic, each crime so random and intermittent that no one is ever caught.

My mother exits the house, concern settling into the fine lines of her face as she catches sight of us in the driveway. She approaches my father slowly, gently placing a hand on the small of his back as she stands next to him in silence. I hate seeing my parents like this, both of them exhausted and stressed out, doing their best not to worry me. "I'll take Avery to school," my mom says, her hand falling away, the two of them barely looking at each other. She turns, putting on a brave face as she gestures toward her car. "Come on honey, let's go."

My mom drops me off at school and I spend the rest of the day thinking about my parents. My father's empty gaze, my mother's light touch, their connection a fraction of what it used to be. They've changed so much in just the last six months, their playful interactions now stale and awkward, the tension between them as tight as a tripwire. I hear them arguing most nights now, frazzled voices behind their closed bedroom door, a bottle of whiskey tucked beneath my father's pillow when I find him on the couch the following morning. Everything I've ever known them to be is unraveling, breaking apart until there's nothing left for either of them to hold onto.

Walking toward my mother's car after school, I open the rear door, only to find the backseat filled with grocery bags. "Sorry, honey," she says, her mood about the same as it was this morning. "Things got a bit hectic today. I need to run by the shop before we head home."

"Okay," I say as I buckle my seatbelt, somewhat relieved not to be heading straight home.

"It won't take long, I promise," she says, looking over her shoulder before pulling out into traffic.

We make our way toward my mother's bakery, an old flower shop in the historical district that she's been renovating for almost a year now. It's set to open in a few weeks, hence the large pile of groceries in the back seat. She parks in her designated spot in the alleyway, each of us grabbing a couple of bags as we enter through the back door. There's plywood and construction materials everywhere, a group of handymen still working as they install her custom shelving in the front of the store.

My mom sets her bags on one of the stainless steel tables, pushing several loose strands of hair away from her face. "I'm gonna pop up front real fast, make sure the guys are done for the night. Do you mind unloading these for me?" I shake my head, pulling a box of sugar out of the bag in front of me as she kisses me on the temple. "Thank you, sweetie, it'll only be a few minutes." She disappears into the front of the store as I slowly unload the bags, my mind elsewhere as I pull out sprinkles and other tasty confections.

After I put everything away, I fold up the reusable bags and set them next to my mother's purse, my anxiety creeping in as I lean against the table. *I hope Dad got his truck fixed today*, I think, desperate for a night off from them arguing. I wait a few more minutes but she doesn't come back, the front room seemingly quiet. Walking toward the swinging silver door, I push it open and step into the showroom, sawdust still lingering in the air, catching the warm afternoon light. The room is empty, no construction workers in sight, just my mother and a man standing at the cash register.

Both of them turn toward me as I enter the room, the space eerily silent, the noise from the door reverberating to the far wall as neither of them speaks. I don't recognize this man but there's an obvious tension between them, like I just walked in on a very bad conversation. He's wearing a dirty, rumpled t-shirt, the corners of his mouth tilting upward as he studies my face, his light hazel eyes fiercely green. "Like I said, we aren't open yet," my mother says, her voice cutting, downright rude even as she turns back toward the man. "There's nothing here for you."

The man slowly nods his head, his gaze lingering on me before turning toward my mother. "I'll just have to come back then," he says, his tone remarkably chipper. He gives her a huge smile, his straight teeth a perfect, pearly-white. "You have a good day, ma'am." He walks out the front door, the bell ringing overhead as he turns right and strolls down the street.

My mother sighs, bowing her head as she leans into the marble countertop. "Are you okay, Mom?" I ask, stepping closer to her.

"I'm good, baby," she says, standing up straight. She marches around the counter and locks the front door before turning around to hug me, her grip fierce as she kisses me on the top of my head. I hug her back, squeezing her tighter when I realize that she's shaking. "Let's get out of here," she says, close on my heels as she ushers me toward the kitchen.

***

I've been asleep for a couple of hours when I wake to the sound of my parents arguing, hushed, angry whispers coming from the front of the house. Slipping out of bed, I run across the room and press my ear to the door, my heart racing as I listen to my father's unmistakable disdain, my mother's voice in the background. Gently twisting my doorknob, I carefully crack the door open a quarter of an inch, just enough to see what's going on.

Peering through the imperceptible slit, I watch as my dad stands near the front door, struggling to put on his work boots, clearly inebriated. "What do you want me to do, just sit here?" he asks, swaying on his feet a little as he bends down to tie his other boot.

"Well, I'm not sure you should be driving in your condition," my mother says, standing in front of the door. I can tell by her stance that she's trying to prevent him from leaving the house.

"Someone needs to go down there, talk to the police," my dad says, his face grim. "If it's gonna be anyone, it should be me. It's dark and it's dangerous, there's glass and debris and God knows what else."

"And then what?" my mom says, stepping toward him, her voice shaking. "We talk to the police, we clean up the mess... how's that going to fix anything?"

"There is no fixing it!" my dad hisses, standing up to face her. He looms over her, pushing into her personal space. "It's done, my hands are tied, Penny. We can't do any more than what we've already done, not without making things a whole lot worse."

My mother covers her mouth with her hand, silent tears trickling down her face. "I can't believe this is happening," she whimpers, hugging herself with her other arm.

My father looks down at the floor, defeated. "Stay here, lock the door. I'll let you know what the damage is." He steps forward, pulling her into a hug, his lips pressing into her hair. He whispers something in her ear that I can't hear, then squeezes past her and walks out the door.

The next day, my parents inform me that my mother's store has been burnt to the ground.

CHAPTER 26

"Miss, are you okay?"

I roll over, shielding my eyes from the sun as I struggle to see who's talking to me. There's a middle-aged man in a patrol uniform standing near the fire pit, his aviator sunglasses reflecting the not-so-pretty picture of what I look like right now. "What time is it?" I ask, leaning back as I close my eyes again.

"It's 8 AM, ma'am," he says, sliding his sunglasses down to get a better look at me. "Are you alright, do you need me to call someone?"

I groan, the world spinning violently as I attempt to sit up. After Graham left, I sat out here for what felt like hours, tears staining my satin dress as I poured my misery into what was left of the champagne. "I must have dozed off," I say, reaching down slowly for my discarded heels, one of which is lying in a small puddle. I tilt forward a little too far, losing my balance as my stomach rolls and buckles. The patrol man catches me, a heroic gesture that incidentally gives him a generous glimpse of my chest. "I'm fine, thank you. I just need to go get cleaned up." Rising to my feet, my legs wobbling beneath me, I grab my things and stagger toward the hotel.

Absentmindedly rummaging through my purse, I pull out my phone, my eyes burning as I squint at the missed calls and text messages on the screen. One is from my mom, her nightly check in, but a few are from Rachel, wondering where I am:

You ok?
Let me know you're safe.
You better be banging Cooper right now.

I laugh, wincing as white-hot pain rockets through my temples, the simplest movement sending my hangover into overdrive. I need coffee, and a bagel, and enough aspirin to tranquilize a horse. Shuffling my way through the lobby, I press the button for the elevator, slipping on my semi-wet shoes as the door opens and I step inside.

As the elevator rises to my floor, I see that I have a new email from Cynthia:

Avery, I saw your latest updates and they are not at all what we discussed. I understand you're on vacation, but I am a long-term ***invested*** *client and I expect more from you, considering what I pay you. Please make the following changes ASAP, our continued business arrangement depends on it.*

I glare at my phone, frustration outweighing my exhaustion as I reread her email. There's no thank you, no recognition of the extra work I've done for her, no respect for my time off, just a message full of criticisms and a threat, to boot. I send off a quick response as I exit the elevator, reassuring her that I'll get the changes made, then I tuck my phone away. Grabbing the room key from the bottom of my bag, I swipe it across our door's sensor and let myself inside.

"Thank God," Rachel says, rushing over to greet me. Her hair is curled and pinned to the top of her head, her locks already stiff from too much hair spray. "Where have you been?"

"I crashed a wedding last night," I say, kicking off my soiled shoes. Slipping out of my wrinkled dress, I throw my hair in a high bun and stumble into the bathroom. "Then I got drunk and fell asleep next to the fire pit downstairs."

"Sounds exciting," Rachel says, crossing her arms, a smile spreading across her face as she leans against the wall. "Was anyone with you?"

"Just the guys, and Graham," I say, partially closing the door as I turn on the shower. I wonder how much I should tell her, what I can get away with keeping to myself. I'm not a good liar and while I don't want to delve into the details of last night, I don't like keeping things from her, either. "Tim and Connor discovered the party, they invited us down after you passed out on the bed."

"Figures," Rachel says, her words muffled by the running water. "I woke up around ten and couldn't find you. Watched TV for a couple hours, hoping you'd come back, but I eventually fell asleep again."

"Sounds like your routine back home," I say, stepping into the shower. Hot water streams down my face and I inhale, breathing in the thick, muggy air as my body relaxes

"I know, right?" Rachel says, her voice clear as a bell, evidence that she's stepped into the bathroom. "So, are you sure you didn't run into anyone else last night? Maybe Cooper?"

"No, no Cooper," I say. "And I don't want to run into him, remember? He's here with Victoria, who knows who I am. The last thing I want is to spend more time with either of them."

"That's true," she says, the excitement deflating from her voice. "It's a damn shame, he's one hunky dude."

Turning off the shower, I reach for a towel on the towel rack, wrapping it around my body as I throw open the curtain. "We need to hurry, I have to be downstairs by 10 AM for the judges' critique panel. Then there's the meet and greet with attendees to discuss our work individually. Hopefully it will get me a couple more votes."

"Don't worry, I've got you," Rachel says. "I've already ordered us pancakes and coffee, it's on the way up as we speak. There's a dress laid out for you on your bed, and I've already gotten your bag ready for the meet and greet." She smiles, handing me a makeup wipe for my face, my eyes still smeared with mascara. "You just need to get yourself ready. If you do your makeup, I can help you with your hair."

I smile at her, swiping at my soiled face as I step out of the shower. "What would I do without you?"

"Good thing you never have to find out," she says, winking at me. "Now get dressed, maybe we can have you ready by the time the food arrives."

***

By some miracle, we walk into the convention center ten minutes before the panel starts, both of us polished and full of pancakes. Hurrying through the throngs of people, Rachel blows me a kiss as she takes her place amongst the crowd, a whisper of red lipstick staining her fingertips as she waves me off. I rush forward, my stomach churning with every step, my head pounding as I join the other contestants near the stage.

"I'm impressed," Cooper says as I approach. "You're really good at being precisely on time."

"It's a gift," I mutter, my politeness evaporating along with the alcohol on my breath. "Did you have a nice evening?"

"Yeah," Cooper says, shifting awkwardly from side to side. I can tell he's a little embarrassed, since both of us know I never texted him. "Vicky and I came back from dinner and saw some people walking through the lobby wearing top hats and ball gowns. Turns out there was a 19th century-themed wedding in the Grand Ballroom, how crazy is that?!"

"That sounds amazing," I say. "Wish I could have seen it."

"It would have been more fun if you were there," he says, a glimmer of hope still shining in his eyes.

I smile stiffly, deflating at the thought of having to turn him down yet again. I have to give him credit, though; for being a good-looking guy, he certainly puts in a lot of effort. "Rachel was jet lagged, so we stayed in our room," I say, my response completely sidestepping his comment. "Plus, my job has been nonstop. I still have work to do before we fly home tomorrow."

"I understand," Cooper says, not pressing any further. He looks past me toward the crowd, smiling and waving at attendees as they push closer to the front of the stage.

Following his gaze, I look around at the sea of people, strangers shuffling back and forth, curiously watching us from afar. Even with my makeover and new wardrobe, I feel exposed, each person a potential threat, an unknown gateway to my past. Turning to the right, I catch sight of Victoria, her arms folded over her black Van Halen t-shirt, her dark eyes piercing beneath her smokey, smudged-out eyeliner. She's looking at me, her face shifting between annoyed and confused, a peculiar expression that chills me to the bone. My eyes dart towards Graham's booth but he doesn't notice me, his attention on the new customer in front of him. I stare at him, my chest tightening as I remember the press of his lips against my throat, the feel of his hand on my thigh, the way he worshiped my body last night with every touch, every kiss. It's been five years since I last touched him but I feel like I'm an addict, unable to fully turn the cravings off now that I've had a taste.

Music blasts out of the overhead speakers, snapping me back to reality. "Ladies and gentleman, please welcome our finalists for the 'Photo of the Year' competition!"

We walk single file onto the stage, taking our seats like before. This time, however, there's five chairs in the middle, forming a semi-circle: one for each judge, one for the featured contestant, and one final chair for our host, David Hermann. As soon as we're seated, David takes the stage and begins calling the judges up individually, the crowd going wild with each name that is called. Anthony Freeman walks up last, the entire arena erupting with genuine fervor as he smiles and waves at the crowd. Everyone takes a seat, silence sweeping over the room as the judges' panel begins.

The first two finalists are called up to present their work, each receiving a tough but fair critique from the judges. Cooper goes up next and, to my surprise, gets an overwhelmingly positive review. As he walks back to his seat, he glances over at me, a stunned smile spreading across his face as he flashes me a subtle thumbs up.

"Next up, Avery Walters!" our host bellows through the loud speaker. Applause ripples through the crowd, the shouts and cheers deafening.

I stand up, my knees weak and wobbly as I move toward the center of the stage. I shake everyone's hand, lingering on Anthony Freeman as I give him a proper greeting, then we all take our seats. Looking down, I notice my submission on the monitor in front of us, something for the judges to look at as they critique my work.

"I truly enjoyed this submission," Linda Thomas says, a prominent architectural photographer. "The colors are absolutely exquisite. The image is pulsating, it has a life of its own."

"I agree," says George Burman, well known for portraiture back in the 90's. "Even though it's mostly a landscape shot, there's something about it that evokes some very strong emotions. We aren't being told what those emotions should be, either, which may be what makes it so interesting. As the observer, you end up projecting your own ideas and meaning onto it."

"That's so true," David chimes in, nodding his head. "My favorite thing has always been the coloration of this image, from deep, dark blues and purples, to yellows and fiery reds. Everything blends together so beautifully, there's a lot of technical mastery in this photograph."

"I agree," Anthony Freeman says, quickly glancing over at me. "Unfortunately, the decision to rely so heavily on technical skills is also my biggest criticism of this piece."

My smile falters, his words slicing through me. *This doesn't make any sense*, I think, as I try to compose myself. *I thought he liked my work?*

"Ms. Walters is showing us something beautiful, something important to her, but this image doesn't reveal the whole story. What is so significant about this place, and why don't we, as the viewer, get to experience it with her?" Anthony looks at me, his eyes fierce and unapologetic. "This work is magnificent, and yet it's confusing. You've layered the image with meaning through color and movement but removed the true subject. It may be bold in terms of our craft, but it doesn't share anything with us... it doesn't tell me what I want to know."

"Okay," David says, laughing to dispel the tension. "Thank you, judges, for sharing your thoughts. Any final words from you, Avery?"

I stare at Anthony, my chest heaving as his harsh words echo through my mind. I need to get off this stage, I need for this to be over. "No, I don't think so," I say, subtly shaking my head.

"Thank you, Avery—please take your seat," David says, giving me a sympathetic smile as he releases me from the judges' circle.

I get up and walk back to my chair, too embarrassed to look at Rachel or even Cooper. One of my favorite photographers just gutted me in a room full of my colleagues, in front of hundreds, if not thousands, of people. Even in disguise I want to hide, to crawl under the stage and disappear.

CHAPTER 27

I SLUMP OFF THE stage, my chest heavy, my confidence shot as I slowly descend the stairs. There's no way I'm going to win the competition now; I probably won't even place in the top five. As soon as I hit the floor, Rachel rushes over to me, wrapping me in a tight hug, the smell of honeysuckle and vanilla emanating from her overly-processed hair. "I'm sorry, Avery," she says, squeezing me tighter. "That was pretty rough."

"I feel like someone just put me through a spin cycle," I say, laying my head on her shoulder. Everything aches, my head still pounding as I lie cocooned in Rachel's soft hair, her hand moving in soothing circles over my back. Pulling away from her, I grimace as I watch the other contestants file past me toward the meet and greet. "And now I have to go mingle with a bunch of strangers. Could this day possibly get any worse?"

As Rachel consoles me, the judges step down from the stage, walking right past us. Breaking away from her, I storm after Anthony Freeman, my defeat turning into rage as I grab him by the arm. "I thought you said you liked my work?" I say, coming around to face him.

Anthony adjusts his jacket, looking past me at the other judges. He nods his head, a cue for them to continue on without him, before turning back to me. "I do," he says, the wrinkles around his eyes creasing as he gives me a mournful smile. "Your work is very good."

"Then what the hell was that?" I cry. "Your critique just killed any chances I had at winning, or even placing for that matter! Saying that my work is confusing, that it doesn't 'tell you what you want to know'? It's freakin' landscape photography, what exactly were you expecting?"

Anthony tilts his head forward, his dark, hooded eyes taking on a serious tone. "Your photograph is exceptional, Avery, easily one of the best submissions this year. But it is *not* your best work. I've seen your portfolio, you are capable of more than this." He smiles again, his face softening. "You are very talented, but you are not a landscape photographer or a product photographer. Quite frankly, you don't know what you are yet and that's the problem."

I glare at him, frustrated and confused. "You don't know me, you don't know anything about me."

"That's the point," he says. "I *want* to know you, I want you to show us who you are through your work. I'm not just here to placate you, I'm here to challenge you, to push you forward. Your technical abilities are way beyond your years, but I *know* you have more to give than this." He stares at me, his eyes searching my face, eyes that seem to see me more clearly than most people ever do. "You're hiding behind your talent, Avery—it's time to show us who you are, what moves you, what matters to you."

Tears spring into my eyes, my mind reeling as his words sink in. His actions, however poorly timed, were meant to help me, to give me strength and make me better, not just as a photographer but as a person, too. I blink my tears away, refusing to cry in front of him. "You have no idea what it took for me to come here," I say, the remaining anger in my voice building to not much more than a whisper.

Anthony nods, his expression apologetic as he reaches forward, taking my hand in his. "What we do… it's about honesty, it's about transparency. Our most beautiful work will always be the things that move us, the images that say more about us than the subject in the frame." He smiles, scanning my face, his brown eyes warm and sincere. "When you figure out what that is, call me. I can't wait to discover all the things you have to say." With that, he pats my hand affectionately before turning and walking toward the exit.

"Well I have a few things to say," Rachel chimes in, walking up to stand beside me. "Mostly that you're an asshole." She turns me towards her, grabbing me by the shoulders as she scrutinizes my face, her green eyes assessing the damage. "You okay? Just say the word and we'll ditch this whole meet and greet. I'll have you in bed with room service watching a pay-per-view in thirty minutes."

I glance toward the exit, swallowing my emotions as Anthony and I's conversation plays over in my mind. I'm too upset and tired right now to know whether his words are true, if what he said about my work is actually valid. As much as I hate to admit it, I have a sinking suspicion that he's probably right. "No," I say, shaking my head. "I need to go, I need to get more votes. With or without his support, I have to try."

"Attagirl!" Rachel says. She throws her arm around my shoulders, bumping me with her hip. "He did say your work is exceptional, and you're a total hottie right now with that red hair. I bet if you work the crowd a bit, you'll still have a decent shot."

***

Walking toward the back side of the stage, we join the other contestants, each person setting up his or her own table to meet and mingle with guests. Every table boasts a vast collection of photographs, signifying each artist's work, in addition to their submission photos and smaller prints for signings. Grabbing my bag from Rachel, I pull out my laptop, bringing up my website and social media pages as people gather around to speak to me.

I glance over at Cooper, his table set up next to ours, Victoria slouching in the chair beside him, looking bored. She notices me staring, her dark eyes assessing me for a moment before turning away, ignoring me completely. *Fine by me*, I think, shoving her out of my mind as I smile and greet the first guest at my table.

Within ten minutes it's a frenzy, brands and journalists and photography enthusiasts rushing over to meet us, gushing about our portfolios and our work. People hurl questions at me rapid fire, and I deep dive into what cameras I have, what techniques I use for indoor versus outdoor photography, what tips I have regarding different software. I sign photos, take pictures, shake dozens of hands, the stream of fans and fanatics apparently endless.

As things begin to die down, I glance over at Rachel as she fidgets in her chair. "Is it over yet?" Rachel asks, leaning on the chair's hind legs. "My butt is starting to cramp."

"Almost," I say, smiling at passersby as the crowd thins out. "We'll be done in about 30 minutes."

"Fine," Rachel says, closing her eyes. "Wake me up when it's time to go."

"Oh my gosh, it's you!" someone screams, a shriek so deafening that Rachel rockets forward in her chair, its metal feet crashing into the ground, causing me to jump.

A young girl runs up to our table, her Hello Kitty t-shirt and rainbow-colored braces indicating she's most likely in her early teens. I half expect her to jump over our table and clobber me, but then I realize that she's not talking to me—she's talking to Rachel. "I *love* your home makeover videos, they're so creative! You could totally be a comedian, except you'd probably have to leave Selene to do that. Can I get a picture with you?"

I freeze, my anxiety skyrocketing as I glance over at Cooper's table. Cooper is distracted, smiling for the camera as he takes pictures with a couple of fans, but Victoria is watching us, her head cocked to the side as the girl continues gushing over Rachel. We lock eyes again and I turn away quickly, not wanting her to see my obvious panic.

Rachel clears her throat, smiling politely at the girl as she tries to play it cool. "I'm sorry sweetie, I'm not sure what you're talking about."

"You're 'Rachel_Recycled89', from Arkansas," she says. "Sorry to freak out, I just didn't expect to see you here. It's a photo convention, not a flea market!" She laughs, her nose crinkling as she lets out a little snort. "This is so wild, do you come to this every year?"

Rachel gets up and throws her arm around the girl's shoulder, aggressively leading her away from the table. "You know what, how about we go check out some of the booths together? I haven't had a chance to see all the vendors?" She glances back at me, mouthing "I'm sorry" as she pulls the girl away, their feet moving as fast as the teenager will allow. I try to compose myself, smoothing out my dress before reaching forward to tidy up my table.

"Hey," Victoria calls out from her chair, her interest clearly peaked from Rachel's conversation. "I thought you said you were from Arizona?" she asks.

"I am," I say, fighting to remain calm. I adjust the pictures on the table, pulling my hands back quickly when I notice that they're shaking. "I mean, we are. We grew up near Phoenix, but we live in Sedona now. That's where I took my submission pictures, near South Rim."

"Then why did that girl think that she's from Arkansas?" she presses, her dark eyes searching my face, trying to see past my obvious lie.

I let out a nervous laugh, my throat tightening as anxiety grips my insides. "I honestly have no idea," I say. "Rachel doesn't do thrift stores, she doesn't even like to shop."

"Huh," Victoria says, leaning back in her chair. She stares at me, her eyes scanning my face, assessing my features in a way that makes me very nervous. Grabbing her phone off the table, she looks away, slouching down in her chair as she begins doom scrolling once again.

I start packing up my table, grabbing my laptop and the smaller prints and shoving them into my bag. I couldn't possibly get out of here any sooner, the fact that I haven't sprinted out of the room by now somewhat shocking. Just as I'm finishing up, Rachel walks over, a wide-eyed grimace plastered on her face. "Wow, that girl was a *little* nuts," she says, loud enough for Victoria to hear. "I told her

I didn't even have a house, and she burst into tears and ran away. Anyway, you ready to go?"

"So ready," I say, snatching my bag off the table, my pulse racing as we scurry toward the exit. I look back, relieved to see Victoria still scrolling through her phone, oblivious to our departure. Cooper gives me a half-wave, his face falling as we leave without saying goodbye.

Once we're far enough away, Rachel groans, covering her face with her hands. "I'm so sorry! Of all people to be here, why did I have to run into some nerdy teenager obsessed with vintage teapots? I mean, I have like fifty measly subscribers.... how did this happen?"

"I know," I sigh. "It's okay, I played it off. I told her you don't even like to shop."

"Well, that's a terrible lie," Rachel says, twirling in a circle. "I mean, look at me... I have impeccable taste."

"You do," I say, letting out a small laugh. "Next time, I'll let you come up with a better excuse."

"Good idea," she says, giving me a wink. "Now let's steal some food from the contestant's lounge, go veg out on the beach."

I smile at her, shaking my head. "You read my mind."

CHAPTER 28

We spend the rest of the afternoon on an uneven blanket of beach towels, sipping fruity cocktails and eating tiny finger sandwiches. Rachel runs back inside several times for drink refills until the contestant's lounge closes, and I pay a hotel employee forty bucks to let us steal a beach umbrella from the pool. Spreading out on the warm sand, we drink in the cool, salty air, listening to the ocean beat against the shoreline, churning up seashells and little pockets of sea foam. It's the first time all day I feel good, my stomach full and settled, my mind at peace as I relish the quiet movement of the water

"I needed this," Rachel says, placing her drink back into a small hole she had dug in the sand.

"The trip, or the complimentary beverages?" I ask, snapping a quick picture of our hotel, my warm peach bellini strategically placed in the foreground. Condensation slowly rolls down the sides of the glass, sparkling in the sunlight as I take another picture.

"Both," she says. "The more free food I eat, the more I can justify the plane tickets."

I laugh, shaking my head, my hair full and frizzy from the salty ocean breeze. Tucking my camera away, I stretch out on the makeshift blanket, my toes squishing into the sand as my feet inch past the edge of the towels. "I should have brought my mom. She would have loved this."

"No, Avery," Rachel says, her expression serious beneath her dark sunglasses. "I'm sorry, but this was meant to be a girls' trip, just you and me. No family allowed."

"Except for Graham," I say, giving her a pointed look. "Seriously, this could have easily been a group trip! We could have brought our moms, and Daniel could have flown in from his travel job in Jersey, taken some time off work."

"Yeah," Rachel says, turning away as she flips over onto her back. She sits up, dusting sand off of one of her legs before glancing over at me. "I just wanted some time with you, though, just the two of us. I hope that's okay."

"Of course," I say, squinting up at her as I turn onto my side. "Apart from my multiple hangovers and running into Victoria, I've had a great time. It's honestly been really nice, having some time away to ourselves."

"We needed it," Rachel says, grabbing her drink and hoisting it into the air. "We've gonna do something fun tonight, hangovers be damned! We need to show Miami what we're made of."

"Sounds good to me," I say, raising my own glass. We cheers, sunlight refracting through our tumblers as we drink, casting geometric patterns across the sand. Beads of condensation splash across my bare belly, the spatter of cool water welcome in this heat. "One more night."

We stay out on the beach a little longer, the sun slowly descending toward the horizon, its light eventually obscured by the looming shadow of the hotel behind us. Picking up our towels and umbrella, we head inside to our room, stripping off our sand-caked bathing suits to shower and freshen up for dinner. Combing through my remaining dresses, I choose a simple, lavender sundress, its flowered skirt swishing gracefully as I move about the room.

I'm in the middle of putting my mother's necklace on when I hear a knock at the door, its sound almost obscured by Rachel's loud dance music. Rushing across the room, I peer through the door's peephole, my heart skipping with excitement when I see Graham standing on the other side. "Hi," I say as I open the door, half shouting as our music spills into the hallway. "What are you doing here?"

"I thought I'd take you both to dinner," Graham says, his hands stuffed lazily into his pockets. He's wearing khaki slacks and a loose-fitting dress tee, its fabric covered in vintage Hawaiian caricature art. There's a slight scruff along the edge of his jawline, and his hair is styled in asymmetrical, messy waves. I breathe in, his scent intoxicating, a combination of cardamom, pepper, and sea salt so strong that I have to remind myself not to lean out the door toward him.

Rachel pops her head out of the bathroom, simultaneously turning the music down on her phone. "As long as we can sit down somewhere," she says, her words echoing against the tile walls as she continues getting ready. "No street tacos or anything like that."

"No, no street tacos," Graham says as he looks back at me, his eyes sparkling. "Grab your camera, you're gonna want it tonight."

***

"This is not a restaurant," Rachel says, her mouth twisting into a sour expression as she steps out of the car, her stiletto heels clicking against the pavement. We're standing in a marina, seagulls drifting on the wind overhead as yachts and sailboats bob gently back and forth in the water, their hulls making ripples in the waves. We'd driven down the coast about thirty minutes or so, the sun's brilliant light blazing through the windows as it sank lower on the horizon, preparing to be swallowed up by the sea.

"I know," Graham says. "But luckily, we have dinner waiting for us." He gestures toward the end of the dock and I gasp, noticing the massive yacht anchored in the water, its shiny white paneling gleaming in the afternoon sun. From what I can see, there's at least three separate levels, its polished front and upper decks giving passengers an incredible view of the sea. Excitement ripples through me as I watch crew members move around on board, deck hands and servers preparing for our departure.

"Damn bro," Rachel says, glancing over Graham in astonishment. "This is a lot for dinner."

Graham shakes his head, his cartoon-riddled dress tee almost comical now, considering the circumstances. "One of the convention's showrunners owns it," he says. "He offered it to our team for the night." As if on cue, Tim and Connor pop up from below deck, their boisterous laughter echoing off the nearby boats. Tim spots us on the dock and they both wave eagerly, shielding their eyes from the sun as they yell for us to come onboard. "I thought we could make a night of it, sort of a final 'bon voyage' before we all head home tomorrow." Graham smiles down at me, and I'm not sure if I'm imagining it or not but his eyes seem sad, like our departure isn't something he truly wants to celebrate.

"You're not the one cooking, are you?" Rachel cuts in, giving her brother a serious look. "Because if that's the case, I'd rather have the street tacos."

Graham laughs. "It's fully staffed, the guy loaned us his private chef for the evening. And we aren't going that far, they're just taking us for a trip down the coast and back. It's basically enough time to watch the sunset, eat dinner, and have a few cocktails together."

"This guy must really like you," I say, surveying the impressive ship. "This is pretty generous."

"It's a perk of the job," he says, shrugging his shoulders. "Our company was a big sponsor this year." Graham waves at the guys then graciously steps aside, motioning for Rachel and I to lead the way. "We better get going, we need to be out of the bay before sunset."

We make our way down the dock, Rachel swaying considerably in her inappropriate dress shoes, cursing under her breath as Graham steadies her with his arm. I cover my mouth with my hand, giggling as I watch them shuffle forward, their unique sibling playfulness on full display. As we carefully step aboard the vessel, Connor rushes forward, offering each of us a drink. "It's charcuterie and cocktail hour till sundown, and then we'll have dinner," he says.

"I think I'm going to hold off on the booze for a bit," I say, raising my hand in protest. "At least until we start moving and I get my sea legs under me."

"I'll take one," Graham says, coming up beside me, his hand brushing across the small of my back. My skin prickles, gooseflesh crawling down my arms as he grabs a drink from Connor with his other hand, taking a small sip. He glances down at me as his hand falls away, the imprint of his warm touch still lingering on my skin. "Are you ready to go?" he asks.

I stare at him, his question churning like a rip tide in my mind. The truth is, I'm not ready. The sooner this little excursion starts, the sooner it will end, and I'm not ready for this weekend to be over. I'm not ready for us to part ways and fly off to other parts of the country. I'm not ready to go back to my modest life without his quiet laugh, his intoxicating scent, and his pale honey-colored eyes. Grief floods through me as I smile at him, determined to enjoy our night together in spite of my misery. "Yeah, I'm ready," I say.

The ship pushes away from the dock, slowly drifting out of the harbor and into open water. Within ten minutes, we are gliding down the coast, crashing through billowing waves as the sun sinks into the ocean, its fiery rays of red and orange streaking across the sky. Moving to the front of the boat, I pull out my camera, compulsively snapping photos as the sea melds with the sky, the horizon a dazzling masterpiece of pinks and purples and blues. I take dozens of pictures, mildly aware of the salsa music blaring from the back of the ship, my friends' voices echoing through warm air as they dance and laugh in the summer heat.

Footsteps approach from behind me, a slow, melodic rhythm that rumbles through the polished wooden deck. Lowering my camera, I glance back to see Graham walking up the port side, his approach intentional so he doesn't obstruct my shot. He quietly leans against the railing behind me, salty sea air whipping across his now-rumpled shirt, his eyes set ablaze by the setting sun. I stare at him for a moment, desperate to remember him this way, his beauty and confidence glowing in the late afternoon light. His gaze shifts toward the sunset and without thinking, I turn the camera and snap a photo of him, then another. "Sorry," I say, lowering the camera once again, my cheeks warm and blotchy. "I should have asked first."

"It's okay," he says, seemingly unphased. Turning back around, I refocus my camera on the horizon, my embarrassment subsiding as I take another series of photos. "What do you see?" Graham asks, his words floating toward me on the wind.

"Light, colors, movement." Pulling back from the viewfinder, I look out at the sparkling water, at the cascade of colors bursting across the sky. As much as I love photography, there is nothing like an unobstructed view, the image right in front of you that is pure euphoria, that sinks into your soul. "It's just... magical," I say.

"It is," he agrees. I hear his footsteps once again and without warning, his arms wrap around me, his peppery, warm body cradling my frigid skin. I freeze, my heart pounding against my chest as his fingers curl around mine, his warm breath tickling my ear. Without a word, he quietly takes my camera, stepping back from me as he lifts the strap over my head. He places the strap around his own neck and steps to the side, angling the lens toward me to take my picture.

I hold up my hand, my heart still racing as I attempt to block his shot. "I don't do pictures, remember? I'm the artist, not the subject."

"Maybe it's time to change that," he says, his gaze steady as he waits patiently for me to lower my hand. "Maybe it's time to let someone see you." All at once, I hear Anthony Freeman's words echoing through my mind, crashing around me like a tidal wave. *It's time to show us who you are*. I stare at Graham, cool air catching in my lungs as I manage an almost imperceptible nod, my heart racing as I turn to face the sea.

I stare at the horizon, focusing on the shimmering waves as Graham buoys around me, snapping photos from multiple angles. His movements are painfully slow, as though any sudden shift will spook me, scaring me away. I hear the *click, click, click* of the shudder and think of our morning atop the canyon, his tender kiss under the rising sun. It feels like a lifetime ago and yet, here we are, orbiting each other beneath a golden sky, our undeniable chemistry so strong my bones ache. I sneak a glance at him and he instantly stops, firing off a rapid series of shots, a drumline-beat so fast it does actually surprise me a little. Feeling my bravery wearing off, I reach out to take the camera from him but he recoils, shaking his head. "Not right now," he says, capping the lens and tucking the camera into my bag. "Later."

He turns toward the sunset, the wind pushing through his hair as we continue our journey through the water. I admire him for a moment, wondering what he's thinking, if he feels as conflicted about us as I do beneath his calm exterior. Following his gaze, we stand still for a moment, looking out at the water together, neither of us speaking or touching as we take in the incredible view.

"My dad reached out to me," Graham says, breaking the silence.

I turn toward him, unable to hide the shock on my face. "He did?"

"Yeah," he says. "He found me through a mutual friend, saw some of my travel photos. Asked if he could come visit me sometime in LA."

My mind is tripping over itself, unsure how to talk to him about this. It's such a sensitive subject for him, I can't help but wonder why he's telling me. "Does Rachel know?" I ask.

"No," Graham says, "neither does my mom. I'm not sure I want them to know."

I nod, carefully asking him the most difficult question. "Do you want to see him?"

Graham bows his head, his face wrought with pain. "A part of me does," he says. "I just have so many questions. Like, if I hadn't said anything, would things have just fizzled out, gone back to normal? Would he have stuck around?" His voice cracks and he breathes out, struggling to maintain his composure. Even in his sorrow, I can't help but notice how unbelievably beautiful he is, his golden eyes swimming in a glossy pool of unshed tears.

I can tell how difficult this is for him, and every fiber of my being wants to hold him, and kiss him, and tell him it will be okay. Instead, I shake my head, then reach forward and grab his hands in mine. "What happened with your dad... it wasn't your fault, Graham," I say, ducking down a bit until he looks at me, his tortured gaze latching onto mine. "He was the adult, not you. Whether you said something or not, he made his own choices. One to cheat, the other to leave."

"I know," Graham says, releasing a shaky breath. "It just felt like everyone blamed me, whether they said so or not." His shoulders slump a bit, and he squeezes my hands tighter. "I just want to know how his life turned out, I guess. I want to know if anything good came from all of it, if any of our pain was worth it."

I think about my dad, about our Sunday mornings together, about our silly jokes and breakfasts filled with laughter. I think about my mom's broken face, about our car riddled with boxes and clothes as we left everything behind. I would never dare to find my father, to try and track him down, but I often wonder the same thing. Was his need to express his anger worth what we had as a family? Does he think about the enormity of what we lost? And was leaving Graham worth it, shattering our future just so I can sleep at night under the same roof as my mother, secure in the knowledge that she's safe. "I understand," I say, my throat thick with emotion as I give him a sad smile. "More than you know."

We hear footsteps approaching and we pull back from one another, each of us composing ourselves as Connor pops his head around the helm of the boat. "Come on, you two," he says. "Dinner's ready." As he walks away, I glance toward the horizon, surprised to find the sun tucked away for the night, its final rays casting a mural of hazy pastels across the water. I smile, and when I turn to face Graham, he's smiling too, his shy, boyish grin that I adore so much. Without hesitating, I step forward once more, softly kissing his cheek and hugging him with all the love I have to give. Then I release him and nod toward the back of the boat, leading the way as we join the others for dinner.

CHAPTER 29

Eighteen years old, six years after "The Incident"

Wind swirls through my hair from the open window as we pass over the state line into Arizona, no clear indication of the crossing except for a red, blue, and yellow sign that reads, "The Grand Canyon State Welcomes You". We'd spent the previous night in a sketchy motel outside of Albuquerque, watching *I Love Lucy* reruns on a staticky TV with no sound and eating vending machine popcorn, our bed sheets so musty that we were afraid to sleep under the covers. Graham slept on the bed closest to the door, and when we woke to the sound of drunken, incoherent shouting at 5 AM, we decided it was time to get up and move along.

We'd been on the road for three days now, stopping at every ridiculous place Graham could think of. He'd taken us to a rattlesnake museum, we spent an afternoon spray painting trippy art installations made from old cars, we even visited a folk art museum filled with hundreds of animated, hand-carved toys. We'd stayed our second night at Big Texan Steak Ranch, stuffing ourselves with barbeque ribs and Texas toast, taking turns at the lobby's shooting gallery while sampling handcrafted beer, compliments of Graham's new fake ID. We even tried a bit of line dancing, both of us failing miserably, laughing in a tipsy haze as we tripped over one another on the sticky, beer-stained floor.

I look out at the scorching desert, the hot sands punctuated by cacti and dry shrubbery, wondering how long someone could survive out here without food or water. Next to me, Graham hums along to the radio, singing the bits he likes before abruptly flipping to another song. While I don't consider him to be a particularly good dancer, I do enjoy listening to him sing. "So, what's on the agenda for today?" I ask, turning around to face him, swooning a bit as he continues singing till the end of the song.

"Well, I wanted to make a stop at the Petrified Forest National Park because, rocks," Graham says, reaching over to turn down the music. "And then, I figured we'd stay near Flagstaff for the night."

I perk up a little, knowing that Flagstaff is very near the Grand Canyon. "Really? Do we have time to see South Rim?" I ask.

Graham glances over at me, a smile creeping across his face as the music plays on without him. "We're going to *stay* at South Rim," he says. "I reserved us a camping spot on the east side of the ridge, we just need to grab some supplies before we go up there. I figured we could stay there a day or two, give us some time to explore."

I grin, my face practically splitting in two at the thought of seeing the Grand Canyon for the first time. Settling into my seat, I stare at the open road ahead of us, silently wishing we would move faster. "We'll need sleeping bags, and bug spray, and s'mores! We can't forget the s'mores."

***

We cruise into Flagstaff before lunch time, stopping at the local big-box store for supplies. After loading up on food and drinks, we hop over to the camping section, each of us picking out a cheap sleeping bag and blanket while Graham decides on the best tent for his truck. Within an hour, we are headed north on Interstate 180, sparse pine trees flanking either side of the road as we wind our way toward South Rim.

Graham pulls off the main highway into the Grand Canyon Visitor Center, maneuvering around tourists and other vehicles as he finds a spot to park. "So I figured we'd spend most of the day here," he says, throwing the Jeep in park and killing the engine. We step out into the smoldering heat, groaning as we stretch our stiff muscles. "We can have lunch, check out the vistas, whatever you want to do. We just need to get to the other side by nightfall so I can set up the tent."

I open the rear hatch to grab my backpack and my cameras, eager to start taking photos. "Let's just walk around a bit, see what we find," I say as I throw my backpack over my shoulder. We take off on foot, stopping at the visitor center for a map before moving on to Mather Point, the nearest vista location. Moving west along the cliffs, I stop repeatedly, snapping photo after photo, each location more brilliant than the next. Even in the daylight it's breathtaking, the vast ruggedness of the valley melding with the raw, unobstructed beauty of nature. Moving on to Yavapai Point, we take a break to eat lunch, the two of us cowering beneath a batch of scraggly trees as we munch on deli sandwiches and chips.

"Is it what you imagined?" Graham asks, taking a sip of water from his water bottle. He's sweating profusely, the collar of his shirt dark around the edges.

I look around us at the swarms of people, the wooden benches flanking us all occupied. "It's more crowded than I thought it would be," I say, watching as a group of children sprint past us, kicking up a cloud of loose dirt into the air.

Graham chuckles, a deep, throaty sound that sinks deep into my belly. "Well, you aren't the only one who enjoys beautiful scenery, even if you do capture it better than most." He tucks his water bottle away, my skin prickling as his leg accidentally brushes against mine. This trip has been amazing so far, but it hasn't exactly been easy for me to maintain our friendly boundaries. "Are you excited for college?" he asks, his amber eyes sparking in the warm daylight.

"Yeah, I think so," I say, glancing away, my longing for him mostly hidden behind my thick sunglasses. "I'm sure it'll be great, but I don't know... it's just far from home."

Graham tilts his head, frowning. "I thought you couldn't wait to get out of there?" he says. "You're always talking about traveling, experiencing new places."

"I know," I say, looking around at the steady stream of people walking past us. I notice a lady staring at me and I look away, my anxiety around strangers fading but still present. "It's just a lot, being around so many new faces. And it's hard being away from my mom."

"You'll get used to it," Graham says, nudging me with his shoulder. He's so close to me, his scent mingling with the smell of bug spray and dust. "College will change that, you'll see." He pulls the canyon map out of his bag, studying the vista points. "It looks like we can hike along the trail for another mile or so, but a lot of these places are much further away. Might be best to double back, take the car to the west side."

"Sounds good to me," I say, crumpling up my sandwich wrapper and tossing it in my bag. Graham jumps up, dusting off his pants before offering me his hand, our dusty fingers intertwining for a second before we set off along the South Rim Trail.

We drive around the park for the rest of the afternoon, hitting location after location, my memory card full of pictures. Graham lets me work, only chiming in when I show him a photograph or he sees something interesting on the horizon. Around six o'clock we start heading east, the canyons glowing behind us as we make our way to the Desert View campgrounds. We stop several more times before we get there, Graham waiting patiently as I run to the nearest vista, capturing as much of golden hour as I can.

As soon as we park at the campgrounds, I jump out of the car, grabbing both my digital and my film cameras and sprinting toward the Desert View Watchtower. "I'll be right back!" I call over my shoulder, running away from our campsite, the last of the sun's rays peeking through the trees.

"I'll be right here," Graham says, laughing as he unloads the car.

I sprint across the dusty ground toward the tower, slowing down a little as I get closer, looking for the perfect spot. Stepping around a couple of onlookers, I find a large rock near the tower's base and scramble onto it, breathing heavily as I adjust my camera settings. I start taking pictures with my digital, the canyon a sea of reds and golds, the Colorado River snaking through the center of it, its water a shimmering blue against the dry desert rocks. I switch over to my film camera and take a couple more pictures, each shot more dazzling than the next, the wild beauty of this place so overwhelming that I begin to tear up behind the lens. I'm so happy that we came here, this place more incredible than I could ever have imagined, the pinnacle of the best trip I've ever been on. I eventually put my cameras away, sitting down to watch in wonder as the sun sinks into the horizon, the clouds above tipped in gold. People start packing up, the sun all but gone, and after a couple more minutes I follow suit, a gentle smile on my face as I slide off the rock and head toward the campground.

When I get back to our campsite, Graham has already attached the tent to the back of the truck, the smell of hot dogs and roasted corn thick in the air. "I hope you don't mind," he says, setting a couple of drinks on the table, his sweaty hiking clothes replaced by a fresh t-shirt and sweatpants. "I went ahead and got things set up."

"Fine by me," I say, peeking inside the tent, my sleeping bag rolled out in the cargo area of the hatchback while Graham's is on the ground. "How long till dinner's ready?"

"It's done," he says, gesturing behind him, our dinner already laid out on the table. He smiles, my favorite toothy grin lighting up his face, and I know instantly that coming here has been his plan all along. As soon as he thought of this road trip, he decided to bring me here, an opportunity to check off something on my bucket list, not just some wild, pre-college excursion.

I smile at him, my feelings for him throbbing behind my cool exterior, pounding on it, desperate to break free. "Ready when you are," I say.

We eat our meal under the stars, the voices of nearby campers floating around us on the breeze, loud conversations and laughter echoing through the cool summer night. After a while the voices die down, the hum of crickets and the far-off cries of coyotes the only sound left. Graham packs up what's left of our dinner, tossing our soiled plates into the nearby dumpster as I duck into our tent, careful not to hit the tailgate as I crawl onto my sleeping bag. It's soft, the surface beneath me cushioned by a thick, foam mattress.

"I have something for you," Graham says, turning on a small camping lantern as he steps inside the tent, zipping it shut. He reaches beneath his pillow and pulls out a notebook, the outside of it a worn leather, a thin cord tied around it to keep it closed. He sits down near the foot of my bed, handing it to me, his face a mixture of anticipation and nervousness.

"What is this?" I ask, taking it from him.

"It's your graduation gift," he says, watching me intently as I carefully open the book. I draw in a breath, the first page an eerily accurate sketch of me, my fourteen-year-old self dancing wildly in my nymph Halloween costume.

"You drew this?" I say, tilting the page forward toward the light, the details of my costume exactly how I remember them. This must have taken him hours, if not days.

"Yeah," he says, his expression sheepish as I evaluate the picture. "You always said I should do portraits, so I thought I'd draw yours."

I flip through the pages, each drawing a different picture of me, snapshots in time from our many years of friendship. I feel like I'm going to cry, the amount of effort he put into this becoming more obvious with every turn of the page. "These are incredible, Graham," I say, the fingers lightly skimming over each drawing, scared I'll somehow ruin them. "I love it."

"I started drawing when I was pretty young, it was the only thing I ever wanted to do," Graham says, looking down at his hands, his demeanor changing as he becomes quiet, smaller somehow. "Like most kids, I started drawing pictures of the people in my life. Me, my sister, my parents... and my mom's best friend, Monica. Blake's mom." He pauses, shifting uncomfortably. "She and Blake were always around, hanging out at our house, so I drew them. Sitting in our living room, playing in the backyard... sleeping in my parents' bed." He exhales, my stomach bottoming out as his face takes on an anguish I've never seen. "She and my dad were having an affair, but I didn't realize that's what was happening, I was just drawing what I saw. My mom asked me to explain one of my drawings one day, and everything just spiraled from there. My dad and Monica skipped town, leaving all of us behind. It was a huge scandal, the whole town gossiped about it for years, and Blake pretty much hated me after that, blaming me for what happened. I stopped drawing at home, convinced that I did something wrong, that it was my fault that my dad left us." Graham looks up at me, his eyes glistening in the dark, his sadness lifting slightly as he studies my face. "I felt like everyone in Selene hated me, judged me, but then you moved to town and you didn't know about any of that stuff. I could be myself around you, you saw me the way I wanted to be seen—just some nerdy kid who loves to draw. You literally saved me from going crazy in that place, Avery, and I just wanted you to know that it meant something, that you will always mean something to me for what you did."

I stare at him, my heart swelling with anger and grief and sadness all at once. I want to wipe his pain away, my desire to comfort him as urgent as my need to breathe. All the nights he spent in our apartment, drawing in our home as he avoided his own finally makes sense. There's so much I want to tell him, so much I wish that he knew, that for the first time I open up about my past, the truth revealed but still hidden. "When we moved to Selene... I never thought I'd feel whole again," I say, looking down at the notebook in my lap, running my hands over the smooth leather. "We left behind a life that I loved, and it shattered me. But you and Rachel... you changed everything, you brought joy into my life again. I know it isn't the same thing, but trust me... you saved me too."

He stares at me, his eyes glowing in the lantern light. He puts his hand on mine, the notebook beneath both of our palms, his face so serious that it feels like he's taking an oath. "I don't know what will happen with college or afterward, but I'll always be there for you, Avery, in any way you want me to be. No matter where you go, you will always have me. I promise."

My heart swells, the love I have for him bubbling to the surface, propelling me forward as I lean in and press my mouth to his. Graham jumps a little, my kiss surprising him before he melts into me, his lips warm and languid. I pull away quickly, my face red with embarrassment. "I'm sorry, I just..." I say, tripping over my words. I look at him, thinking about all the time I've loved him, unable to deny how I feel any longer, the dam finally broken. "It's you, Graham. For me, it's always been you."

Graham cups my face in his hands and kisses me, his touch incredibly gentle as his lips move over mine. He grabs the sketchbook, tossing it onto his bed before pulling me in close, his strong arms wrapping around me as he lowers us onto my bed. I reach for him, our bodies sweltering in the cool night, every touch sizzling with heat. His kiss grows deeper, his tongue caressing mine, hungry lips trailing along my jaw and pressing into my neck. His hand caresses my arm, swims through my hair, but he doesn't go any further, even as I feel him stiffen, his body wanting more. I pull at him, curiosity and greed and hunger overcoming me as I twist my hands in his shirt, drunk on desires I didn't know were possible. Sitting up quickly, I push him down on the sleeping bag, throwing my leg over his thighs as I strip off my shirt, the moonlight illuminating my pale skin as I kneel over him wearing only my bra.

Graham looks up at me, eyes wide as he stares at my body, his groin impossibly hot. "Are you sure?" he asks, his arms still, his hands resting motionless on my thighs. I nod, certain that I want this, that I want *him*. He sits up slowly, his amber eyes boring into mine as he removes his shirt, our chests now inches apart. He pauses, waiting for me to stop him, to change my mind, but I don't. I love him, I've always loved him; I don't want to hide that anymore. His hands move up my thighs, brushing over my sides, skimming along the sides of my breasts. I shudder, my breath catching but I don't look away, the two of us face to face as he slowly explores my skin. His hands come up, gently brushing my hair back over my shoulders, my chest exposed as he slides his hands down my back, unclasping my bra. It falls away, landing between us, his eyes growing dark as he looks at me bare. We just sit there, staring at one another, our breathing heavy as we examine each other in the lantern night.

Graham's hands are on my thighs once again but one of them creeps up, pressing into my belly, his groin twitching as his palm makes contact with my bare skin. It moves up a little more, his thumb reaching out, whispering over my nipple. I sigh, my heart pounding beneath his hand, neither of us moving except for the slow rotation of his thumb, agonizing circles that I feel all the way down in my toes. I let him do this, over and over again, the pressure building between us until I can't take it anymore. I kiss him, pressing my body into his, his full lips and warm skin the only thing I want to know. He reaches down, wrapping my legs around his waist before laying me on my back, my head facing the tail end of the truck. He kisses me deeply, pressing me into the sleeping bag, and then his mouth is everywhere, trailing over my body in a pattern I cannot follow. I groan as my nipple slips into his mouth, my body tensing, the feel of him new and electrifying. He slips a hand past my waistline and I gasp, his thumb working slow circles again, his palm rubbing against me in a way I've never felt before. His mouth crashes back into mine but his hand stays where it is, exploring deeper, my belly rigid as his fingers sink into me. He pushes and pulls, a slow, steady rhythm as I moan into his mouth, unable to breathe. He breaks away from me, his mouth exploring my chest again as he moves his way down my body, my sweatpants bunching around my ankles as he tugs them down, his tongue trails up and down my thighs. I tense, fighting for control as his mouth latches onto me, his face hidden between my legs. I gasp, crying out, arching into everything he's doing, my body numb as it buzzes with desire, this moment pure ecstasy. After several minutes of agony he backs off, and I lie in wait as he opens his glove box, the sound of torn foil echoing through the truck as he grabs a condom. He crawls back to me, trailing kisses up my body, the two of us face to face again as his erection presses into me.

"We can wait, Avery," Graham says, gently caressing my face, pushing wet pieces of hair off my brow. "We have time, we don't need to do this now."

"I know," I say, admiring his handsome face as I comb my hands through his hair. I know we could stop right now, that I'd be fine with waiting, but I just don't want to—I've waited long enough. I slide my hands down his body, his skin quivering as I position myself beneath him. Neither of us says anything, we just kiss each other, a deep kiss of love as he slowly pushes into me.

I sigh, pain and exhilaration rippling through me all at once. He goes slow, his movements gentle, an easy rocking that doesn't hurt too much. The pressure builds and we speed up a little but just barely, Graham holding us steady, the two of us moving as one. I kiss him over and over, my heart exploding, my body aching, every fiber of my being knowing that this is right. I am fractured, my body coming apart at the seams but he doesn't stop, the steady rhythm continuing, breaking me anew. I am a sweaty pile of nothing by the time he finishes, both of us spent, my blankets a matted mess of sweat. I pant heavily, my naked body glistening in the moonlight, Graham's chest heaving up and down beside me.

He sits up for a moment, quickly cleaning himself up before grabbing my pillow and bringing it to the foot of the bed. He gently lifts my head, setting it beneath me before grabbing his blanket off the ground, draping it over my warm body as he turns off the camping lantern. His hand trails up my arm, tracing over my skin, his face calm and distant, almost like he's in a trance. "I love you, Avery," he says, brushing strands of hair away from my sweaty skin.

It's the last thing I remember before I fall asleep.

CHAPTER 30

WE SPEND THE NEXT few hours gliding up and down the Florida coast, lights from the shore rippling across the water, beams of pink and blue neon stretching across the restless sea. We laugh and eat and drink, the evening turning into a bittersweet farewell, each toast solidifying our newfound friendships as much as they say goodbye. At some point, the music comes back on and we dance freely under the stars, our inhibitions cast aside as the cocktails sink deeper into our veins. Graham grabs me during a slow song and we sway together, his rough cheek resting against my hair, his hand pressing against the small of my back, pulling me in close. Even when the music changes, he doesn't let me go, just holds on tight as we move together, each of us silently clinging to the remainder of the day.

Around ten o'clock, the ship drifts back into the harbor, its music subsiding as the captain announces our impending departure. One by one we exit the yacht, thanking the crew as we hop off the back of the boat and stumble up the teetering dock. Our car is waiting where we left it, and within no time, we're back in the lobby of our hotel, buzzed and exhilarated from our night out on the open sea.

As we walk toward the elevators, Tim stops us, throwing his hands into the air like a stage performer. "How about a night cap?" he says, an earnest smile spreading across his face. "We can grab drinks at the hotel bar, take them out by the pool."

I angle myself away from Graham, my face on fire as I recall our escapades from the night before. "I don't know, it's pretty late. I should probably go inside, get a little work done before bed."

"Come on, Avery," Rachel begs, tugging on my hand like a child. "It's our last night! You'll have plenty of time to do it in the morning." I look around at my friends' eager faces, at Graham's steady gaze, my heart pinching at the thought of leaving him. "Okay," I say, leaning toward Tim with a playful scowl across my face. "*One* drink."

Grabbing our round of cocktails, we walk out onto the moonlit patio, cool ocean air sweeping over us as we take a seat around the blazing fire pit. We chatter on about the conference, the company the guys work for, our individual plans for the summer. Graham sits next to me, and while he doesn't outright touch me, he does drape his arm across the couch behind us, his fingers intermittently caressing the back of my shoulder. It feels nice, every brush of his hand smooth and sensual, a single point of contact that's devastating and exhilarating all at once.

Determined to avoid a hangover, Connor runs back inside to grab us a couple of waters and returns with none other than Cooper and Victoria. My face falters at the sight of them, our perfect evening tarnished by their unexpected arrival. "Hey guys," Cooper says, beaming at us with his signature megawatt smile. "Can we join you?"

"Sure," Rachel says, eagerly patting the cushion beside her. I shoot her a look, a little surprised by her blatant flirting but she ignores me, angling herself toward Cooper as he plops down next to her.

Victoria, on the other hand, does not sit down right away. She stares at me, her dark eyes examining my face, scanning every detail. She seems kind of off, even for her, but I'm not really sure why. After a beat, she slowly moves toward Cooper, her gaze still locked on me as she passes by him and takes a seat.

"Well, big day tomorrow," Tim says, nodding toward me and Cooper. "You two nervous?"

"A little," Cooper says. "It would be great to win, I'm hoping to use the money to buy a house." He shrugs, looking toward me, his smile deflating when he notices Graham's arm around my shoulder. "How about you, Avery?"

"I'm just glad I could be here," I say, fiddling with my mother's necklace. "I mean yeah, I could use the equipment and the prize money, but what I really needed was this. Some time away, a little bit of adventure." I glance at Graham, our eyes catching once again as he lightly strokes my shoulder.

"Well, you know," Connor says, "you can work anywhere. I've seen your portfolio, you could easily get a job in New York or Chicago—wherever you want, really. The adventure doesn't have to be over."

"We'll see," I say, smiling at his kind words. "I hope not." Setting my drink down, I slowly stand up, teetering a bit as I smooth out my dress. "I'm gonna run inside real quick, use the restroom."

"I'll come too," Victoria says, standing up so quickly that she splashes some of her drink on Cooper's leg. He cries out in protest but she ignores him, setting her glass down before beelining toward the hotel without me. Surprised again by her strange behavior, I follow her inside, careful to keep some distance between us as we both walk into the lobby bathroom.

After relieving myself of hours worth of alcohol, I exit the bathroom stall, wobbling a bit as I walk to the nearest sink. I feel tired and woozy, the lights above the mirrors taking on a hazy, ethereal quality. To my surprise, Victoria is still in the bathroom, apparently over drying her hands on a disposable towel. "So, are you ready to head home? To Arizona?" she asks, slowly turning the towel over in her hands, the criss-cross motion that's eerily mechanical. Her voice has a weird edge to it, like her words are more of an accusation than a question.

I shrug, reaching forward to turn on the faucet. "I'm ready to see my mom, and my dog."

She nods, discarding her soiled towel in the wastebin. "Is your mom from Arizona?" she asks, crossing her arms over her chest, her dark brown pupils almost black beneath the moody, overhead lights. This question, while innocent, seems completely out of the blue, especially considering our surroundings. Alarm bells start ringing through my fog of exhaustion and alcohol, a sixth sense that something about this conversation is very wrong.

"Yeah," I say, trying to hurry through the motions without raising any red flags. I quickly wash and dry my hands, my heart somersaulting in my chest as I attempt to nonchalantly check my makeup.

"What about your dad?" Victoria asks.

I keep my eyes forward, careful not to look at her, my hands shaking as I comb them through my hair. This is not normal bathroom conversation, she stayed in here to interrogate me because she knows something. "What about my dad?"

"He isn't in the picture?" she asks, clearly pressing me for more information.

"No," I say, mustering up the courage to turn and face her. I need to get out of this bathroom, even if it means running her over. "He left when I was a kid."

"Where did he go?" she asks, her body planted firmly between me and the door. She's staring at me intently, studying my every feature and movement, looking for the truth. I don't want her dragging this conversation back to our table, but I can't stay in this bathroom another second.

"I don't know," I say flatly, "and I don't care to know. He wasn't a good guy. I'm going back out, I'll see you in a minute." With that, I step around her, my breath shallow and ragged as I rush to push open the door.

"Avery!" she calls, her voice cut off by the closing door. I keep moving, the erratic clicking sound of my heels following me as I stumble down the narrow hallway, trying to get away from her.

"Avery," she calls again, racing after me, her footsteps not far behind my own. But I don't stop, I can't, this can't possibly be happening. And then, I hear it.

"Anna," Vicky says, her voice echoing around me, that single word stopping me dead in my tracks. I'm frozen, gutted, her voice nearly bringing me to my knees. I haven't heard that name in over a decade and yet, I can't help but to acknowledge that it's mine.

I turn toward her, my composure all but gone. "It's Avery," I say, my words shaky and weak.

"No, it's not," Victoria says. "I looked into your friend, 'Rachel_Recycled89'. It's definitely Rachel, and she definitely lives in Arkansas. Seems like she has for quite awhile."

"I can explain," I say.

"So then I looked up 'Avery Walters' and 'Arkansas', and guess what I found." She holds up her phone and on the screen is the website of our local paper, my picture smack in the middle of the front page under the title, "Local Photographer Enters National Photo Competition." It's the picture from the day we celebrated my nomination, my mother and I smiling into the camera, surrounded by our friends. "That's you," Victoria says, pointing at the picture. "And that, right there, is your mother."

"I don't know her," I lie, an absurd statement considering I'm clinging to her in the photograph.

"Bullshit!" Victoria cries. "You're wearing her necklace!" I clutch it instinctively, as though hiding it makes any difference at this point. Panic surges through me, my chest aching and tight as I try to grapple with what's happening. "I remember her wearing it," Victoria says, emotion rising up in her voice. "Everyday when she would pick you up from school, she'd be waiting in her car, fidgeting with it. And then after that day, you were both gone, disappeared." She stops, waiting for me to confirm what she's saying, to verify the undeniable truth of the situation.

Letting go of the necklace, I reach forward, pleading with her to calm down. "Victoria..."

"I knew it, I knew it was you!" she exclaims, her words caught somewhere between vindication and fury. There are tears in her eyes, this revelation clearly upsetting her. "I thought I was going crazy, I didn't even question your story at first. The name, the hair, the secrecy... what is all this?"

"It's complicated," I say, desperately looking around us, afraid someone will hear.

"Yeah, apparently," she scoffs. "Cause you definitely went to a lot of trouble to lie to everyone about it. We were best friends, Anna—I practically lived at your house for half of middle school."

"I know," I say, bowing my head. "I'm sorry, I didn't want to lie to you, or to anybody for that matter. But who I am has to stay a secret, okay? It's important, for my mother and me."

"Do you know how much I cried when you two never came back?" she says, wiping at her face as her tears spill over the edge. I stare at her, my lip quivering as guilt and sadness ricochet through me. I always thought about how hard leaving was for me; I never considered how much it affected the people I left behind. "You were like family to me... your parents took care of me."

"I'm sorry, Victoria," I say, shaking my head as I look down at the floor. "We didn't mean to hurt you. If there was any other option, we would have stayed."

"Well, you didn't need to come here," she says, looking at me with disgust. "If whatever drove you away was that big of a deal, maybe you should have just stayed in hiding."

"I know," I say, tears bubbling up and spilling down my cheeks. "I told my mother it was risky, that I was terrified to do this. But I've also been hiding for *ten years*, Victoria, and I'm tired, I'm just so damn tired of it."

She looks at me, her anger subsiding into pity. "I really don't care anymore," she says. "It was a long time ago, it's none of my business why you left. But maybe next time you run into an old friend, just be honest instead of lying through your teeth." She looks away, shaking her head. "I am capable of keeping a secret, especially if it's really that important."

"It is," I say, wiping at my eyes, my face a sunken mask of misery. "It's really, *really* important. He would kill her if he ever finds her."

Victoria stares at me, my words slowly sinking in, their implications both sad and terrifying. "Okay," she says, nodding her head, her long hair swaying back and forth. Her eyes sweep over me, marveling at her discovery, the shock of it all still playing across her features. "It's been a long day, I'm going to go to bed. Goodnight, Avery," she says, sighing as she turns on her heel and walks toward the lobby.

I breathe out, flattening myself against the wall, my body shaking as I process our conversation. *Will she tell anyone? Can I trust her? How do I fix this?* I take a deep breath, holding it in, my heart slowing to a normal rhythm as I let out a long, raged exhale. Standing up straight, I'm about to return to our table when Graham comes around the corner, his eyes dark, full of anger. I know instantly that he's heard every word.

"We need to talk," he says.

CHAPTER 31

Eighteen years old, six years after "The Incident"

By noon we're floating down the Colorado River, the sun high in the sky as we skim over the water, its gentle current winding us through the canyons. Sunlight kisses my skin as Graham and I drift lazily back and forth, each of us navigating our own paddle board, waving at other groups as they relax on the shoreline. It's surprisingly quiet, the steady flow of water buffered by rocky cliffs on either side of us, their faces steep and magnificent, rising straight into the sky.

I'm sitting cross-legged on my board, my paddle across my lap as I take pictures with the water-resistant disposable camera I bought at the Lee's Ferry gift shop. "What a gorgeous day," I say, my board drifting sideways with the current.

"It is," Graham agrees, his paddle dragging through the water as he stares up at the cloudless sky. He kneels down and jumps into the river, his paddle floating freely as he disappears into the murky water. He quickly resurfaces and scrambles onto his board, his wet skin glistening in the sun as he lies face up, his paddle board twirling in circles.

I watch him, my face flushing as I think about how warm he is, what his body feels like on mine. After watching the sunrise together, we had returned to the privacy of our tent, exploring each other's bodies until it was time to pack up and leave. My skin prickles as I watch beads of water roll off his toned belly onto the board, his glittering figure radiant under the desert sun. Turning myself toward him, I snap a picture.

Graham looks over at me, an amused smirk lighting up his face. "You're pointing that in the wrong direction," he says, squinting through the harsh daylight. "You're supposed to be photographing the scenery, something memorable."

I tilt my head to the side, my eyes sweeping over his lanky body, his muscles tanned and lean. "It's memorable, Graham," I say, giving him a coy smile. "Trust me."

Graham watches me for a second, his eyes locked on my face. Then he abruptly rolls off his paddle board, disappearing under the water. I look around, trying to find him, the ripples from where he entered the river fading into the current. Suddenly he pops up on the other side of me, standing in the shallow water. He wades forward, his body cool and slick as he grabs my face and kisses me, his warm mouth sliding over mine as tiny beads of water trickle down my chest. I feel breathless, whole, a happiness blooming between us that I can't put into words. He takes the leash from his paddle board and ties it to mine, waves forming around us as he scrambles onto my board. He faces me, pulling me in close, my legs around his waist as he looks down at me, river water dripping from his hair. "I want to go everywhere with you," he says, his hand lightly trailing over my shoulder. "Backpacking, ski trips, Europe, I don't care."

"Well, I think we need to go to college first," I say, teasing him.

His hand skims over my jaw, his golden eyes warm and sincere. "If that's where you are, I'll be there." He leans down and kisses me, his board bumping into mine as we drift down the river, the scenery around us lost as we hold onto one another, our focus entirely on each other.

After an hour or so we're back at Lee's Ferry, our wet clothes tossed in the back seat as we climb into the truck. Graham starts the engine, classic country music drifting out our windows as we pull out of the parking lot. As we near Highway 89, the GPS signals for us to take a right but Graham goes left, heading east. "Where are you going?" I say, glancing over at him.

"Don't worry," he says, his thumb moving over my knuckles as he holds my hand. "You're gonna love it."

An hour later we're parking at Antelope Canyon, Graham taking my hand as we walk toward the check-in booth, a camera around each of our necks. Graham gives them his information, a reservation he apparently booked weeks ago, then we step aside, taking a seat on a nearby bench as we wait for our tour group to be called. "You didn't tell me about this," I say, watching as a different group of people is led away, a large family consisting of adults and teenagers.

"It was a surprise," he says, squeezing my hand. "You'll see, this place is the reason for the entire trip." Ten minutes later our group is called forward, a dozen strangers standing in a circle as our guide walks over to welcome us. "Hey folks! Just wanted to go over some quick safety rules and let you know that we might see a bit of rain today. According to the weather reports it's nothing to worry about, but if things get a little dicey, just stand below an overhang if you want to to protect your belongings." He rattles off a couple of ground rules, tells us what to expect once we're in the canyon itself, and then we're off, our tour group moving as one across the scorching desert.

We trudge across the hot, dry sand, the rocks narrowing as we approach the entrance to the canyon. Our group merges into a single file line as we push forward, the path beneath us sloping downward until we disappear beneath the desert surface. As soon as we're below ground, the canyon opens up, caverns spiraling around us as flights of stairs take us deeper underground. I can feel Graham behind me, watching my reaction as the canyon walls vibrate with color, rays of light spilling through the cracks in the earth, the sandstone warm washes of pinks, oranges, and purples. We go deeper and deeper, each level more vibrant than the last, the view above us breathtaking as we finally reach the bottom. I am speechless, my eyes cast upward, my heart swelling as I stare in awe at the layers of colored earth.

Graham comes up beside me, his hand on the small of my back. "Do you like it?" he asks. I nod, unable to tear my eyes away.

We move forward and I start shooting, finding angles where the light shines through to the floor, slivers of sunshine pushing through the darkness. After about ten minutes our guide stops us, listening to the walkie in his ear while looking toward the sky. "Looks like we're about to get that rain," he says. "Stay close to the wall, it should be over in a minute or two."

The rain starts trickling down, a gentle mist at first that turns into a monsoon, fat droplets of water that instantly sink into the desert floor. Graham spins toward me, mist swirling around us as the rain falls hard against his back, my cameras safely cocooned between us. I look at him, sunlight refracting off the rain behind him, a rainbow of colors dancing in the light. I am completely in awe of this man, relishing the fact that he brought me here, that he knows me well enough to do this for me. Pulling him toward me, I kiss him passionately, ignoring the onlookers as he presses me against the canyon wall, his hand on my waist. The rain starts to let up, the deafening roar of the downpour subsiding, and we break apart, grinning at one another.

"Okay, everyone, let's move," the guide says, scowling at Graham and I as the group starts wandering forward. They walk past us, the space becoming quiet as people slowly disappear, moving into the next cavern. The sun comes out again, the desert walls as vibrant as ever, a drizzle of rain still falling from above. I grab my film camera and start walking in a circle, pointing it toward the sky, trying to find the perfect combination of rain and light.

Graham comes up behind me, wrapping his arms around my waist, kissing my shoulder. We stand like that for a few more minutes, a light mist swirling around us, him cradling me in his arms as I tilt my camera toward the sky.

***

I open my eyes, fluorescent lights blinding me from outside the window. Sitting up slowly, I realize that we're parked at a gas station, the smell of gasoline diffusing through the air as it pumps into the side of the truck. A bell dings nearby and I look over to see Graham exiting the station, wind rippling across his t-shirt as he walks toward the car. I roll down my window, yawning as he approaches. "Good morning," he says, bending down to kiss me on the cheek.

"Where are we?" I ask, looking around. It's dark outside but there's plenty of buildings nearby, their lights twinkling against the night sky.

"We just got to Vegas," Graham says. "On the outskirts, at least. You were out cold."

I shake my head, yawning again. I remember driving through the Kaibab Indian Reservation, but anything beyond that is a blur. "Sorry, didn't mean to crash out on you."

"It's fine," he says, groaning as he bends over, stretching his legs. "You mind taking over? It's only twenty minutes to the motel." He hands me a cold water and I smile, his simple bribe proven effective as I unbuckle my seatbelt and hop out of the truck.

I slowly walk around the Jeep, taking a sip of water as I jump into the driver's seat. Graham puts the coordinates in his GPS, setting it on the dashboard. "Where are we staying?" I ask, squinting at the location on his phone.

"Bandit Bob's Wild Vegas Resort," Graham says, chuckling at the goofy name. "It's not exactly five stars, but it's cheap. It'll give us a chance to shower and change, and then we can check out the strip."

I nod, pulling the truck out onto the road. I make another turn and we're on the highway, the lights of Vegas shining in front of us. "By the way, you need to call home," Graham says, leaning his seat back as he props his feet on the dash. "I got a text from my mom once we had cell service again but you were already asleep."

"Can you grab my phone?" I ask, my eyes on the road as I point toward the backseat. "It's in my backpack." Graham reaches for my bag, digging through the pockets until he finds my phone, handing it to me. I turn it on, the screen dusty even though it's been in my bag for days. As soon as it lights up, a slew of text messages come through, including a voicemail from Frank. Frowning, I click on the voicemail, holding it to my ear as Frank's familiar voice comes through the phone.

Hi, Avery... I'm sorry to be the one delivering this message, but your mom's hurt, kiddo. Time stops, my body suddenly weightless, the car decelerating as my foot eases off the pedal. Words come through in short bursts, tidbits my brain catches as her face flashes through my mind, her cheeks bloodied and bruised. *Car accident... hospital... fire... critical condition.* Emotions swirl through me, the whole car going dark as panic sets in. *He found her, he found her, he hurt her again.* Then the worst thought comes crashing through, eviscerating me completely. *I wasn't there.*

A horn blares to my left and I shriek, dropping the phone in my lap. "Jesus, Avery, be careful!" Graham cries, sitting upright in his seat. He turns toward me, his face falling when he notices my hysteria. "Avery, what's wrong?" he asks.

I shake my head, words escaping me as tears stream down my face. "M-m-my mom, my mom, s-s-she's..." I cry, my vision blurring as I look out at the road in a daze.

"Okay, calm down," Graham says, glancing at the cars around us. He gently sets his hand on mine, my knuckles white as they grip the wheel. "Let's just pull over, okay? We'll call my mom, figure out what's going on."

My mind is broken, fractured, my vision a kaleidoscope of painful images from my past. My mother, my beautiful mother, beaten beyond recognition, her gorgeous face sliced to the bone. *He found her, he found her, this is all my fault.* Guilt slams through me and I can't believe this is happening again, that I wasn't there for her not once but *twice*. I look up at the signs overhead, my brain latching onto the words *Harry Reid International Airport*. I speed up, quickly merging to the right, cars honking around us as I swerve violently through traffic.

"What are you doing?" Graham says, holding onto the door as I skid around another car.

"Home," I say, speeding up even more. I swerve again, barely missing the car in front of us.

"Jesus, Avery, calm down," Graham says, bracing himself as I veer to the left. "We can figure this out, just pull over."

I keep going, speeding around semis and cars, flying toward the airport like my life depends on it. Graham is speaking to me but I can barely hear him, a vision of my mother overtaking my mind, the skin on her face replaced with grisly, burnt flesh. I take the airport exit, the Jeep screeching as I speed through the turns, looping around and around until we're at the arrivals bay. I brake hard, the front passenger tire jumping over the curb as I throw the Jeep in park and climb out, ripping the back door open to grab my things. A security guard rushes over, yelling at Graham as he steps out of the truck, telling him to move his vehicle. I'm halfway to the airport entrance when Graham grabs me, turning me around.

"Avery, stop," he says, looking back at his Jeep, the security guard already on the radio. He turns back to me, his face lined and hollow. "Just hold on for a second, okay? Let's go park the truck, then we can go inside and talk."

"No," I say, shaking my head, pulling away from him. "I have to go, she needs me."

"We don't even know what happened yet," he says, holding onto one of my bags as I struggle to break free. "Just take a moment, breathe."

"No!" I cry, yanking the bag away from him. The handle rips and it falls to the ground, my stuff scattering on the pavement. Graham bends down to scoop up my things as tears stream down my face, my breathing ragged and shallow. "This is all my fault, I never should have left her."

"What are you talking about?" Graham asks, clearly confused. He shoves my stuff back in the bag, tying the handles together so it doesn't spill open. "Avery, you didn't leave her, we just... went on a trip. You're headed to college, anyway."

"I know," I say, shaking my head, my chest burning, all the things I want disintegrating in front of me. I can't protect her and have the life I want, and I can't have him while he's thousands of miles away, living the life we've both dreamed about. I back away from him and the blood drains from his face, the distance growing between us as I take another step. "It's just... I was wrong. I can't do this, it's too much."

Graham steps forward, tossing my broken bag onto the ground. He cups my face in his hands, his amber eyes flashing. "It's not too much," he says, his thumb scraping over my cheek. "Going to college, this trip, you and me... none of it is wrong. We can do whatever you need to do—hell, I'll drive us all the way home, just... come back to the truck with me. We can figure this out together." A security vehicle pulls up to Graham's Jeep and a few men jump out, the original guard pointing at us. Graham glances over his shoulder before turning back to me, his hands clutching my face, his expression hopeful.

I stare at him, the man I love, the distance between us expanding even as we stand perfectly still. I can't go to college but I can't take him home with me, a realization that cuts me to the core. If he takes me back to Selene, he'll stay with me, he'll never leave. He'll be stuck in a town he hates, parts of him rotting away as we live a life that I can't escape from. I think about his first two years of college, all the places he's visited, the joy he's experienced, living a life we both want. But *he's* the only one who can have it, and I love him too much to take it away from him.

I step back, his hands falling away from my face. Bending down, I scoop up my bag, tears splashing against the canvas material as I retreat another step. I can feel my heart shredding in my chest as I pull away from him, the look in his eyes one of pure devastation. "Avery," Graham says, frozen in place as a guard comes up, grabbing him by the arm. He handcuffs Graham and forces him onto the ground, his eyes still on me as he kneels on the pavement.

"I'm sorry," I say, then I turn and flee into the airport.

CHAPTER 32

"GRAHAM, I CAN EXPLAIN," I say, instinctively reaching toward him. He turns to the side, ripping his arm away from me, and I immediately draw back, the fury in his eyes potent and electric. I've never seen him so upset, an unexplored side of him that actually frightens me a little.

"Can you?" he says, pacing the corridor like a caged beast, his fingers digging crevasses through his hair. He's agitated and erratic, his once-calm features disfigured by a cascade of emotions. "Can you honestly explain this? I knew that something was off after Arizona, but this is a whole 'nother level. You've literally been lying to me since the day we met!"

"I only told Rachel a few years ago," I say, my words tumbling out in a rush. "I couldn't—"

"She knew?!" he cries, fresh, unbridled anger ripping through the last of his composure. His voice explodes through the lobby and the evening receptionist turns to look at us, craning her neck to see what is wrong. Summoning what little courage I have left, I look up to meet Graham's gaze, his eyes ablaze with confusion and hurt. I swallow, my mind spinning as I scramble to find the right words, desperate not to make the situation any worse than it already is.

"I told her," I say gently, "after I missed her twenty-first birthday. We had a big fight and she wouldn't talk to me. I had to explain why I missed it, why I've missed a lot of things."

"What about *me*?" Graham hisses, his voice seething with anger. "When were you going to explain this to *me*, Avery? Anna?! Jesus, I don't even know your name!"

"I just, I couldn't risk it," I say, my eyes brimming with tears, tiny droplets catching in my lashes as I struggle not to cry. "It wasn't a choice, Graham. My mother and I, we've kept our identities a secret for our safety. No one in Selene knows about our past."

"Except Rachel," he says, disdain punctuating each word as he looks away in disgust.

"She knows that we changed our names," I say. "That we left our old home. That's all."

Graham starts pacing again, his anger quickly transforming into sheer disbelief. "I just can't believe this," he says, turning once again to face me. "The last five years, all this time I've been pining for a girl who doesn't even exist."

"I'm still me," I say, stepping closer to him, pleading with him to understand, "You know me, Graham, better than anyone. You've always known who I am, the parts of me that really matter."

"But you kept this from me," he says, his face falling, his disappointment giving way to genuine hurt. Even in his misery, I can't help but marvel at how handsome he is, the way the light plays on his somber features in the dimly-lit hallway. "You didn't tell me why you left, why you went home. You just took off and let me think it was my fault."

"I'm sorry," I say, my voice catching as I begin to cry, hot tears falling freely down my face. "When I heard about my mother's accident, I just panicked. I was so afraid that my father had found her, that he'd hurt her again. I had to go home, I had to make sure she was okay."

"But what about afterwards?" Graham presses. "You could have called me. Hell, I would have come back just to be there for both of you, if that's what you really wanted. Instead, you dropped out of college and disappeared. You didn't say anything."

"I know," I say, casting my eyes downward in defeat. "I wanted to call you so many times but I didn't know how to explain everything, I didn't know what to say. By the time my mom recovered, it just felt like it was too late."

"Jesus," Graham says, covering his face with his hands. For a moment I think he's softening, that he's starting to calm down, but when he lowers his hands again his eyes are cold, any hint of love or warmth locked tight behind his rigid features. "I feel like such an idiot—I never should have come here."

"Graham— ," I say, shaking my head, my heart shattering as I realize that my words, coming clean about my past, had next to no effect.

"You were never honest with me about anything," Graham says, his mouth drawing into a thin line as a wry laugh escapes from his lips. "I entered you in this contest, just for a chance to see you, and you couldn't even trust me enough to tell me your fucking name."

I step back, his words slapping me across the face, tearing through everything I thought I knew about the last few weeks. "*You* entered me in the contest?"

"Yeah," he says, his voice flat and lifeless. "I did. Because I wanted to see you." His hard exterior cracks for a split second, his golden eyes glistening with fresh tears, the raw pain of my betrayal on full display. "I know you were Rachel's best friend, but you were mine. The years I spent being bullied, being hated by everyone in that town for what happened. You were everything to me, and then you just up and abandoned me like my dad did—" He looks toward the bar, his jaw tight as he quickly blinks away his unshed tears.

"Graham, I'm so sorry," I say, the events of the past few days finally becoming clear. The contest, the dinners, the parties, our kiss... everything he's done to reach out to me, to bring us together again, to show me that he still cares. I feel like I'm going to be sick, my entire world tilting onto an unstable axis, my stomach convulsing as I realize how badly I've screwed this up.

Graham shakes his head, continuing to look away. "It's fine," he says. "It all makes sense now. I finally know why you left, I got my answer." He looks at me, his emotions under control once again, his cool indifference pulling the air from my lungs. "I won't tell anyone about Victoria, but I have to go. Good luck, Avery." And with that, he turns and walks away, his silhouette moving swiftly through the lobby before disappearing into the bar.

I stand there, frozen in place, my body motionless except for the tears still trickling down my face. I want to scream or chase after him, but I'm afraid it will make things worse, if not cause a scene. Another guest eventually passes by me, her concerned expression snapping me out of my stupor. Pulling my phone out of my purse, I immediately call my mother, my hands shaking as I press the phone tightly to my ear, desperate to hear her voice.

The call rings and rings before eventually going to voicemail. I hang up and try again, each failed attempt pushing me further into a full-on frenzy. By the time Rachel finds me, I am cowering in a corner of the lobby, my face a red, blotchy mess, my cheeks stained with runny mascara and tears.

"Hey, Avery—what's going on?" she says, gently touching my arm as she kneels down in front of me.

I shake my head, unable to look at her. "It's Graham—he knows."

"Knows what?" she asks, tilting her head to the side in confusion.

I glance at her, my voice cracking. "He *knows*, Rachel."

I watch as her expression shifts, my words slowly sinking in. "Oh," she says, staring off into the distance, dumbfounded. "I don't understand, did you tell him?"

"Of course not," I say, pinching the bridge of my nose as I close my eyes, the harsh lobby lighting making my head ache. "Victoria realized who I was and confronted me. Graham overheard us talking."

"Victoria?" Rachel says, her voice laced with confusion. "How did she figure it out?"

"She saw my necklace," I say, opening my eyes to look at her. "She recognized it as my mother's. Oh, and she looked up your thrifting profile, found our picture in the local paper." I start to cry again, quiet sobs wracking my body, my chest already tight and heavy.

"It's okay, Avery," Rachel says, squeezing my hand. "We will figure this out. We just need to find Graham and Victoria."

"No," I say, tugging my hand away to wipe at my face. "I need to get out of here, I need to leave." I stand up and side-step around her, my head pounding as I lurch toward the nearest elevator.

"Wait," Rachel says, catching up to me, blocking my path. "You can't leave, the winner is announced tomorrow! You can't accept the prize money if you aren't here."

"I don't care," I say, brushing past her. "I can't be here anymore. I mean, my mother and I will probably have to move once we get back."

"Move?!" she cries, her face etched in worry as she steps in front of me again. "Okay, let's just take a beat and figure this out. I can talk to Graham, and we'll call the paper first thing in the morning, have them take the article down. It's going to be okay, there's no need to panic."

"You don't know that," I say, wincing as white-hot pain rockets through my temples. "I shouldn't have come here, this was such a huge mistake."

"It wasn't a mistake," Rachel argues. "You deserve to be here—you're so talented, Avery! Your mom sees it, too, she *wanted* you to do this. She was supportive of me submitting your work, regardless of the consequences."

"Don't you mean she was supportive of *Graham*?" I say, my words dripping with sarcasm as my frustration transforms into anger. "Considering he's the one who entered me in this contest, a little detail you failed to mention."

Rachel bows her head, her cheeks turning red as she realizes she's been caught in a lie. "Yes, he entered you in the contest. I had sent him some of your pictures on a whim, showing him how good you've become. I didn't even know he'd submitted them until you got in, until he asked me to take credit for it." She looks up at me, her green eyes apologetic and sincere. "He offered to pay for our flights, our hotel room, everything. But this wasn't just about the contest or some dumb girls' trip, Avery. I needed some time away with you, too."

"We're together all the time," I say, throwing my hands in the air. "Sipping cocktails on a beach isn't any different."

"It is to me," Rachel says, sighing. "I know we're best friends, and I know you'll always be there for me, but you miss things, important things."

"Like what?" I cry, my mind reeling from this sudden shift in conversation.

"You missed summer camps, field trips, spring breaks. Hell, you missed my twenty-first birthday in Atlantic City. You say you're my best friend, Avery, but you're never there when I really need you."

"Are you kidding me?" I say, my pulse skyrocketing. "I've been trapped in our dinky little town for over a decade, watching my life pass me by as I hide from my abusive father, and somehow you're the victim?! I explained why I wasn't there, why I *couldn't* be there. You are the only person I've ever told the truth about my life to, I thought you understood."

"Well maybe I'm tired of understanding," Rachel says, crossing her arms over her chest, her posture rigid. "Maybe I need you to stop hiding, to open your eyes and see what's actually going on around you."

"And what's happening that I need to see?" I ask, crossing my own arms as I challenge her statement.

"That Daniel left me," she says, her words flat and to-the-point, like she's discussing the weather. I stare at her, my mouth hanging open in utter shock, her sad, lifeless expression reminding me so much of her brother. Tears begin accumulating along her lash line, her eyes glistening pools of emerald green, but they don't fall. "He left three weeks ago. He started his new travel contract, but he isn't coming back this time."

"Rachel," I say, lowering my arms, my defenses crumbling as I gape at her, speechless.

"I thought you would notice," she says quietly, "but you didn't. You're so preoccupied with keeping you and your mother safe that you miss it when anyone else gets hurt."

"I'm sorry," I say, scrambling to find my words. "I didn't mean to—"

"I know, you never do," she says, sniffling. "You weren't there when I was lonely and miserable at summer camp. You weren't there when some dude tried to assault me during spring break. You weren't there when I got arrested in Atlantic City. You weren't there for me then, and you clearly don't want to be here now, so just go." Rachel straightens, adjusting the purse on her shoulder. "I'm going back out to the patio, to try and salvage my last night here. Do whatever you want, Avery... you always do." And with that, she walks away, her stiletto heels clicking on the polished floor as her blonde hair swings gracefully behind her.

I watch her leave, my entire body aching as I absorb everything that's happened tonight. Graham, Rachel, Victoria, each of them a witness to my inconsistencies and lies, contending with demons they shouldn't have to endure. I glance down at the phone in my hand, praying to see a reply from my mother, but it's silent, my desperate calls still unanswered. Gutted and exhausted, I move toward the elevator, mindlessly pressing the button to take me to my room. As the elevator doors close, loneliness settles in around me, the agony of my isolation weighing me down like a heavy blanket. Sinking to the floor, I instantly burst into tears.

CHAPTER 33

The next morning, I wake to the bitter taste of alcohol and stale morning breath, whispers of daylight peeking through the edges of our curtains. I roll over, untangling myself from a mess of blankets, last night's dress still on, its flowy fabric bunching around my waist. My eyes feel dry and puffy, their irritation surpassed only by the steady pounding in my head. Discarded shoes and soiled tissues litter the other side of the bed, the far pillow stained with makeup from where I fell asleep crying.

I glance over at the other mattress, its sheets unkempt but empty. Rachel isn't there.

Slowly rising to my feet, I slip out of my crumpled dress, my stomach churning in protest as I stagger toward the shower. Cranking up the heat as high as I can take it, I stand beneath the scalding water, my body relaxing a little as the remnants of the evening wash away. I close my eyes, the memory of Graham's face flashing through my mind, his pain and disappointment captured in a single image that I can't unsee. I stay in the shower for a long time, not wanting to face this wretched day, the hot water washing away my tears and heartbreak.

Stepping out of the shower, I towel off my hair and inspect my face in the mirror. My eyes are bloodshot and ringed with mascara, not exactly a great look for today's big announcement. Grabbing a makeup wipe, I carefully remove the last of my makeup, then I pop in some eye drops before retreating to my bed.

I sit down next to the nightstand and pick up my phone, which has several missed calls and texts from my mother. *Sorry honey, I didn't mean to miss your call. Text me when you get up.* I also have an email from Cynthia, a message I know is coming before I even open it:

> *Hi Avery,*
> *I see that you haven't made any progress on the changes I requested yesterday. Again, I understand that you're currently away and preoccupied, but your recent work is not reflecting the quality I require for my business. After you complete this project, I think it would be best if I continue on with another designer.*
>
> *Hope you understand,*
> *Cynthia.*

I sigh, Cynthia's email the cherry on top of a spectacularly awful morning. I knew this was coming, that she would ditch me in order to hire her niece, but she wouldn't have had grounds to fire me just yet if I'd kept up with my work. Now I'll have to scrounge for new clients the second I get home, other businesses to fill the gap in my paycheck.

I close the email and pull up my mom's number, turning the volume down as I call her on speakerphone. She answers on the second ring, the quiet thrum of country music playing in the background. She must be baking, her voice light and airy as she greets me. "Hi sweetie! I'm so sorry, I forgot to text you last night. Susie and I were in the middle of an 80's movie marathon!"

"It's okay, Mom," I say, my quiet voice still hoarse from crying.

My mother notices the peculiar edge to my voice, her cheery tone quickly shifting to concern. "Avery, what's wrong? Are you okay?"

I shake my head, my chest instantly tightening. "Not really," I say.

"What happened?" she asks, the music in the background coming to a halt.

"Just a bad night," I say, a lump building in my throat as I delay the inevitable. "I ran into someone here.. an old friend, from Seattle." The line goes silent, the only available sound being Hank as he barks at birds or passersby in the next room.

My mother finally clears her throat, the effort behind her nonchalant tone noticeable. "Did they recognize you?" she asks.

"Not at first," I say. "But she eventually figured it out."

"Oh," she says, Hank's barking ringing through the phone line as she goes silent once again.

"I'll be home tonight," I say, trying to reassure her. "We can figure out what to do next."

"Okay," she says, her words distant, like she's not even listening. After a moment, she says, "It's okay, honey, really. Everything's going to be fine, you don't need to worry."

"I'm so sorry, Mom," I say, my words coming out in a rush as tears spring into my eyes once more. "I tried to be careful. This whole thing was so stupid, I never should have come here."

"Yes, you should have," she says, her voice firm. "I am so proud of you, Avery—you are the best thing about my life, now and always. Don't you ever regret how brilliant you are, ever."

"Okay," I say, tears flowing freely as I awkwardly happy-cry into the phone. "I get it, Mom."

"We'll chat when you get home, okay? I want to discuss a couple things with you anyway." Hank starts howling in the background, a sure sign that someone is at the front door. "I have to go, I'll see you tonight at the airport. Don't worry, honey, everything will work itself out."

"Ok Mom," I say, smiling into the phone. "I love you."

"Love you too," she says, her cane thudding against the floor as she walks toward the door. "Good luck today! Let me know what happens with the competition."

"I will," I say, my heart feeling a little lighter as I wipe my tears away. "Talk to you soon." Hanging up the phone, I turn to see Rachel standing in the doorway, her arms overflowing with two giant ice coffees and a paper bag that says *Espresso Yourself*. "Hi," I say, giving her a half-hearted smile as I turn toward her, my face still wet with tears.

"Hey," she says. She walks around the foot of my bed, her expression hesitant as she offers me one of the plastic cups. "I grabbed us some coffee from downstairs, and some pastries."

"Thank you," I say, accepting the cold drink. She sits down on the bed, her eyes on me as I stare at the floor, unable to look at her. "I'm sorry," I say, my face burning with embarrassment and shame. "I should have realized about Daniel."

"It's not your fault," Rachel says. "He left for work like he always does, he just took more stuff with him this time." Rachel takes a long sip of her coffee, her face drawn as she lets out a sigh. "Well, he put it in storage, but you know what I mean."

"Why didn't you just tell me?" I say, angling toward her on the bed. "You're my best friend, you can come to be about anything."

"I don't know," she says. "Probably because I didn't want to accept it. Talking about it would have made it real, you know?"

"Did he say why?" I ask.

"He just said he's gone too much, that our lives are too disconnected." She shakes her head, her beautiful golden hair swishing back and forth. "He didn't want either of us waiting for the other, trying to piece together our lives in the minimal time we have together."

"How do you feel about that?" I ask, sorrow flowing through me as I scrutinize her gloomy face, the joy and exuberance that is Rachel sucked right out of her.

"I was mad at first," she says, "but I honestly think he's right. He loves his new job, and I love my life in our sleepy little town. I think we both need to focus on what's working in our lives instead of trying to fix something that's not." Rachel bows her head, silence wrapping around us as I process her words, the truth of them not making the conclusion any less sad.

"Well, even if you're okay with it now, I still wish you would have told me," I say, setting down my coffee to grab her free hand. "I know I've got some pretty heavy stuff on my plate, but I'm here for you, always. And I want to be there for you in the moment, not weeks or years afterwards." I squeeze her hand, my voice catching as my love for her bubbles to the surface. "You are my sister, Rachel... you are my family. Besides my mom, I've got you—that's it."

"What about Graham?" she asks, taking a sip of her coffee as she waits for my answer.

"After last night, I doubt he'll ever talk to me again," I say, slumping forward, my chin resting on my hand. "Neither will Cynthia, who decided to fire me this morning."

"She's such a bitch," Rachel says, setting her coffee next to mine. "You're better off without her. Now you can take on more creative projects, do something new."

"Maybe," I say, giving her a little shrug.

"I talked to Graham last night," she says. "He was pretty upset, with both of us. He's been wanting to see you for a long time, especially after that rendezvous you two had in Arizona."

I jerk upright, spinning toward her as my face practically melts off with embarrassment. "You knew about that?!" I ask.

"Oh please," Rachel says, giving me a little shove. "You two were never subtle. I pretended I didn't notice, but it was pretty obvious you liked each other."

I laugh, throwing my hands over my face. "I thought I was being discreet," I say.

"Not so much," Rachel chuckles, enjoying my humiliation. I playfully shove her and she shoves me back, both of us tumbling around my bed, laughing hysterically. After a bit she rolls onto her side, facing me as she props her head up on her hand, her expression serious. "He loves you, Avery," she says, her green eyes warm and sincere. "He always has."

"But he doesn't know me," I say. "He said so himself last night."

"Give him time," Rachel says. "He knows deep down that that isn't true."

I nod, smiling at her, my love and admiration for her deeper than it's ever been. "Love you, Rach," I say, nudging her with my foot.

"You'd better," she says. "I made out with Cooper last night, just to keep him distracted for you. Would not recommend, by the way—he kisses like a drunk fish." I cry out, laughing uncontrollably as I roll around the bed again, nearly squishing our bag of pastries. Rachel jumps up, snatching up the bag and tossing me a croissant. "I love you, too. Okay, it's time to get you ready—the big announcement is in T-minus two hours, we need to get moving!"

"Ugh, do I have to go?" I say, tossing the croissant aside.

"Yes," Rachel says, pointing the bag at me. "Because even if my best friend, Avery Walters, isn't a winner, she's a fighter."

CHAPTER 34

Excitement ripples through the crowd as we enter the convention center, meandering patrons buzzing with enthusiasm in anticipation of today's final event. Loud, trendy music plays overhead, the volume only increasing as we push through the throngs of people toward the main stage. As we get closer, I catch sight of Graham's booth, my desire to see him, to apologize, ringing through me to my very core. I tug on Rachel's arm, nodding in that direction, and she follows me, gently squeezing my hand as we move in closer.

As we emerge from the crowd we catch sight of Tim, who runs over immediately, his smile practically splitting his face in half. "It's the big day!" he cries, giving me a massive hug. "You feeling okay? Rachel said you were a bit under the weather last night."

"I'm fine," I say, glancing over at Rachel. "Just ready to get this over with."

"Well, you look fabulous, honey!" Tim says, admiring my outfit. "Even if you don't win the contest, you've won the hearts of the people."

I laugh, peering around the busy booth. "Is Graham here?" I ask.

"No," Tim says, his brow pinching together as he looks back and forth between us. "He moved his flight up last night. He's boarding a plane back to LA as we speak."

My smile collapses, my insides shriveling into raisins. "He left?"

"Yeah," Tim says, tilting his head to the side. "He said he wanted to get a jump on some new extension packages for our software. I thought he told you?"

I look toward Rachel, who gives me a small shrug. Apparently, she wasn't made aware of these last-minute plans, either. "We must have missed the memo," I say, fresh pain crackling through my ribs as I try to force a smile. "Well, wish me luck! We'd better get over to the stage." I pull Rachel away from Tim, my breath shallow as we move through the shifting sea of people, none of them the man I desperately want to see. Rachel puts her arm around me but doesn't say anything, the two of us drifting in tandem, clinging to each other for support.

As we near the stage, I spot Cooper and Victoria huddled together, each nursing a coffee as they chatter back and forth, waiting for the conference to start. "Hey," Cooper says, his charming smile on full display as we approach. "How are you this morning? Still feeling sea sick?"

I shake my head, my current nausea having nothing to do with last night's boat ride. "Just your standard nervous jitters," I say, trying to sound chipper. "I can't believe the conference is already over, it went by so fast."

"I know," Cooper says, nodding in agreement. "It feels like we just got here. Although, I will admit, I'm dying to get home so I can sleep in my own bed. The mattresses here are killing me."

I give him a polite smile, his complaint seeming rather trivial, considering the night I had. "You'll be home before you know it," I say. Lightly bumping Rachel's hip, I quickly glance toward Victoria, discreetly signaling that I'd like a moment alone with her.

Rachel steps toward Cooper, flashing him her own signature smile. "Do you mind if I talk to you?" she asks, her voice light and playful. "It'll only take a second."

"Sure," Cooper says, grinning at her as she pulls him away. They meander through the thick crowd, Rachel laughing as she loops her arm through Cooper's, her lively, flirtatious energy pulling him in like a moth to a flame. *So much for liking me*, I think, happy to hand over the reins to Rachel.

Once they're out of earshot, I turn to Victoria. "Did you tell him anything?" I ask.

Victoria studies me for a moment, contemplating whether or not she wants to answer my question. Eventually she shakes her head, her long, dark hair sweeping against the sides of her coffee cup. "No, I didn't," she says. "It's not really something you discuss over breakfast."

I let out a breath, her answer giving me some relief. "Do you *plan* to tell him anything?" I ask, pressing her further.

"No," Victoria replies, visibly annoyed by my question. "You clearly went to a lot of trouble to... change your look. And your name, for that matter." Her eyes trail over me, both of us a far cry from what we looked like as kids. "I'm not going to tell anyone," she says firmly. "You have my word."

"Thank you," I say, my heart swelling with gratitude. "It's just really important that... certain people don't find us."

Victoria's face scrunches, her brown eyes studying me. After a moment, she nods, resisting the urge to ask me any more questions. "I understand. But just so you know, your dad left town years ago. I'm not sure where he went, or if anyone even stays in contact with him anymore."

I sigh, shaking my head. "I don't know if that makes me feel better or worse," I admit.

"All I'm saying is, he won't hear about this from me," she says. "It's not my secret to tell. If you say there's a good reason to keep this under wraps, I believe you."

I smile at her, unsure what I did to deserve her kindness. "Thank you, Victoria," I say. "I know it's been a long time and that you don't owe me anything, but I really appreciate it."

"Well, like I said, you and your mom looked out for me." She smiles, the first real smile I've seen from her since the conference started. It transforms her face, the girl I knew shining behind her eyes. "I think keeping this to myself is the least I can do," she says.

Cooper and Rachel saunter back over, grinning playfully at one another as they rejoin our group. "Everything good?" I ask, acting like I wasn't the one who sent them away in the first place.

"Yep," Cooper says, grinning at Rachel, clearly unaware that I know about their late-night makeout session. "We were chatting last night and I asked for her advice regarding an old weight-lifting injury. She was just following up, that's all."

"You lift weights?" Victoria quips, clearly teasing him.

"Well someone has to be strong enough to lug all our heavy-ass equipment around," Cooper says. "Considering you live off of snack cakes and coffee, it isn't going to be you." Just then, the house music comes up, the stage lights glowing as the crowd begins to cheer.

"Okay, you two," Rachel says. "Go make us proud!" She gives us a thumbs up then scurries away, taking Victoria with her, both of them weaving through the rowdy crowd to find a good spot next to the stage. Cooper and I line up with the other finalists and ascend the stairs one last time, the crowd going wild as we smile and wave. I spot Anthony Freeman off to the side, standing side by side with the other judges, his brilliant gaze locked on me as he nods in my direction. Our host, David Hermann, eventually takes the stage, a hush falling over the crowd as everyone eagerly awaits the final announcement.

"Thank you, everyone, for being here," David says, waving at the crowd. "And now, the moment you've all been waiting for... the *winner* of our 'Photo of the Year' competition!" The crowd cheers wildly, the sound deafening as it ricochets off the glass walls. "Our grand prize winner will receive $50,000, plus the newest line of Canon mirrorless camera equipment, in addition to a ten-page photo spread in *Aperture Magazine*. So, are you ready to know who won?" The audience roars once again, David beaming at them as he holds up the final envelopes.

"So, our third place winner, who receives $5,000 and a one-year subscription of *Aperture Magazine* is... Avery Walters!"

I gasp, throwing my hands over my mouth as I step forward, my heart bursting with excitement. I barely register shaking David's hand as he relinquishes my envelope, the crowd going wild all around us. We smile for a quick photo before I return to my seat, my hands shaking as I examine the envelope in my lap, dumb-founded. I look out at the audience and find Rachel, laughing as I watch her jump up and down, her face practically splitting in two. I look past her, expecting to see Graham but he isn't there, and in the middle of one of the greatest moments of my life, I realize that the prize in my hands isn't worth a fraction of what I lost.

"Our second place winner is... Myles Barlowe!" People shift around me, another series of gasps and applause, pictures and prizes. They finally announce the grand prize winner, the photographer from Ohio who took a stunning black-and-white picture of his children, his work admittedly very good. I watch as he accepts his prize, cameras flashing from every direction, confetti raining down, a layer of colorful tissue paper littering the stage. I see it all and yet I can't ignore what's missing, who I desperately wish was here with me, cheering me on.

The audience starts to disperse and Cooper runs over to me, his smile proud but a little sad. "Congratulations!" he says, clapping me on the back. "Not exactly what *I* was hoping for, but I'm glad you won something."

"Yeah," I say, looking around at the room, trying to take in the moment. Even without Graham, I know that being here is a victory, a small step toward healing the fear in me that has dominated my life for so long. "I definitely won something." We turn and walk down the stairs together, me proudly waving my envelope as Rachel rushes toward me, giggling as she pulls me in for a hug.

"I'm so happy for you!" she squeals, squeezing me with all her might. "You won third! It's your first competition and *you won third,* that's so great!"

"Thanks," I say, slowly pulling away from her. "I couldn't have done it without you."

"Please," Rachel says, giving me a little nudge. "You did all the work, I just made you look fabulous." We laugh and I hug her again, her soft hair pressing against my cheek. "You ready to get out of here? Go get packed up?" she asks.

I mull it over for a second, an idea popping into my head. "Maybe we should grab one more cocktail, have a little more girl time on the beach," I suggest.

Rachel grins, a look of genuine delight spreading across her face. "You read my mind," she says. We say goodbye to Cooper and Victoria, me embracing Victoria in a long hug before reluctantly pulling away. Then Rachel throws her arm around my shoulders, the two of us walking side by side as we head for the exit.

CHAPTER 35

After a couple more hours out in the sticky Miami heat, we go back to our hotel room, pack up our belongings, and head to the airport. Once we're through security, we stop at a couple of gift shops, grabbing cheesy knick-knacks for our families before rushing toward our gate. We walk up just as they're preparing to board, the gate agent announcing our on-time departure over the airport intercom.

"Ready to go home?" I ask, pulling up my digital plane ticket on my phone.

"Yeah," Rachel says, "I am. This trip was exactly what I needed, just a little time away with my bestie."

"Good," I say, giving her an affectionate smile. "Maybe when we get back, we can look into getting you a new place. Something with some character that you can call your own."

"Maybe," she says, looking down at her empty ring finger, not quite sold on the idea. "How about you? Are you ready to go home?"

"Sort of," I say. "Part of me wants to go home, but the other part wants to just take off, go somewhere unexpected. Chase the horizon for a while, you know?"

"Yeah," Rachel says, giving me a coy smile. "Maybe take a trip west—to California, for example?"

I playfully push her away, swatting her with my purse. "I didn't mean Graham," I say, laughing. "I mean, yeah, I want to see him. But there are a lot of places I want to visit, things I want to see and experience. I don't know, I just wish it wasn't over, that I could keep going."

"You can," Rachel says. "And you should. If that's what you really want, find a way to make it happen." The gate agent announces our boarding group so we line up, shuffling forward in single file to scan our plane tickets. Cruising down the jetway, we hop on board the plane and quickly find our seats, stowing our suitcases in the storage bin above us. "I don't know about you," Rachel says as she buckles her seatbelt, "but I am sleeping the *entire* trip home. Who knew I'd need a vacation from my vacation."

"That's how you know it was a great trip," I say, tucking my backpack under the seat in front of me.

"The best," she replies, her eyes already closed. She burrows into my shoulder, her hair smelling like salt water and hairspray, her expression relaxed and peaceful. Within minutes, she is out cold, her light snoring eventually drowned out by the rumbling of the plane's engines.

Try as I might, I can't fall asleep. After tossing and turning for a good hour, I open up social media, scrolling through my saved travel photos, all the places I want to see. Before I know it, I'm looking up Graham's page, his public profile something that I've ignored for years. I'm shocked to see how many new pictures he has, candid shots from all over the globe, kayaking down foreign rivers and eating exotic foods. Places that I've wanted to see for years, adventures we said we would experience together. My chest aches, scrolling through his memories, moments I wish I had been a part of. But more than that, I ache for him, one of the few people in my life that I can call home. After a while I close the app, stowing my phone away, my spirit battered and bruised as I stare out the window.

We land in Bentonville a few hours later, our bodies stiff as we grab our bags and head for the exit. My mom is waiting outside baggage claim, leaning on her cane, the opposite arm spread wide as I slam into her. "There's my girl," she says, hugging me tightly. She hugs Rachel too, lovingly patting her on the shoulder as she pulls away. "I'm so happy to see you two! Did you have a nice flight?"

"Flying is always nice in business class," Rachel quips.

"I can imagine," my mother says, pivoting around to shuffle toward our car. "You girls are so fancy, jet-setting around the world in style!" We walk slowly to where my mother is parked, throwing our bags in the back as she scrambles into the driver's seat. Bluesy country music plays over the radio as she merges into traffic, her headlights slicing through darkness as we make our way home. "So, tell me about your trip!" she says. "I got the picture Rachel took of you on stage, I can't believe you won third!"

"Yeah," I say, feeling a bit bashful. "Obviously it's not first—"

"Oh that doesn't matter," my mom says. "You went and had fun, that's what's important."

"We did," I say, smiling at Rachel in the rearview mirror. "We had a great time."

"Speaking of time together," my mother says, glancing back at Rachel, "how is Graham? I heard from your mom that he was at the convention, too."

"He's good," Rachel says, her voice a bit too chipper, like she's telling a lie. "He really loves his job, and living on the West Coast. It seems like he's pretty happy there."

"That's good," my mom says, smiling. "He's such a nice boy, I'm glad to hear he's doing so well."

"Yeah," I say, looking out at the night sky, thinking about the fact that he's on the other side of the country. "Me too." We jabber on for another half hour or so, talking about the restaurants and our trip down the coast, and before we know it we're parked in front of Rachel's house. I get out to help her with her bags, then walk with her to the front door. "Thank you for coming with me," I say, setting her suitcase down. "It was a really fun trip."

"Of course," Rachel says, unlocking the door and tossing her purse inside. "No way I'm going to let my bestie run off and be a rockstar without tagging along."

I chuckle, shaking my head. "Call me tomorrow, we can grab coffee in the square."

"Will do," she says, giving me a quick hug before stepping inside and closing the door. I stand there for a moment, wondering what her life has been like without Daniel, how empty this house must feel. *It's my turn to be there for her,* I think as I walk back to our car. I hop back in the passenger seat and we take off down the road, turning left toward home.

"So," my mom says, glancing sidelong at me, "someone recognized you at the conference?"

"Yeah," I say, surprised that she wants to immediately dive into this. " Victoria, she lived down the street from us. You used to give her rides home from school."

"Yes, Victoria," she says, nodding her head. She stares straight ahead, her eyes fixated on the road. "She was always a very sweet girl."

"She promised she wouldn't tell anyone," I say, wringing my hands in my lap. "She seemed sincere. Plus, she said that dad moved, that he left town years ago."

My mom stiffens in her seat, this news regarding my father catching her off guard. "I see," she says, her voice barely a whisper.

"So, either way, I think we're okay," I say, watching her closely, hopeful that she thinks so, too. We pull into our driveway, the car going quiet as she kills the engine. She sits still for a long time, the silence interrupted by crickets chirping outside our windows, singing in the warm summer night. "Mom, are you okay?" I ask, leaning toward her.

"Yes, sweetie... I'm okay," she says, gently patting my hand. "Let's go inside, Hank has been dying to see you."

I grab my bags from the trunk and we walk to the front door, the crickets chirping louder now, the evening alive with bugs and other critters. I can hear Hank trotting up to the door, howling at the top of his lungs as he catches our scent. My mother unlocks the dead bolt and we step inside, but the alarm doesn't go off. When I turn to check on it, I catch a glimpse of a man sitting on the couch, his face partially in the shadows. I freeze, blood pooling in my veins, certain that it's my father. But then he turns, his warm smile familiar and welcoming.

I exhale, setting my stuff down. "Oh gosh, hi Frank! What are you doing here?" I ask.

My mother walks over to the couch and sits down next to him, her eyes on me as she quietly grabs his hand. I look back and forth between them, my mind churning as I try to understand what's happening. "Sit down, honey—we have a lot to talk about."

CHAPTER 36

Twelve years old, the day of "The Incident"

"Okay class—today we're learning about the desert, specifically the plateaus, canyons, and sedimentary rock layers that make up the Grand Canyon." Resting my head on my desk, I listen to my teacher as she dives into the vast history of this region, the land formations and ecosystems that were created from millions of years worth of land erosion. As she begins scrolling through images on the overhead projector, I sit up a little, my eyes squinting through the dark at the vast, colorful desert landscape.

I stop listening to her after the third slide, the wild imagery of the desert truly taking my breath away. *We should go there*, I think, watching in wonder as picture after picture rolls across the white canvas. I can see myself there with my parents, the three of us watching the sunset together, my mother decked out in sunscreen and big hats while my dad wears tall socks with flip flops, rambling off factoids in a Grand Canyon pun t-shirt. It's so real that I can taste it, the heat and the salt and the sunscreen, the smell of earth. I know things haven't been great at home lately but maybe this could be a good ice breaker over dinner, something to talk about with my dad.

The bell rings and the lights come up, the spell immediately lifting. Shaking my head, I stand up with my classmates and hustle toward the door.

I weave through the hallways, moving with the crowd until I'm out in the afternoon sunshine, students pouring onto the sidewalk at the end of a long day. I see Victoria standing in our usual spot and I scurry over to her, bumping into a few people as I make my way through the crowd. "Hey," I say, adjusting my backpack as I come to stand next to her.

"Hey," she says, pulling on the hem of her shirt. It's an older t-shirt, probably a size too small, the fabric dull from multiple rounds in the washer. "How was class?"

"We learned about the desert," I say, my enthusiasm not reflected in her reaction. "Think I found another place to add to my bucket list."

"That's cool, more interesting than my math class," she says, pulling on her shirt again. I can't tell if she's embarrassed because it's too short or she's nervous about something. "My mom might be a bit late, she texted me that she's getting groceries."

I know what that means, that she's busy watching soap operas and won't be here for another hour. I try not to make her feel bad about this when it happens, her home life isn't exactly that great. As we've gotten older, she's been spending more and more time at my house; she even has a drawer with pajamas and some deodorant. "Well, let's pop around the corner, we'll go play basketball for a while or something," I say.

Victoria nods, looking down at her feet as we walk to the end of the block. Before we get too far, I notice my mom's car parked near the corner, a familiar dent on her back bumper glistening in the sunlight. As we get closer, I notice a laundry basket sitting in the backseat, another box piled with clothes. I can see her sitting in the driver's seat, wearing a long jacket even though it's pretty warm outside. "Mom?" I say, ducking down to peer into the car.

She jumps, turning toward me a little before facing forward again. "Hi, sweetie," she says, carefully adjusting her sunglasses.

I stare at her, her mannerisms somewhat off. "What are you doing here? Victoria's mom will be here soon, it's her day to come get us."

"Oh, I know, but I need your help running a few errands." She glances at me sidelong but keeps her face straight, her movements strangely robotic. "Get in, would you?" she asks.

I glance over at Victoria, unsure what to do. "Mom, I don't want to leave Victoria here alone."

"Victoria, why don't you run inside, honey—wait for your mom in there, okay? Anna, get it." She doesn't ask, her usual kindness sapped from her voice.

I look over at Victoria and shrug. "See you tomorrow?" I say. She nods, still looking down at her feet as she walks back toward the school. I watch her go inside before turning to open the squeaky car door, a scowl across my face as I slide in next to my mother. This whole thing feels wrong, especially the fact that we're leaving Victoria here by herself. Throwing my bag on the floor, I turn to argue with my mom but stop, my blood running cold as I take a real look at her.

She almost looks normal, her curly hair softly settling around her slim face, but there's a cut on her lip and it's quivering. Her skin is pale, green even, a faint sheen of sweat dotted across her brow. Her chest looks bruised, and while she's clearly wiped most of it off, there's a significant blood stain on the collar of her blouse. Parts of her face are swollen, her cheek disfigured by inflammation, her features distorting even more as I begin to panic, trying to make sense of what I'm looking at. "Mom, what happened to you?" I say. She looks down, her hands clenched in her lap. I glance at the backseat and recognize our clothes in the laundry basket, bags and boxes strewn about the car. I look back at her, trying to focus as I struggle to breathe. "Mom... talk to me."

"I'm sorry, baby," she says, her face still tilted downward. "I'm just a little fuzzy right now." She carefully removes her sunglasses and I gasp, the cut across her face a gnarled, angry crevice, her left eye socket swollen shut. I lean toward her but stop, terrified to touch her.

"Mom, who did this to you?" I say, horror and rage pulsing through my veins. When she doesn't answer, I lean forward, urging her to tell me. "Mom, *talk to me*. Who did this to you?"

She turns toward me, tears falling from her uninjured eye. "Your f-f-father..." she says, shaking her head as a cry crackles out of her, her sobs instantly causing pain to her injuries. She weeps and winces, reaching for her ribs, desperately trying to stop her tears. "We need to go," she chokes out, leaning back in her seat, her sobs fading to rigid sighs. "He'll find us... he'll find you."

"What?" I say, drawing back from her. I look around at the messy car, my stomach bottoming out as I come to understand the full gravity of the situation. "Where?"

"East," she says, letting out a breath. She points to her phone, a destination already plugged into her GPS. "Just east." She braces herself, starting up the engine, the car rumbling beneath us.

"We can't just leave!" I cry, looking around us at the school, at students as they stroll past us on the sidewalk. "I don't understand, why can't we just go to the hospital, talk to the police? What about my friends, our home—"

"We can't stay here, Anna," my mother says, turning to face me, grimacing as her grisly wound seeps fresh blood. "We aren't safe here anymore, okay? We need to leave, we need to go—now." I cry, tears spilling down my face for the first time as I buckle my seatbelt, leaning back into the leather seat as my mom carefully pulls out onto the road. We pass houses and small businesses, familiar landmarks that I watch fade into the distance, realizing that I'm looking at them for the last time. As we approach the highway, we hit a pothole, my mother wincing as the car unexpectedly jolts.

I look over at her, my misery subsiding as I stare at her broken face. Her swelling has gotten worse, the left side of her face ballooning into one, giant mass. "Are you okay, Mom?" I ask, a stupid question but I ask it anyway.

"I don't know," she says, turning right onto the highway. She shakes her head, her pain most likely excruciating. "Just keep an eye on the road for me, baby. Make sure I stay in my lane."

We pull onto the highway, trucks and semis roaring around us as we merge onto the busy three-lane road. My mother gets behind a minivan and turns on her cruise control, setting our speed to match theirs. She carefully adjusts her body, trying to get comfortable, the car swerving slightly as she settles into her seat. I am scared and sad and angry all at once, grappling with what's happening while trying desperately to trust my mother. If she says my father did this, I have to believe her, even if I don't want to. If she says we need to go, we need to go.

I don't look back until we're outside of the city, the bulk of the heavy traffic far behind us. The road is getting dark, headlights turning on all around us, my mother still wincing here and there but mostly calm. I look in the rearview mirror, the sun blazing low in the sky, the most beautiful sunset descending on our old life. I think about the Grand Canyon, about the vistas and the wild sands, about the conversation I wanted to have with my dad. I decide right then and there that I'll go there someday, but he won't be a part of it. After what he's done, he doesn't get to be in our lives anymore.

We drive for a few more hours, the radio gently humming between us as we look out at the long, dark road. I hold onto my mother's hand, watching as stars appear above us one by one, guiding us forward as we move across the salted plains.

CHAPTER 37

Lowering myself onto the oversized armchair next to the couch, I wait for someone to speak, my foot tapping incessantly against the hardwood floor. I glance back and forth between my mother and Frank, trying to process their intertwined hands, the closeness with which they sit, their legs touching. My mother looks at Frank, her nervous gaze met with a reassuring nod, before turning to face me.

"We've obviously known Frank since we moved here, and he's become a big part of our lives over the years," my mother says, pausing to gather her thoughts. "But what you don't know is that I've been seeing him romantically for quite some time now."

"For how long?" I ask, leaning toward them, teetering on the edge of the chair.

My mother swallows, holding my gaze. "Five years," she says.

"Five years?!" I cry, jumping back into the armchair like I'm retreating from a rabid dog.

"Well, it's actually closer to six now," Frank says, his face apologetic as he gives me a slight shrug.

"How is that possible?" I ask, my mind sifting through memories from the last six years, looking for clues, trying to make this revelation make sense. "How did you keep this from me for so long?"

"Well," my mom says, "since we have no family here, we've done most of the major holidays and town functions with our neighbors, including Frank. Plus, you stay at Rachel's place from time to time, and I try to spend time with him on the weekends if you're working."

I look away for a moment, mulling over her words. "So, you weren't over at Susie's house, planting flowers and getting wasted?" I ask.

She laughs, clearly relieved that I'm poking fun at the situation. "No, at least not as often as I said I was. I do visit her quite a bit, but I admittedly pop over to Frank's place, too, spend Saturday afternoons with him. We usually do similar activities, like baking or gardening, making fresh jam. Things I could bring home so my absence wouldn't seem suspicious."

"Sorry to keep this from you, kiddo," Frank says, gently patting the top of my mother's hand. "We didn't mean to hide this for so long, it just kind of happened. We were afraid that our relationship might freak you out a little, a new man dating your mom and all."

I stare at him, the implications of his words clear. "You know? About my dad?"

"He's known since the beginning," my mother says, her eyes becoming misty. "Charles reached out to him after Donna died, asked for his help to keep their program afloat. They started working together to find homes for survivors, provide them with basic employment. I didn't know any of that until much later, but that's why he had the apartment available above his restaurant, just in case someone needed it. It's difficult to secure housing or a job when you abandon your identity, when you don't have credit or a job history."

Leaning forward again, I cover my mouth with my hands, my brain overwhelmed by all this new information. "Why didn't you tell me this sooner?" I say, looking back and forth between the two of them.

"We planned to," Frank says. "We'd only just started seeing each other when you graduated from high school. As soon as you left for college, we agreed to tell you when you came home for Christmas, or during summer break. But then your mom had her accident and you moved back so suddenly, we didn't want to spring it on you during her recovery."

"But then you hid it," I say, challenging their explanation. "For *years*."

"I know, sweetie," my mom says, reaching out with her free hand to gently touch my knee. "I'm sorry, we never meant to keep you in the dark for so long. I just kept thinking you would take off one day, go back to school, and we could tell you then. But you never did..." She cuts herself off, the room going silent except for the ticking of a clock in the next room.

"So, what now?" I ask, glancing back and forth between the two of them. "Do we make an announcement in the local paper or something?"

Both of them laugh, smiling at one other. "Not exactly," my mom says. "Frank and I have discussed it, and we're ready to take our relationship to the next level. We want to live together."

I gape at them, another announcement I didn't see coming ."You want me to move out?" I ask, my voice coming out in a high-pitched squeak.

"Oh no!" my mother cries, waving her hands in the air. "Not at all, you can absolutely stay here. The house is paid for besides utilities, and I'll leave all the furniture, the decor, everything. I'm just going to move my personal items to Frank's place, that's all."

"Okay, wow" I say, my pulse returning to a reasonable rhythm. "You've really thought this through, huh?"

"I have," she says, the lines of her face crinkling with joy as she smiles, no hint of fear or doubt in sight. "It's been a long time coming, we're ready to move forward. But we don't need to rush anything, I want you to feel comfortable with it."

I shake my head, chuckling at how overprotective she is. "I'll be fine, Mom," I say. "I want you to be happy. Safe and happy."

"I know you do," she says, reaching forward to squeeze my hand. "I am happy, very happy."

"Well, that settles it then," I say, relaxing into my chair. My mother beams at Frank, clearly ecstatic to be starting the next chapters of their lives. I watch them for a moment, the way they look at each other, how Frank is so gentle toward her. The love they have for one another is so obvious, I'm not sure how I ever missed it. "Do you plan to get married?" I ask, cutting into their excitement.

They stare at each other, nervous smiles on both of their faces. "I don't know," my mother says, her eyes lingering on Frank before turning back to me. "I know that we've technically been together long enough, but for now, we're just taking it one step at a time."

"She may come running home after a month or so, who knows," Frank says, giving her a playful wink. "I do make quite a mess sometimes, might drive her crazy."

"I like your messes," she says, lightly kissing him on the cheek. It's so bizarre to watch her behave this way, but also really refreshing. I haven't seen her this happy in a long time. "They usually involve cooking us dinner, which I'm always a fan of."

As I mull over my question, my thoughts latch onto a slight snag. "Can you even get married?" I ask her, interrupting their playful antics. "I mean, you were never divorced... is it even possible?"

My mother's forehead crinkles, her face overcome with doubt once again. "That's the other thing I wanted to talk to you about," she says. She rises from the couch and walks toward her bedroom, her cane still thumping against the floor as she disappears out of sight. When she returns, she's carrying a thick, white envelope, her hand shaking as she sets it on the table in front of me. On the front is my old nickname, *Annabean*, written in my father's sprawling, cursive handwriting. I look up at her, my heart plummeting into my stomach as I realize who this is from. "What is this?" I say, my eyes darting toward the envelope once again, afraid to even touch it.

"I received this a few months ago," she says, her expression somber, the lines on her face etched with concern. "I've been trying to figure out how to give it to you... it's from your father."

I stiffen, her acknowledgement of him enough to truly frighten me. "He found us?" I ask, my voice barely a whisper.

"Not exactly," she says, settling back onto the sofa. She takes a deep breath, her hands clenched in front of her, her fingers flexing and releasing as she continues. "I told you on the day that we left that we had to leave immediately, that it was my idea to start over, to disappear. The truth is, it was *father's plan*—he was the one who told me to take you and go."

"I don't understand," I say, the air around me growing thin, my breath shallow. *This makes no sense, he would never do that.* "You said that he hurt you, that we had to hide from him."

"You're right," she says, looking down at the floor. I catch sight of her scar, the memory of her gnarled, bruised face flashing through my mind, like pictures from a crime scene. "I did say that, that your father hurt me. What I didn't tell you is that he wasn't... that your father isn't your father."

I stare at her, dumbfounded, unable to move, to speak. I feel like I'm in an alternate universe, conversing with someone I've never met before. Confusion and anger boil up inside of me as I sit there, staring at this petite, frail wisp of a woman, the woman I've clung to and trusted my entire life. "That's not possible," I say, blood rushing through my head, my words sounding a thousand miles away. "He was at the hospital with you, on the day I was born. There were pictures of the two of you, I saw them."

"He was there," she says, her voice cracking as she slowly nods her head. "I met your dad at my job, working in a small Mexican restaurant, while I was still dating your biological father. Your real father had a temper right from the start, he was pretty unpredictable. Your dad saw me come in a few times with bruises, small cuts on my face. When I found out I was pregnant, your real father screamed at me and beat me up pretty badly, then stole my car and skipped town." She shakes her head, her eyes cast downward. "Your dad took care of me, helped me during the pregnancy, drove me to the hospital when you were born. We didn't even start dating till you were more than a year old. By then, he was such a big part of your life, and he loved you so much..." She pauses, her eyes distant, scanning the room as she relives the memories. "It wasn't till years later that your real father showed up again. For whatever reason, he came back to town and decided to track me down."

My mind is a vortex, her words slipping into my brain, disappearing into the void. There's so much to process, I don't know if I'm angry, or sad, or just plain heartbroken.

My mom watches me for a moment, gauging my reaction before she continues. "All he wanted was money, a place to crash. When I refused and he found out I was with your dad, he started harassing us, following us around town. He lashed our tires, left threatening notes, vandalized our home. We reported everything to the police but it didn't do any good. Your dad and I talked about it so many times, unable to come up with a real solution. We started fighting, arguing about how to handle it without involving you. Then one day, your biological father walked into my shop to confront me face to face and he saw you."

I think back to that day, the man standing at the counter in his rumpled white t-shirt, the strange look in his haunting hazel eyes. "He's the one who burned down your store?" I say, recognition rocketing through me, that brief moment in time suddenly very clear.

"Yes," she says, her face shrouded in sadness. "He was convinced that I wronged him somehow, that I deserved to suffer. And then he saw you, and it only got worse." She stops for a second, breathing heavily, clearly overcome by emotion. Frank lightly rubs her back, comforting her, reassuring her she's not alone. "On the day of the incident, I was home alone, you and your dad had just left for the day. I was walking out the door to go clean up the shop when he showed up at the house. He threw me back inside, beat me, trashed the entire living room. Your dad had forgotten something and just happened to come home, they both threw a few punches before your real father fled. We didn't know what to do, his behavior was completely out of control."

I stare at her, my hands digging into the chair below me, my breathing short and ragged. I concentrate, pushing down my emotions, trying to stay focused on her story as she continues. "We knew we could go to the cops again, try to have him locked up, but that would take time and they would have to catch him first. We were terrified he would try to hurt me again, or worse, attempt to hurt you." She begins to cry. "Your dad told me I needed to leave, that it... that it was the only real option at that point. He went into our room, started throwing things in duffle bags and laundry baskets. He had everything ready—money, divorce papers, the deed to my car, Charles' contact information. He packed up our things while I tried to clean up my face, then he put me in my car and told me not to come back." She wipes at her tears, fat droplets falling freely down her cheeks. "That was the last time I saw him."

My heart breaks, thinking about my father sending her off, our home shattered. Anger starts rising in me, fury at how little I knew about my own life. "How could you not tell me all of this?" I cry, standing up, pacing the floor. "All these years, you let me think he was a monster! That he was capable of hurting you, of hurting us!"

"I did it because he *knew* it was the only way to get you to leave," she says. "It had to be a clean break or we'd never escape. If you thought your dad hurt me, you wouldn't want to see him, you wouldn't try to contact him." She shakes her head, burying it in her hands. "Neither of us were willing to risk your safety, especially him. And to be honest, I didn't want you to know your real father, because he *was* a monster. I was terrified he'd abduct you, or try to get custody, or simply hurt you just to spite me."

Tears start streaming down my face, anger and hurt and pain leaching out of me. I glare at the floor, unable to look at her, the life I loved being stripped away from me all over again.

"So, after he packed up our car, I found you at school and we left. I never talked to him again, not once. I called Charles from a rest stop in Idaho, he gave me his address, and we made our way here. He and Frank helped to get us settled, and Charles walked me through changing our names, getting our legal paperwork sorted out. After that, it was just you and me, on our own."

"I just can't believe this," I say, looking up to meet her eyes. "You kept this from me for so long! We could have fought, we could have figured it out as a family! We didn't have to leave Dad!"

"It was the only real way to keep us safe," she says. "He knew that. That's why he was drinking, why we were arguing so much near the end. Your dad knew your real father like I did, knew what he was capable of. He loved you so much, he'd rather you hate him for something he didn't do than let you be anywhere near him."

I shake my head, tears falling freely now. "All you've done since the day I was born is lie to me. Everyone... you, Dad, Frank." My jaw quivers, a tsunami of emotions threatening to burst free. "So what's this? Something else you've kept from me? I don't know if I even want to read it, it's probably full of more bullshit."

My mom sighs, gesturing toward the letter on the table. "A few months ago, I was contacted by a private investigator," she says. "Your dad hired him to find us. Not to reveal our location or interfere in our lives, just to reach out. He informed me that your biological father went to prison several years ago but recently passed away inside from an unknown illness. He also gave me two letters, one for each of us, as well as a check for half the sale price of our old home. Your dad didn't have to do that, considering the deed was in his name, but he wanted to give it to us. Make sure that you had money for a wedding or to go to college."

I look down at the letter, curiosity getting the better of me as she continues. "He told me in my letter that he moved to another state, that he's married now with two little boys. That he thinks about us often and hopes that we made a good life for ourselves. I don't know what your letter says, but the main point is that it's over—we're safe now. Everything and everyone is okay, there's no reason to be afraid anymore."

I look down at the letter, taking in the fact how long she's had it in her possession. "So that's why you told me to go through with the contest? Because my real father is dead?"

"Yes," she says. "That's why I told you to go. I understand if you're angry, if there's a part of you that wanted to know him. But I promise you, your dad was your parent in every way that really matters. He was the one who protected you, who kept us safe. He's the reason we made it out of this thing with the few scars that we have."

I glance back and forth between her and Frank, look down at the letter. "I just need some time to process all this," I say, fixating on the sloppy, cursive writing, my old nickname. "It's kind of a lot to take in."

"Of course," my mom says. "Take all the time you need."

I walk around the chair, grabbing the letter, my fingers trembling as I slide my hand over the handwriting. I start to walk toward my room but stop, the weight of all the revelations weighing on me, the implications daunting. Knowing my sweet mother was harassed, stalked, beaten on multiple occasions, having her marriage and dreams shattered over and over again. I walk back into the living room and kiss her on the side of the head. "I love you mom," I say.

"Love you too, sweetie," she says, her tear-stained skin pressed into my cheek. "More than you know."

I stand, then turn and go to my room.

CHAPTER 38

WALKING INTO MY ROOM, I gently close the door behind me, leaning on it as the weight of our conversation sinks in. I hear Hank pad up to the door, sniffing curiously near my feet, whining a little at my absence before trotting away. I hold up the envelope, a lump forming in my throat as I feel the weight of it against my palms, my fingers tracing along the worn edges. My mind replays my mothers words, the highlights popping up over and over again like a broken record player. *He isn't your father... He took care of me... it was his plan... he loved you so much.*

Drifting toward my bed, I sit down, scooting backward until my back hits the wall. Scrunching my legs against my chest, I carefully open the envelope, my hand shaking as I pull out several pages of folded paper. I set the envelope aside, my thumb trailing over my name once more. Taking a deep breath, I unfold the papers, transporting back to childhood as my father's scribbled handwriting explodes off the page.

My dearest Anna,

As I write you this letter, sitting at my old wooden desk in my new home, miles from our old life, I can't help but think of you as a little girl, my sweet angel, immortalized at the tender age of twelve when you left. But, after seeing recent photos of you, a beautiful young woman looking so much like your mother, I know that you're not a little girl anymore. You are an adult, and as such, you deserve an apology, especially from me. First of all, I want to tell you how sorry I am that our lives separated in the way that they did. It was quick and painful and it wasn't fair. If I had known any other way to protect you, any option to keep us together while shielding you from a life you didn't ask for, I would have taken it. Letting you go, watching your mom drive away that day, was the hardest thing I've ever had to do. My heart was in that car, tucked away between the two of you, a piece of me gone forever. As much as it killed me, I've found peace in knowing that you've held onto one another, that your bond hasn't been broken by the chaos we all endured.

I also want you to know that none of this is your fault. We made many choices, your mother and I... some of them stupid or immature or selfish. But the one thing we always agreed on was putting you first, no matter the cost. If that meant hiding you from an abusive man, taking the burden of his rage upon ourselves, then so be it. I do not apologize for keeping you from him... in my eyes, he was not what a man ought to be, what a father and a partner is supposed to be. Those duties are sacred, a privilege that too many take lightly or squander altogether. I do apologize for not being honest about my role in your life, but for me, there was no truth to tell. You are my daughter - every good part of me is in you, the kindness and goodness you have from my role in your life is as real as flesh and blood. Whether I ever see you again or not, there is nothing stronger than my conviction in that one simple truth. So, Anna, my sweet daughter whom I love dearly, do not take what happened upon yourself. If I had to do it all over again just to achieve the same outcome, to see you become the woman you are today, I would. That's what being a father and a parent is all about.

The last thing I really need to say is, don't be upset with your mother. She has survived and endured way more than most people have or ever should, and she's done it with grace. I was always in awe of her, how gentle and compassionate she is, even when life tried so hard to be cruel. I don't regret meeting her or helping her after your father left, it was an honor to be her husband and I will always miss her. She is an extraordinary woman who deserves your love, respect, and gratitude, and I can only hope you've grown to embody her many gifts. Love her, be gentle with her, give her the grace that she deserves. There were many occasions where she very nearly died just to protect you.

I love you so much, Annabean, I hope you have the big, beautiful life we always talked about, that I dreamt for you to have. If you haven't traveled much yet, take some of the money I sent and go someplace incredible, somewhere that will make you happy. I only hope you think of me while you're there, looking up at the stars, knowing that I love and miss you.

I will always be your dad, always. I think about you every day when I make breakfast for my boys, when I tell them stories about pirate ships and adventure. If you ever want to contact me, I've put my business card in this envelope, please reach out anytime. You are so loved and missed, forever and ever.

All my love,
Your dad

My shirt is soaked with tears by the time I finish his letter, my chest tight as I struggle to breathe. Everything that I've missed about him, everything I knew him to be, is in this letter, proof that it was real, that I wasn't crazy to love him, to miss him. I think of all the moments we missed out on together, the things I wish we could talk about, that he should have been there for. I close my eyes, hearing his voice as he calls my name, his loving call echoing across time and space. My heart shatters, the distance between us cutting through me, fresh slices that go all the way down to the bone. I fall over onto my bed, sobbing into my pillow.

***

When I wake up the next morning, the house is quiet, the smell of coffee drifting under my door. I grab the throw blanket off my bed, tossing it around my shoulders as I open the door and walk out toward the living room.

I catch sight of my mother right away, sitting on the couch as usual, thumbing through a cooking magazine. As I get closer, I can see that she's made cinnamon rolls, thick icing piled high on each twisting pastry. She hears me approach, turns, catches me eyeing the cinnamon rolls. "Figured I'd make breakfast, it's a good morning for something comforting." I sit down beside her, nodding as I pick up a ceramic mug. I don't look at her, I merely feel her eyes on me as I pour myself some coffee. "Did you read the letter?" she asks, tilting her head to the side. I nod, blowing on the steaming beverage before taking a small sip, the aromatic drink comforting after a long night of crying. "And?" she says, still waiting.

Remembering my father's words, I turn toward her, meeting her gaze for the first time. "He said that he loves me, that he misses us. That he hopes I have a big, beautiful life."

My mother nods, smiling. "That sounds like him," she says.

"He also said not to be angry with you," I say, watching her as I take another generous sip.

My mother shakes her head, her frizzy hair skittering over her shoulders. "No one gets to decide that but you, Avery. If you want to just be angry for a while, be angry. I don't blame you, I dropped a lot on you last night."

"You did," I agree, setting down my drink. "I mean, you lied about a lot of stuff, good intentioned or not, for a long time." She nods, absorbing my words, not arguing at all. "I just hate the way it all went down, you know? You're all I've got, I need to be able to trust you."

"You can trust me," she says, setting her hand on my knee. "You can trust that I love you, you can trust that I'll put you first, always." She sits back, frowning. "And I'm not all you've got, not anymore. You have Rachel and Maggie and Frank, Graham. Even your dad would be on the next plane here, if you asked him to be. You have so many people worthy of your love and your trust, honey... you have an entire town behind you!" I nod, mulling over her words. "Did the letter say anything else?" she asks.

I chuckle, reaching out for a cinnamon roll, its frosting sliding over the edge. "He told me to take a trip," I say, grinning as I bite into it.

"That is *definitely* something he would say!" my mother cries, shaking her head. "Well, between the check he sent us and your prize money, you have plenty of money to do it. Did he say where you should go?"

I nod, the warmth of his letter filling me up. "Somewhere that makes me happy," I say.

"Any ideas?" my mother asks, grabbing her own pastry.

"Yeah," I say, looking over at her, smiling. "I think I know exactly where to go."

CHAPTER 39

Six months later

WIND WHIPS AROUND ME as I step out onto the upper deck of the ferry, a rush of cool air blowing south from the Norwegian Sea. I look out across the water, a myriad of island coastlines encrusted in snow and ice, red houses and blue rooftops popping against the snowy backdrop. Pulling my hat down over my ears, I stroll along the upper deck, passing couples and small families, everyone bundled in heavy coats and scarves against the bitter cold. After making a full lap around the ship, I take a seat on an empty folding chair near the bow, its wind-battered wood creaking in protest as I settle in, my eyes fixed on our destination.

Torshavn. The only pitstop on the ship's way to Iceland.

I take in a deep breath, coughing as the dry air hits my lungs, the breeze so cold that it's like my chest is on fire. My skin feels chapped and raw, my body stiff from weeks worth of travel. I gaze out at the ocean, the surface like glass, birds swimming through the crystal blue water in a perfect reflection of the sky. My scarf still high over my mouth and nose, I peer once again at my fellow passengers, analyzing their faces, every man and woman a stranger to me. I turn back to the sea, something in my gut telling me to just be patient.

Just a little further, I think as I stare at the island in the distance. *Just one more day.*

The following morning, the ship docks in Torshavn just after sunrise, a majority of its patrons disembarking to explore the frozen capital city. Walking down the ramp amongst the other passengers, I glance around me as people slowly begin to scatter, dispersing in all directions as soon as we hit the pier. I have no idea where I'm going, just a stubborn determination pushing me forward as I pass tourists and fisherman, the smell of seaweed and raw fish punctuating the air. After a stretch, the harbor falls away, the city opening up before me as I walk up and down the side streets, looking, searching.

I weave through a labyrinth of avenues, passing old and new buildings alike, small boutiques and quaint restaurants that smell of meat and beer. I listen to locals as they stroll past me, speaking languages I don't understand, smiling politely as they continue down the street. I wander to and fro, searching desperately for the right location, a place that just makes sense. With only a few hours left, I turn down Tórsgøta to return to the harbor when suddenly, I see it.

A crowd has gathered near a large stone building, parents bundled up in heavy parkas as their children glide past them, their laughter turning into condensation as they wave in earnest beneath the overhead Christmas lights. *Ice skating*, I think, stepping closer, searching the fence line for his face. After a couple of sweeps I finally spot him, ducking behind groups of people as I slowly move around the perimeter, terrified that he may take off if he sees me.

He's standing on the far side of the rink, draped in a long, dark coat, his silhouette noticeable among so many colorful jackets.

He isn't skating, just watching, his face sunken and empty as he absentmindedly observes the skaters flying past him. I swallow, summoning my courage as I walk toward him, my body practically weightless as adrenaline courses through my veins. I walk up beside him, not saying anything at first as I lean against the fence, letting him see me. He finally turns, his eyes vacant, not cold but certainly not the man I love. "Hi, Graham," I say, taking a breath as I turn to face him.

He stares at me, his eyes so distant that I wonder for a moment if I have the wrong person. He's disheveled, a burly beard covering his jaw and chin, though I can tell that he's lost weight. He doesn't say anything, just turns to face the rink again. "What are you doing here?" he finally asks, his tone less than welcoming.

"I came to see you," I say, my heart pounding as I stand my ground, determined not to turn away from him. I feel like he's a stranger right now, like I don't know him in this new identity he's created for himself, but I keep going. "Tim told me you'd be here."

"Tim," he says, nodding his head. He keeps his eyes on the ice skaters, his face drawn and emotionless. "Did he call you?" he asks.

"No," I say, taking another deep breath. "I saw him, when I was in LA."

Graham glances at me, a flicker of curiosity in his eyes, his attention piqued for a fraction of a second. He turns away again, trying to appear disinterested. "I guess five years too late is better than never," he says, his voice still flat, like it's a statement rather than an insult.

I bow my head, my heart aching as his words pierce through my chest, my courage waning as I try a different tactic. "Rachel says hello," I say, raising my head high to look at him, determined to break through this facade. He nods, still ignoring me as I continue. "She moved out of her and Daniel's place, took over my mom's old room. She's basically planning to tear the place apart, I think, which is good... it'll help keep her busy for a while."

"That's great," Graham says, sneering at this new information, his jaw tensing as he shakes his head in disgust. He hasn't talked to her since Florida, so I'm not really surprised by his attitude. "I'm glad things are working out for *her*. I'm sure you two will be very happy together."

"Well, I'm sure we would be," I say carefully, "if I still lived there."

Graham's head snaps sideways, his golden eyes burning, his face twitching as he tries not to care about what I just said. "Are you at the studio?" he asks.

"No," I say, tilting my chin a little higher, defiant against his relentless animosity. "I don't really live anywhere at the moment, except for in hostels and on trains."

Graham stares at me, his anger melting to something more tired and weary. "What do you want, Avery? It's still Avery, right?" He looks away again, deflating a little as he leans on the wooden fence, bowing his head. "You didn't come halfway around the world to make small talk, just spit it out."

I square my shoulders, my stomach bottoming out as I realize that this is my last chance to get through to him. "I reached out to Anthony Freeman," I say, my voice cracking a little as I struggle to keep my emotions in check. "A few months ago. He's been mentoring me, improving my skills. He made a few calls on my behalf and I'm planning to start a new job...in LA."

Graham stands up, his body finally acknowledging mine, his eyes sweeping over my face. "In LA?" he says, his nonchalance completely shattered.

"Yeah," I say, swallowing. "At the beginning of the year. I flew out to meet my new boss, look at some apartments. But I couldn't settle on anything, not until I talked to you."

Graham looks away, his demeanor a mix of anger and anguish. "I don't see why not," he says, turning back to face me. "I've never factored into your life before, no reason to start now. I've barely been in LA since the contest, I'm not even sure I'll go back."

I nod, trying not to feel defeated. Reaching over into my bag, I pull out my dad's letter, my emotions overwhelming me as I smooth my hand over the white envelope. "My dad sent me this," I say, a tear sliding down my cheek as I hold it up to him. "I got it right after Florida. He told me to have a big, beautiful life, to go somewhere that made me happy. And I did, I tried. I used my prize money to take Rachel and I to Japan, China, the Philippines. All these destinations, all these 'bucket list' places that I thought I needed to see." I stare at him, tears pouring down my face, willing him to look at me. "They were amazing, exactly what I always hoped for. But the only place I *really* want to be, the only place that makes me truly happy, is standing right next to you."

Graham keeps his eyes averted but I watch as tears begin to fall, his body shivering as he starts to weep. I put the letter back in my bag and pull out a medium-sized notebook, the outside made of leather and fastened with a small metal clasp. I take a deep breath, offering it to Graham. He glances at it briefly before looking away. "What is that?" he asks, his voice thick with emotion.

"Please," I say, holding it out to him. "Just trust me." He holds my gaze, tears still rolling down his face, a look of uncertainty in his amber eyes. He reaches out, carefully taking the book, holding it at arm's length for a moment as his hand moves over the leather exterior. Taking a deep breath, he removes the clasp and lifts the cover, a sob squeezing out of him as he examines the first page.

It's a small scrapbook, consisting mainly of pictures of him, images I've taken over the years with and without his knowledge. Tears cascade down his face as he turns the pages, one after another, laughing and crying at the abundance of memories. Pictures of him at the table in our studio apartment, long lens shots of him drawing in the back booth at Buttercrust, his wild, dizzying photos from our night out on the ice. The two of us in our Halloween costumes, pictures of us on the Colorado River, and finally, the image of him on the yacht in Florida, his silhouette vibrant and dashing in the gorgeous sunset. Graham laughs, a smile splitting his face in two, softness returning to his features as he looks over at me, his eyes filled with warmth and relief. He nods his head, flipping through the pages again, laughing when he gets to the pictures of him on the trash can lid. "This was more difficult than it looks," he says, smiling as he wipes his tears away.

"I bet it was," I say, looking toward the ice. I tilt my head toward the busy rink, giving him a sly smile. "Care to join me? For old time's sake?"

Graham closes the book, carefully slipping it back into my bag. He looks down at the ground for a long moment, silence wrapping around us until he finally nods, looking up at me. "Yeah," he says, his voice breaking as he smiles at me, his shy, perfect smile. "I'd love to."

I reach up, stroking his scraggly beard, wiping at his tears as new ones begin to fall. He leans down and kisses me, my face mottled with his tears as he kisses me over and over before hugging me tightly, his face buried in my hair. We hold each other, both of us shaking but not from the cold, relief flooding through us because we know that we are finally home. Graham releases me, a genuine smile on his face as he gently caresses my cheek, wiping away my tears. We both pull ourselves together, laughing a bit at the melodramatic scene we caused, and then he reaches out, his golden eyes on my face as he takes my hand in his.

For the next two hours, we glide over the frozen water together, sunlight and laughter enveloping us as we move around the rink as one. Our spirits whole and rejuvenated, we spin and laugh and twirl under the Arctic sky, a lifetime realized in an afternoon, both of us recognizing that this is it, that we'll never skate alone again.

ACROSS THE SALTED PLAINS: BONUS CHAPTER

SIGN UP FOR MY AUTHOR NEWSLETTER!!

Be the first to learn about Megan Longmeyer's new releases and receive exclusive bonus content, including the BONUS CHAPTER of "Across the Salted Plains".

Click the link below or scan the QR code:
https://BookHip.com/NBWSHHL

Website: https://meganlongmeyerbooks.com/
Socials: @meganlongmeyerwrites
Pre-Orders & Socials: LinkTree

ACKNOWLEDGEMENTS

While there's no one person in particular I want to thank, since I tackled this insane project all on my own, I do want to acknowledge how very blessed and thankful I am for the people in my life. The people who cheer for me, who push me forward, who didn't call me crazy when I set off to complete this project. Writing this book has been one of the hardest things I've ever done, and I never would have gotten through it if it weren't for those closest to me. So thank you to my family and friends, you are what keeps me going, always...

Made in the USA
Columbia, SC
06 August 2024

39705483R10190